THE CHILDREN'S HOUR

The chipmunk stopped in astonishment, still holding the acorn basket.

First Story Book

A BOOK TO GROW ON

Consultant Editor for
First Story Book

MARGARET JONES WILLIAMS
Director of Elementary Education
Cornell College, Iowa

CONSULTANT EDITORS FOR THE CHILDREN'S HOUR

CAROL RYRIE BRINK
Author
Newbery Prize Winner

JULIA CARSON
Author and Biographer

IRVING CRUMP
Editor and Author

HELEN DEAN FISH
Editor and Author

WILHELMINA HARPER
Anthologist, Librarian
Redwood City, California

WILLIAM HEYLIGER
Author,
Editor of Literature for Youth
The Westminster Press

SIDDIE JOE JOHNSON
Children's Librarian
Dallas Public Library

CORNELIA MEIGS
Author and Teacher
Newbery Prize Winner

NORMA RATHBUN
Chief of Children's Work
Milwaukee Public Library

MABEL L. ROBINSON
Author, Associate Professor
Columbia University

MARGARET JONES WILLIAMS
Director of Elementary Education
Cornell College, Iowa

MARJORIE BARROWS, *Editor*

First
Story Book

MATHILDA SCHIRMER
Associate Editor

DOROTHY SHORT
Art Editor

THE CHILDREN'S HOUR

PRINTED IN THE UNITED STATES OF AMERICA

Acknowledgments

The editor and publishers wish to thank the following publishers, agents, authors, and artists for permission to use and reprint stories, poems, and illustrations included in this book:

APPLETON-CENTURY-CROFTS, INC., for "A Good Little Dog" by Anne Stoddard. Copyright, 1930, The Century Company.

JONATHAN CAPE, LTD., for Canadian permission to reprint "Rocking-Horse Land" by Laurence Housman.

CHILDRENS PRESS, INC., for "The Littlest Reindeer" by Johanna de Witt; "Johnny and the Monarch" by Margaret Friskey; "The Littlest Angel" by Charles Tazewell, with illustrations by Katharine Evans.

CONSOLIDATED BOOK PUBLISHERS for "Augusta Goose" by Ruth Dixon; "Tommy the Tugboat" by Betty Martin; "Adventures of a Brownie" by Dinah Marie Mulock, retold by Mathilda Schirmer; "Said the Sandman" by Helen Wing; and illustrations by Bianca, Clarence Biers, Betty Carroll, Hazel Frazee, Miriam Hurford, and Ruth van Tellingen.

COWARD-McCANN, INC., for story and illustrations from "The Funny Thing" by Wanda Gág. Copyright, 1921, by Coward-McCann, Inc.

DODD, MEAD & COMPANY, INC., for "There Was Tammie" by Dorothy M. Bryan, with illustrations by Marguerite Bryan, copyright, 1935, by Dorothy M. Bryan; "The Lost Merbaby" by Margaret Baker, copyright, 1927, by Dodd, Mead & Company, Inc.

DOUBLEDAY & COMPANY, INC., for "The Velveteen Rabbit" by Margery Williams Bianco. Reprinted by permission of the author's estate; "Angus and the Ducks" by Marjorie Flack, copyright, 1931, by Marjorie Flack Larssen; "The Picnic Basket" from *Poppy Seed Cakes* by Margery Clark; "Mr. Murdle's Large Heart" from *A Street of Little Shops* by Margery Williams Bianco, copyright, 1926, by Margery Williams Bianco.

E. P. DUTTON & CO., INC., for "The King's Breakfast" from *When We Were Very Young* by A. A. Milne, with illustrations by Ernest H. Shepard. Published and copyright, 1924, E. P. Dutton & Co., Inc., N. Y.; "In Which Eeyore Has a Birthday and Gets Two Presents" from *Winnie-the-Pooh* by A. A. Milne, with illustrations by Ernest H. Shepard. Published and copyright, 1926, E. P. Dutton & Co., Inc., N. Y.; the story and illustrations from "Twin Seals" by Inez Hogan. Published and copyright, 1940, E. P. Dutton & Co., Inc., N. Y.

HARCOURT, BRACE & COMPANY, INC., for "Rocking-Horse Land" from *Moonshine and Clover* by Laurence Housman.

WILLIAM HEINEMANN, LTD., for Canadian permission to reprint "The Velveteen Rabbit" by Margery Williams Bianco.

HOUGHTON MIFFLIN COMPANY for story and illustrations for "Kit and Kat Go Fishing" from *The Dutch Twins* by Lucy Fitch Perkins; "The Little Steam Engine" from *Riverside Second Reader*, published by Houghton Mifflin Company.

THOMAS NELSON & SONS for story and illustrations from "Down, Down the Mountain" by Ellis Credle.

OXFORD UNIVERSITY PRESS, INC., for "Minnie the Mermaid" by Tom and Elizabeth Orton Jones, with illustrations by Elizabeth Orton Jones, copyright, 1939, Oxford University Press, Inc., N. Y.; illustrations by Helen Sewell for Rachel Field's "All through the Night" from *A First Bible* illustrated by Helen Sewell. Copyright, 1934, by Oxford University Press, Inc., N. Y.

PLATT & MUNK, INC., for "Mrs. Tabby Gray" by Maud Lindsay.

G. P. PUTNAM'S SONS for story and illustrations from "Hercules" by Hardie Gramatky. Copyright, 1940, by Hardie Gramatky.

RAND McNALLY & COMPANY for "Cocky" by Marjorie Barrows (Jack Alden), with illustrations by Clarence Biers. Copyright, 1943, by Rand McNally & Co., publishers; "Goosie Gray" and "The Peaceful Pirate" from *The Jolly Jingle Picture Book* (*Rimskittle's Book*) by Leroy F. Jackson.

A Word to Parents

"Let your child read the best stories," said a wise man long ago. "These will influence him in the finest way all the days of his life."

The purpose of *The Children's Hour* is to provide these best stories. They are stories, a wide selection of the great literature of all time, that fill sixteen volumes and over six thousand pages. They are stories that range from the earliest folk tale to the tales of A. A. Milne, from King Arthur's knights and their venturesome deeds to those who sailed on the "Kon-Tiki." And, most important of all, these stories are the ones that children themselves love. Never before has so wide a selection by the world's finest writers been chosen because, first and foremost, these stories were the boy's and girl's own choice.

Children, when given a fair chance, choose the best. This is a well-established fact among educators today. Young children, exposed to both good reading and shoddy reading, really prefer the good. It must be readily available, of course, and it must ring true, be simply told, and be of genuine interest to them.

The children's own choice is here. Answers to one hundred and twenty-five thousand "favorite reading" questionnaires came to us recently from children, teachers, and librarians throughout the country. They named their favorite stories, and their choice in the main agreed with many other lists of recommended children's books prepared both by experts and by the children themselves. The best of them are in these pages, endorsed also by many other authorities on literature for children, including, of course, the outstanding consultant editors of *The Children's Hour*. Here are the boy's and girl's favorites among the Newbery and Caldecott prize books, here are the children's favorites among all the best writers of yesterday and today.

The Children's Hour thus covers a wide range of boy and girl interests. Its readers will find fun and information and inspiration in imaginative folk and fairy tales, in heroic myths and legends, and in courageous tales of pioneers and days of long ago. They will also find genuine appeal in stories of school and sport, home, adventure, animal and outdoor life, worthwhile mysteries, and wonder tales of tomorrow. Here, too, they will discover beauty, absorbing interest, or humor in poems, in classics that deserve to endure, and in inspiring tales of leaders and heroes.

Just as a list of the authors in *The Children's Hour* is a *Who's Who* among the writers for children, a list of its outstanding illustrators who paint and draw pictures children love is a *Who's Who* among the artists of today. The work of nearly every famous artist who draws or paints for children today will be found among the one hundred and twenty-eight pictures in full color and the two thousand five hundred pictures in two colors in *The Children's Hour*. The pictures help tell the story often with humor, often with action and the details children like. The artists have a real feeling for line and color, a sense of beauty, a sense of drama, and a sense of wonder.

Thoughtful parents realize the importance of surrounding their children with good literature and good art. They know their lasting values. They know the ideas and ideals children gain from them enrich their lives. They know that great literature and great art will expand a child's horizon, will open windows to a world of beauty, of ideas, of adventure, and of high achievement. It is the hope of the editor that *The Children's Hour* will do just that and will lift its readers far above the average in character, intelligence, and culture, as well as give them, during their impressionable years, one of the greatest joys in life—the love of reading when they are young.

Marjorie Barrows

Editor

Contents

Margery Williams Bianco

THE VELVETEEN RABBIT

ILLUSTRATED BY *Elizabeth Orton Jones*

THERE was once a velveteen rabbit, and in the beginning he was really splendid. He was fat and bunchy, as a rabbit should be; his coat was spotted brown and white, he had real thread whiskers, and his ears were lined with pink sateen. On Christmas morning, when he sat wedged in the top of the Boy's stocking, with a sprig of holly between his paws, the effect was charming.

There were other things in the stocking, nuts and oranges and a toy engine, and chocolate almonds and a clockwork mouse, but the Rabbit was quite the best of all. For at least two hours the Boy loved him, and then Aunts and Uncles came to dinner, and there was a great rustling of tissue paper and unwrapping of parcels, and in the excitement of looking at all the new presents the Velveteen Rabbit was forgotten.

For a long time he lived in the toy cupboard or on the nursery floor, and no one thought very much about him. He was naturally shy, and being only made of velveteen, some of the more expensive toys quite snubbed him. The mechanical toys were very superior, and looked down upon everyone else; they were full of modern ideas and pretended they were real. The model boat, who had lived through two seasons and lost most of his paint, caught the tone from them and never missed an opportunity of referring to his rigging in technical terms. The Rabbit could not claim to be a model of anything,

1

for he didn't know that real rabbits existed; he thought they were all stuffed with sawdust like himself, and he understood that sawdust was quite out-of-date and should never be mentioned in modern circles. Even Timothy, the jointed wooden lion, who was made by the disabled soldiers, and should have had broader views, put on airs and pretended he was connected with Government. Between them all the poor little Rabbit was made to feel himself very insignificant and commonplace, and the only person who was kind to him at all was the Skin Horse.

The Skin Horse had lived longer in the nursery than any of the others. He was so old that his brown coat was bald in patches and showed the seams underneath, and most of the hairs in his tail had been pulled out to string bead necklaces. He was wise, for he had seen a long succession of mechanical toys arrive to boast and swagger, and by-and-by break their mainsprings and pass away, and he knew that they were only toys, and would never turn into anything else. For nursery magic is very strange and wonderful, and only those play-things that are old and wise and experienced like the Skin Horse understand all about it.

"What is REAL?" asked the Rabbit one day, when they were lying side by side near the nursery fender, before Nana came to tidy the room. "Does it mean having things that buzz inside you and a stick-out handle?"

"Real isn't how you are made," said the Skin Horse. "It's a thing that happens to you. When a child loves you for a long, long time, not just to play with, but REALLY loves you, then you become Real."

"Does it hurt?" asked the Rabbit.

"Sometimes," said the Skin Horse, for he was always truthful. "When you are Real you don't mind being hurt."

"Does it happen all at once, like being wound up," he asked, "or bit by bit?"

"It doesn't happen all at once," said the Skin Horse. "You become. It takes a long time. That's why it doesn't often happen to people who break easily, or have sharp edges, or who have to be carefully kept. Generally, by the time you are Real, most of your hair has been loved off, and your eyes drop out, and you get loose in the joints and very shabby. But these things don't matter at all, because once you are Real you can't be ugly, except to people who don't understand."

"I suppose *you* are Real?" said the Rabbit. And then he wished he had not said it, for he thought the Skin Horse might be sensitive. But the Skin Horse only smiled.

"The Boy's Uncle made me Real," he said. "That was a great many years ago; but once you are Real you can't become unreal again. It lasts for always."

The Rabbit sighed. He thought it would be a long time before this magic called Real happened to him. He longed to become Real, to know what it felt like; and yet the idea of growing shabby and losing his eyes and whiskers was rather sad. He wished that he could become it without these uncomfortable things happening to him.

There was a person called Nana who ruled the nursery. Sometimes she took no notice of the playthings lying about, and sometimes, for no reason whatever, she went swooping about like a great wind and hustled them away in cupboards. She called this "tidying up," and the playthings all hated it, especially the tin ones. The Rabbit didn't mind it so much, for wherever he was thrown he came down soft.

One evening, when the Boy was going to bed, he couldn't find the china dog that always slept with him. Nana was in a hurry, and it was too much trouble to hunt for china dogs at bedtime, so she simply looked about her, and seeing that the toy cupboard door stood open, she made a swoop.

"Here," she said, "take your old Bunny! He'll do to sleep with you!" And she dragged the Rabbit out by one ear and put him into the Boy's arms.

That night, and for many nights after, the Velveteen Rabbit slept in the Boy's bed. At first he found it rather uncomfortable, for the Boy hugged him very tight, and sometimes he rolled over on him, and sometimes he pushed him so far under the pillow that the Rabbit could scarcely breathe. And he missed, too, those long moonlight hours in the nursery, when all

4

the house was silent, and his talks with the Skin Horse. But very soon he grew to like it, for the Boy used to talk to him, and made nice tunnels for him under the bedclothes that he said were like the burrows the real rabbits lived in. And they had splendid games together, in whispers, when Nana had gone away to her supper and left the night-light burning on the mantelpiece. And when the Boy dropped off to sleep, the Rabbit would snuggle down close under his little warm chin and dream, with the Boy's hands clasped close round him all night long.

And so time went on, and the little Rabbit was very happy—so happy that he never noticed how his beautiful velveteen fur was getting shabbier and shabbier, and his tail coming unsewn, and all the pink rubbed off his nose where the Boy had kissed him.

Spring came, and they had long days in the garden, for wherever the Boy went the Rabbit went too. He had rides in the wheelbarrow, and picnics on the grass, and lovely fairy huts built for him under the raspberry canes behind the flower-border. And once, when the Boy was called away suddenly to go out to tea, the Rabbit was left out on the lawn until long after dusk, and Nana had to come and look for him with the candle because the Boy couldn't go to sleep unless he was there. He was wet through with the dew and quite earthy from diving into the burrows the Boy had made for him in the flower-bed, and Nana grumbled as she rubbed him off with a corner of her apron.

"You must have your old Bunny!" she said. "Fancy all that fuss for a toy!"

The Boy sat up in bed and stretched out his hands.

"Give me my Bunny!" he said. "You mustn't say that. He isn't a toy. He's REAL!"

When the little Rabbit heard that he was happy, for he knew that what the Skin Horse had said was true at last. The nursery magic had happened to him, and he was a toy no longer. He was Real. The Boy himself had said it.

That night he was almost too happy to sleep, and so much love stirred in his little sawdust heart that it almost burst. And into his boot-button eyes, that had long ago lost their polish, there came a look of wisdom and beauty, so that even Nana noticed it next morning when she picked him up, and said, "I declare if that old Bunny hasn't got quite a knowing expression!"

That was a wonderful summer!

Near the house where they lived there was a wood, and in the long June evenings the Boy liked to go there after tea to play. He took the Velveteen Rabbit with him, and before he wandered off to pick flowers, or play at brigands among the trees, he always made the Rabbit a little nest somewhere among the bracken, where he would be quite cosy, for he was a kind-

6

hearted little boy and he liked Bunny to be comfortable. One evening, while the Rabbit was lying there alone, watching the ants that ran to and fro between his velvet paws in the grass, he saw two strange beings creep out of the tall bracken near him.

They were rabbits like himself, but quite furry and brand-new. They must have been very well made, for their seams didn't show at all, and they changed shape in a queer way when they moved; one minute they were long and thin and the next minute fat and bunchy, instead of always staying the same like he did. Their feet padded softly on the ground, and they crept quite close to him, twitching their noses, while the Rabbit stared hard to see which side the clockwork stuck out, for he knew that people who jump generally have something to wind them up. But he couldn't see it. They were evidently a new kind of rabbit altogether.

They stared at him, and the little Rabbit stared back. And all the time their noses twitched.

"Why don't you get up and play with us?" one of them asked.

"I don't feel like it," said the Rabbit, for he didn't want to explain that he had no clockwork.

"Ho!" said the furry rabbit. "It's as easy as anything." And he gave a big hop sideways and stood on his hind legs.

"I don't believe you can!" he said.

"I can!" said the little Rabbit. "I can jump higher than anything!" He meant when the Boy threw him, but of course he didn't want to say so.

"Can you hop on your hind legs?" asked the furry rabbit.

That was a dreadful question, for the Velveteen Rabbit had no hind legs at all! The back of him was made all in one piece, like a pincushion. He sat still in the bracken and hoped that the other rabbits wouldn't notice.

"I don't want to!" he said again.

But the wild rabbits have very sharp eyes. And this one stretched out his neck and looked.

"He hasn't got any hind legs!" he called out. "Fancy a rabbit without any hind legs!" And he began to laugh.

"I have!" cried the little Rabbit. "I have got hind legs! I am sitting on them!"

"Then stretch them out and show me, like this!" said the wild rabbit. And he began to whirl round and dance, till the little Rabbit got quite dizzy.

"I don't like dancing," he said. "I'd rather sit still!"

But all the while he was longing to dance, for a funny new tickly feeling ran through him, and he felt he would give anything in the world to be able to jump about like these rabbits did.

8

The strange rabbit stopped dancing and came quite close. He came so close this time that his long whiskers brushed the Velveteen Rabbit's ear, and then he wrinkled his nose suddenly and flattened his ears and jumped backwards.

"He doesn't smell right!" he exclaimed. "He isn't a rabbit at all! He isn't real!"

"I *am* Real!" said the little Rabbit. "I am Real! The Boy said so!" And he nearly began to cry.

Just then there was a sound of footsteps, and the Boy ran past near them, and with a stamp of feet and a flash of white tails the two strange rabbits disappeared.

"Come back and play with me!" called the little Rabbit. "Oh, do come back! I *know* I am Real!"

But there was no answer, only the little ants ran to and fro, and the bracken swayed gently where the two strangers had passed. The Velveteen Rabbit was all alone.

"Oh, dear!" he thought. "Why did they run away like that? Why couldn't they stop and talk to me?"

For a long time he lay very still, watching the bracken, and hoping that they would come back. But they never returned, and presently the sun sank lower and the little white moths fluttered out, and the Boy came and carried him home.

Weeks passed, and the little Rabbit grew very old and shabby, but the Boy loved him just as much. He loved him so hard that he loved all his whiskers off, and the pink lining to his ears turned gray, and his brown spots faded. He even began to lose his shape, and he scarcely looked like a rabbit any more, except to the Boy. To him he was always beautiful, and that

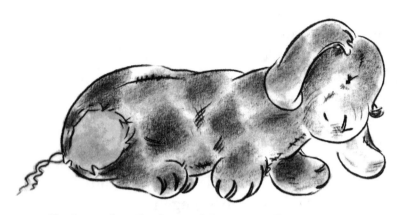

was all that the little Rabbit cared about. He didn't mind how he looked to other people, because the nursery magic had made him Real, and when you are Real shabbiness doesn't matter.

And then, one day, the Boy was ill.

His face grew very flushed, and he talked in his sleep, and his little body was so hot that it burned the Rabbit when he held him close. Strange people came and went in the nursery, and a light burned all night, and through it all the little Velveteen Rabbit lay there, hidden from sight under the bedclothes, and he never stirred, for he was afraid that if they found him someone might take him away, and he knew that the Boy needed him.

It was a long weary time, for the Boy was too ill to play, and the little Rabbit found it rather dull with nothing to do all day long. But he snuggled down patiently and looked forward to the time when the Boy should be well again, and they would go out in the garden amongst the flowers and the butterflies and play splendid games in the raspberry thicket like they used to. All sorts of delightful things he planned, and while the Boy lay half asleep he crept up close to the pillow and whispered them in his ear. And presently the fever turned, and the Boy got better. He was able to sit up in bed and look at picture books, while the little Rabbit cuddled close at his side. And one day, they let him get up and dress.

It was a bright, sunny morning, and the windows stood wide open. They had carried the Boy out on to the balcony, wrapped in a shawl, and the little Rabbit lay tangled up among the bedclothes, thinking.

The Boy was going to the seaside tomorrow. Everything was arranged, and now it only remained to carry out the doctor's orders. They talked about it all, while the little Rabbit lay under the bedclothes, with just his head peeping out, and listened. The room was to be disinfected, and all the books and toys that the Boy had played with in bed must be burnt.

"Hurrah!" thought the little Rabbit. "Tomorrow we shall go to the seaside!" For the Boy had often talked of the seaside, and he wanted very much to see the big waves coming in, and the tiny crabs, and the sand castles.

Just then Nana caught sight of him.

"How about his old Bunny?" she asked.

"*That?*" said the doctor. "Why, it's a mass of scarlet fever germs!—Burn it at once. What? Nonsense! Get him a new one. He mustn't have that any more!"

And so the little Rabbit was put into a sack with the old picture-books and a lot of rubbish, and carried out to the end of the garden behind the fowlhouse. That was a fine place to make a bonfire, only the gardener was too busy just then to attend to it. He had the potatoes to dig and the green peas to gather,

11

but next morning he promised to come quite early and burn the whole lot.

That night the Boy slept in a different bedroom, and he had a new bunny to sleep with him. It was a splendid bunny, all white plush with real glass eyes, but the the Boy was too excited to care very much about it. For tomorrow hc was going to the seaside, and that in itself was such a wonderful thing that he could think of nothing else.

And while the Boy was asleep, dreaming of the seaside, the little Rabbit lay among the old picture-books in the corner behind the fowl-house, and he felt very lonely. The sack had been left untied, and so by wriggling a bit he was able to get his head through the opening and look out. He was shivering a little, for he had always been used to sleeping in a proper bed, and by this time his coat had worn so thin and threadbare from hugging that it was no longer any protection to him. Near by he could see the thicket of raspberry canes, growing tall and close like a tropical jungle, in whose shadow he had played with the Boy on bygone mornings. He thought of those long sunlit hours in the garden—how happy they were—and a great sadness came over him. He seemed to see them all pass before him, each more beautiful than the other, the fairy huts in the flower-bed, the quiet evenings in the wood when he lay in the bracken and the little ants ran over his paws; the wonderful day when he first knew that he was Real. He thought of the Skin Horse, so wise and gentle, and all that he had told him. Of what use was it to be loved and lose one's beauty and become Real if it all ended like this? And a tear, a

12

real tear, trickled down his little shabby velvet nose and fell to the ground.

And then a strange thing happened. For where the tear had fallen a flower grew out of the ground, a mysterious flower, not at all like any that grew in the garden. It had slender green leaves the color of emeralds, and in the center of the leaves a blossom like a golden cup. It was so beautiful that the little Rabbit forgot to cry and just lay there watching it. And presently the blossom opened, and out of it there stepped a fairy.

She was quite the loveliest fairy in the whole world. Her dress was of pearl and dewdrops, and there were flowers round her neck and in her hair, and her face was like the most perfect flower of all. And she came close to the little Rabbit and gathered him up in her arms and kissed him on his velveteen nose that was all damp from crying.

"Little Rabbit," she said, "don't you know who I am?"

The Rabbit looked up at her, and it seemed that he

13

had seen her face before, but he couldn't think where.

"I am the nursery magic Fairy," she said. "I take care of all the playthings that the children have loved. When they are old and worn out and the children don't need them any more, then I come and take them away with me and turn them into Real."

"Wasn't I Real before?" asked the little Rabbit.

" You were Real to the Boy," the Fairy said, "because he loved you. Now you shall be Real to everyone."

And she held the little Rabbit close in her arms and flew with him into the wood.

It was light now, for the moon had risen. All the forest was beautiful, and the fronds of the bracken shone like frosted silver. In the open glade between the tree-trunks the wild rabbits danced with their shadows on the velvet grass, but when they saw the Fairy they all stopped dancing and stood round in a ring to stare at her.

"I've brought you a new playfellow," the Fairy said. "You must be very kind to him and teach him all he needs to know in Rabbitland, for he is going to live with you for ever and ever!"

And she kissed the little Rabbit again and put him down on the grass.

"Run and play, little Rabbit!" she said.

But the little Rabbit sat quite still for a moment and never moved. For when he saw all the wild rabbits dancing around him he suddenly remembered about his hind legs, and he didn't want them to see that he was made all in one piece. He did not know that when the Fairy kissed him that last time she had changed him altogether. And he might have sat there a long

14

time, too shy to move, if just then something hadn't tickled his nose, and before he thought what he was doing he lifted his hind toe to scratch it.

And he found that he actually had hind legs! Instead of dingy velveteen he had brown fur, soft and shiny, his ears twitched by themselves, and his whiskers were so long that they brushed the grass. He gave one leap and the joy of using those hind legs was so great that he went springing about the turf on them, jumping sideways and whirling round as the others did, and he grew so excited that when at last he did stop to look for the Fairy she had gone. He was a Real Rabbit at last, at home with the other rabbits.

Autumn passed and Winter, and in the Spring, when the days grew warm and sunny, the Boy went out to play in the wood behind the house. And while he was playing, two rabbits crept out from the bracken and peeped at him. One of them was brown all over, but the other had strange markings under his fur, as though long ago he had been spotted, and the spots still showed through. And about his little soft nose and his round black eyes there was something familiar, so that the Boy thought to himself:

"Why, he looks just like my old Bunny that was lost when I had scarlet fever!"

But he never knew that it really was his own Bunny, come back to look at the child who had first helped him to be Real.

Dr. Seuss

THE 500 HATS
OF BARTHOLOMEW CUBBINS

ILLUSTRATED BY THE AUTHOR

In THE beginning, Bartholomew
Cubbins didn't have five hundred hats. He had only
one hat. It was an old one that had belonged to his
father and his father's father before him. It was probably the oldest and the plainest hat in the whole Kingdom of Didd, where Bartholomew Cubbins lived. But
Bartholomew liked it—especially because of the feather
that always pointed straight up in the air.

The Kingdom of Didd was ruled by King Derwin.
His palace stood high on the top of the mountain.
From his balcony, he looked down over the houses of
all his subjects—first, over the spires of the noblemen's
castles, across the broad roofs of the rich men's mansions, then over the little houses of the townsfolk, to
the huts of the farmers far off in the fields.

It was a mighty view and it made King Derwin feel
mighty important.

Far off in the fields, on the edge of a cranberry bog,
stood the hut of the Cubbins family. From the small
door Bartholomew looked across the huts of the farmers
to the houses of the townsfolk, then to the rich men's
mansions and the noblemen's castles, up to the great
towering palace of the King. It was exactly the same
view that King Derwin saw from his balcony, but Bartholomew saw it backward.

It was a mighty view, but it made Bartholomew Cubbins feel mighty small.

Just after sunrise one Saturday morning, Bartholomew started for town. He felt very happy. A pleasant breeze whistled through the feather in his hat. In his right hand he carried a basket of cranberries to sell at the market. He was anxious to sell them quickly and bring the money back home to his parents.

He walked faster and faster till he got to the gates of the town.

The sound of silver trumpets rang through the air. Hoof beats clattered on the cobbled streets.

"Clear the way! Clear the way! Make way for the King!"

All the people rushed for the sidewalks. They drove their carts right up over the curbstones. Bartholomew clutched his basket tighter.

Around the corner dashed fifty trumpeters on yellow-robed horses. Behind them on crimson-robed horses came the King's Own Guards.

"Hats off to the King!" shouted the Captain of the King's Own Guards.

On came the King's carriage—white and gold and purple. It rumbled like thunder through the narrow street.

It swept past Bartholomew. Then suddenly its mighty brakes shrieked. It lurched—and then it stopped. The whole procession stood still.

Bartholomew could hardly believe what he saw. Through the side window of the carriage, the King himself was staring back—straight at him! Bartholomew began to tremble.

"Back up!" the King commanded the Royal Coachman.

The Royal Coachman shouted to the royal horses. The King's Own Guards shouted to their crimson-robed horses. The trumpeters shouted to their yellow-robed horses. Very slowly the whole procession backed down the street, until the King's carriage stopped right in front of Bartholomew.

The King leaned from his carriage window and fixed his eyes directly on Bartholomew Cubbins. "Well . . .? Well . . .?" he demanded.

Bartholomew shook with fright. "I ought to say something," he thought to himself. But he could think of nothing to say.

"Well?" demanded the King again. "Do you or do you *not* take off your hat before your King?"

"Yes, indeed, Sire," answered Bartholomew, feeling greatly relieved. "I *do* take off my hat before my King."

"Then take it off this very instant," commanded the King more loudly than before.

"But, Sire, my hat *is* off," answered Bartholomew.

"Such impudence!" shouted the King, shaking an angry finger. "How dare you stand there and tell me your hat is off!"

"I don't like to say you are wrong, Sire," said Bartholomew very politely, "but you see my hat *is* off." And he showed the King the hat in his hand.

"If that's your hat in your hand," demanded the King, "what's that on your head?"

"On my head?" gasped Bartholomew. There *did* seem to be something on his head. He reached up his hand and touched a hat!

The face of Bartholomew Cubbins turned very red.
"It's a hat, Sire," he stammered, "but it *can't* be mine.
Someone behind me must have put it on my head."

"I don't care *how* it got there," said the King. "You
take it off." And the King sat back in his carriage.

Bartholomew quickly snatched off the hat. He stared
at it in astonishment. It was exactly the same as his own
hat—the same size, the same color. And it had exactly
the same feather.

"By the Crown of my Fathers!" roared the King,
again leaning out of the carriage window. "Did I or
did I *not* command you to take off your hat?"

"You did, Sire. . . . I took it off. . . . I took it off twice."

19

"Nonsense! There is still a hat upon your head."

"Another hat?" Again Bartholomew reached up his hand and touched a hat.

"Come, come, what is the meaning of all this?" demanded the King, his face purple with rage.

"I don't know, Sire," answered Bartholomew. "It never happened to me before."

The King was now shaking with such fury that the carriage rocked on its wheels, and the Royal Coachman could hardly sit in his seat. "Arrest this impudent trickster," shouted the King to the Captain of the King's Own Guards. "We'll teach him to take off his hat."

The Royal Coachman cracked his long whip. The King's carriage swung forward up the street toward the palace.

But the Captain of the King's Own Guards leaned down from his big brass saddle and grabbed Bartholomew Cubbins by his shirt. Away flew Bartholomew's basket! The cranberries bounced over the cobblestones and rolled down into the gutter.

With a jangling of spurs and a clatter of horseshoes, the Captain and Bartholomew sped up the winding street toward the palace. Out of the narrow streets, on up the hill! Bartholomew clung to the Captain's broad back. On and on they galloped, past the bright gardens of the wealthy merchants. Higher and higher up the mountain, on past the walls of the noblemen's castles. . . .

Flupp! . . . the sharp wind whisked off Bartholomew's hat. *Flupp Flupp* . . . two more flew off. *Flupp Flupp Flupp* flew another . . . and another. ". . . 4 . . . 5 . . . 6 . . . 7 . . ." Bartholomew kept counting as the hats came

20

faster and faster. Lords and ladies stared from the windows of their turrets, wondering what the strange stream of hats could mean.

Over the palace drawbridge they sped—through the great gates and into the courtyard. The Captain pulled in his reins.

"His Majesty waits in the Throne Room," said a guard, saluting the Captain.

"The Throne Room!" The Captain dropped Bartholomew to the ground. "I'd certainly hate to be in your shoes," he said, shaking his head sadly.

For a moment Bartholomew was terribly frightened. "Still," he thought to himself, "the King can do nothing dreadful to punish me, because I really haven't done anything wrong. It would be cowardly to feel afraid."

Bartholomew threw back his shoulders and marched straight ahead into the palace. "Follow the black carpet," said the guard at the door. All through the long hallway Bartholomew could hear the muttering of voices behind heavy doors. "He won't take off his hat?" "No, he won't take off his hat."

Bartholomew walked on till he stood in the very middle of the Throne Room. The King, in a long scarlet robe, was sitting on his throne. Beside him stood Sir Alaric, Keeper of the King's Records. He wore in his belt, instead of a sword, a long silver ruler. Lords and noblemen of the court stood solemn and silent.

The King looked down at Bartholomew severely. "Young man, I'll give you one more chance. Will you take off your hat for your King?"

"Your Majesty," said Bartholomew as politely as he possibly could, "I will—but I'm afraid it won't do any

good." And he took off his hat—and it didn't do any good. Another hat sat on Bartholomew's head. He took off hat after hat after hat after hat until he was standing in the middle of a great pile of hats.

The lords and noblemen were so astonished they couldn't even speak. Such a thing had never happened in the Throne Room.

"Heavens!" said Sir Alaric, Keeper of the Records, blinking behind his triangular spectacles. "He's taken off 45!"

"And there were three more down in the town," said the King.

"And you must add on 87 more that blew off my head as we galloped up the hill," said Bartholomew, trying to be helpful.

"One hundred and thirty-five hats! Most unusual," said Sir Alaric, writing it down on a long scroll.

"Come, come," said the King impatiently. "Sir Alaric, what do you make of all this nonsense?"

"Very *serious* nonsense, Your Majesty," answered Sir Alaric. "I advise you to call in an expert on hats."

"Excellent," agreed the King. "Ho, Guard! Fetch in Sir Snipps, maker of hats for all the fine lords."

Into the Throne Room marched the smallest man, wearing the tallest hat that Bartholomew had ever seen. It was Sir Snipps. Instead of a sword, he wore at his side a large pair of scissors.

"Take a look at this boy's hat," commanded the King. Sir Snipps looked at Bartholomew Cubbins' hat and sniffed in disgust. Then he turned to the King and bowed stiffly. "Your Majesty, I, Sir Snipps, am the maker of hats for all the fine lords. I make hats of cloth of gold, fine silks and gems and ostrich plumes. You ask *me* what *I* think of *this* hat? Pooh! It is the most ordinary hat I ever set eyes on."

"In that case," said the King, "it should be very simple for you to take it off."

"Simple, indeed," mumbled Sir Snipps haughtily, and standing on his tiptoes, he pushed his pudgy thumb at Bartholomew's hat and knocked it to the floor. Immediately another appeared on Bartholomew's head.

"Screebees!" screamed Sir Snipps, leaping in the air higher than he was tall. Then he turned and ran shrieking out of the Throne Room.

"Dear me!" said the King, looking puzzled. "If Snipps can't do it, this *must* be more than an ordinary hat."

"One hundred and thirty-six," wrote Sir Alaric, wrinkling his brow. "Your Majesty, I advise that you call in your Wise Men."

"A fine idea!" said the King. "Ho, Guard! bring me Nadd. Nadd knows about everything in all my kingdom."

In came an old, old man. He looked at the hat on Bartholomew's head, and he looked at the pile of hats on the floor.

"Nadd, my Wise Man, can you take off his hat?" asked the King. Nadd shook his head solemnly— solemnly no.

"Then fetch me the Father of Nadd," commanded the King. "He knows about everything in all my kingdom and in all the world beyond."

In came an even older man. But when he looked at

24

Bartholomew's hats, the Father of Nadd merely locked his fingers across his beard and said nothing.

"Then bring me the Father of the Father of Nadd!" ordered the King. "He knows about everything in all my kingdom, in all the world beyond, and in all other worlds that may happen to be."

Then came the oldest man of them all. But he just looked at Bartholomew and nibbled nervously at the end of his beard.

"Does this mean there is *no one* in my whole kingdom who can take off this boy's hat?" bellowed the King in a terrifying voice.

A small voice came up through the balcony window. "What's the matter, Uncle Derwin?" To Bartholomew, it sounded like the voice of a boy.

The King stepped out on the balcony and leaned over the marble railing. "There's a boy in here . . . just about your age," the King said. "He won't take off his hat."

Bartholomew tiptoed up behind the King and looked down. There stood a boy with a big lace collar—a very proud little boy with his nose in the air. It was the Grand Duke Wilfred, nephew of the King.

"You send him down here," said the Grand Duke Wilfred. "*I'll* fix him."

The King thought for a minute. He pushed back his crown and scratched his head. "Well . . . maybe you can. There's no harm trying."

"Take him to the Grand Duke Wilfred!" commanded the King. And two of the King's Own Guards led Bartholomew out of the Throne Room.

"Pooh!" said the Grand Duke Wilfred, looking at

25

Bartholomew's hat and laughing meanly. "*That* hat won't come off? You stand over there." He pointed to a corner where the wall curved out. "I need a little target practice with my bow and arrow."

When Bartholomew saw that the Grand Duke Wilfred had only a child's bow he didn't feel frightened. He spoke up proudly, "*I* can shoot with my father's big bow."

"My bow's plenty big enough for shooting hats—especially hats like yours," answered Wilfred. And he let fly an arrow. zzZ . . . it grazed Bartholomew's forehead and nipped off his hat. Away it blew, and over the parapet. But another hat appeared on his head. zzZ! . . . zzZ! . . . zzZ! . . . the arrows flew . . . till the Grand Duke's whole bagful of arrows was gone. And still a hat sat upon Bartholomew's head.

"It's not fair," cried the Grand Duke. "It's not fair!" He threw down his bow and stamped upon it.

"One hundred and fifty-four hats!" gulped Sir Alaric.

"These hats are driving me mad!" The King's voice rang out through all the palace. "Why waste time with a *child's* bow and arrow. Fetch me the mightiest bow and arrow in all my realm—fetch the Yeoman of the Bowmen!"

"Yeoman of the Bowmen," echoed all the lords.

A gigantic man strode out across the terrace. His bow was as big as the branch of a tree. The arrow was twice as long as Bartholomew and thicker than his wrist.

"Yeoman of the Bowmen," said the King, "shoot off this boy's hat . . . and make it *stay* off!"

Bartholomew was trembling so hard that he could

26

scarcely stand straight. The Yeoman bent back his mighty bow.

G—r—r—zibb! . . . Like a mad giant hornet the arrow tore through the air toward Bartholomew Cubbins.

G—r—r—zapp! . . . The sharp arrowhead bit through his hat and carried it off—on and on for a full half mile.

G—r—r—zopp! . . . It plunked to a stop in the heart of an oak tree. Yet there on Bartholomew's head sat another hat.

The face of the Yeoman of the Bowmen went white as the palace walls. "It's black magic!" he shrieked.

"Black magic, that's *just* what it is," sighed the King with relief. "I should have thought of that before. That makes things simple. Back to the Throne Room! Call my magicians!"

In the whole Throne Room there wasn't a sound as loud as a breath. But from the spiral stairs that led down from the southwest tower came the shuffling of slow, padded feet. The magicians were coming! Low and slow, they were chanting words that were strange . . .

> *"Dig a hole five furlongs deep,*
> *Down to where the night snakes creep,*
> *Mix and mold the mystic mud,*
> *Malber, Balber, Tidder, Tudd."*

In came seven black-gowned magicians, and beside each one stalked a lean black cat. They circled around Bartholomew Cubbins muttering deep and mysterious sounds.

"Stop this useless muttering," ordered the King. "I want a chant that will charm away this boy's hat."

27

The magicians huddled over Bartholomew and chanted.

"Winkibus
Tinkibus
Fotichee
Klay,
Hat on this demon's head,
Fly far away!
Howl, men, howl away,
Howl away, howl away,
Yowl, cats, yowl away,
Yowl away, yowl away!
Hat on this demon's head,
Seep away, creep away, leap away, gleap away,
    Never come back!"

"A mighty good chant," said the King, looking very pleased. "Are you sure it will work?"

All the magicians nodded together.

"But," said the King, looking puzzled, "there still *seems* to be a hat upon his head. How long will it take for the charm to work?"

"Be calm, oh, Sire, and have no fears,"

chanted the magicians.

"Our charm will work in ten short years."

"*Ten years!*" gasped the King. "Away, fools!" he shouted. "Out of my sight! I can't wait *ten years* to get rid of his hat. Oh, dear, what *can* I do? What CAN I do?"

"If I were King," whispered the Grand Duke Wilfred, "I'd chop off his head."

28

"A dreadful thought," said the King, biting his lip. "But I'm afraid I'll have to."

"Young man," he said to Bartholomew Cubbins, and he pointed to a small door at the end of the room, "march down those steps to the dungeon and tell the executioner to chop off your head."

Bartholomew's heart sank into his boots, but he did as the King commanded. "I *must* take off my hat," he said to himself as he started down the long black stairway. "This is my last chance." One hat after another he tore from his head ". . . 156 . . . 157 . . . 158 . . ." It grew colder and damper. ". . . 217 . . . 218 . . . 219 . . ." Down . . . down . . . down. ". . . 231 . . . 232 . . . 233 . . ." It seemed to Bartholomew he must be in the very heart of the mountain.

"Who's there?" said a voice from the blackness.

Bartholomew turned a corner and stepped into the dungeon.

The executioner was whistling and swinging his axe idly, because at the moment he had nothing to do. In spite of his business, he really seemed to be a very pleasant man.

"The King says you must chop off my head," said Bartholomew.

"Oh, I'd hate to," said the executioner, looking at him with a friendly smile. "You seem like such a nice boy."

"Well . . . the King says you have to," said Bartholomew, "so please get it over with."

"All right," sighed the executioner, "but first you've got to take off your hat."

"Why?" asked Bartholomew.

"I don't know," said the executioner, "but it's one of

the rules. I can't execute anyone with his hat on."

"All right," said Bartholomew, "you take it off for me."

The executioner leaned across the chopping block and flipped off Bartholomew's hat.

"What's this?" he gasped, blinking through the holes in his mask, as another hat sat on Bartholomew's head. He flipped this one off . . . then another and another.

"Fiddlesticks!" grunted the executioner, throwing his axe on the floor. "I can't execute you at all." And he shook hands with Bartholomew and sent him back upstairs to the King.

The King had been taking a nap on the throne. "What are you doing back here?" he said to Bartholomew, angry at being awakened.

"I'm sorry, Your Majesty," explained Bartholomew. "My head can't come off with my hat on. . . . It's against the rules."

"So it can't," said the King, leaning back wearily. "Now how many hats does that make altogether?"

"The executioner knocked off 13 . . . and I left 178 more on the dungeon steps," answered Bartholomew.

"Three hundred and forty-six hats," mumbled Sir Alaric from behind his scroll.

"Uncle Derwin," yawned the Grand Duke Wilfred, "I suppose I'll have to do away with him. Send him up to the highest turret and I, in person, will push him off."

"Wilfred! I'm surprised at you," said the King. "But I guess it's a good idea."

So the King and the Grand Duke led Bartholomew Cubbins toward the highest turret.

Up and up and up the turret stairs he climbed behind them.

"This is my *last*—my *very last* chance," thought Bartholomew. He snatched off his hat. "Three hundred and forty-seven!" He snatched off another. He pulled and he tore and he flung them behind him. ". . . 398 . . . 399 . . ." His arms ached from pulling off hats. But still the hats came. Bartholomew climbed on.

". . . 448 . . . 449 . . . 450 . . ." counted Sir Alaric, puffing up the stairs behind him.

Suddenly Sir Alaric stopped. He looked. He took off his triangular spectacles and wiped them on his sleeve. And then he looked again. *The hats began to change!* Hat 451 had, not one, but *two* feathers! Hat 452 had three . . . and 453 also had three *and a little red jewel!* Each new hat was fancier than the hat just before.

"Your Majesty! Your Majesty!" cried out Sir Alaric.

But the King and the Grand Duke were 'way up where they couldn't hear. They had already reached the top of the highest turret. Bartholomew was following just behind.

"Step right out here and get out on that wall," snapped the Grand Duke Wilfred. "I can't wait to push you off."

But when Bartholomew stepped up on the wall they gasped in amazement. He was wearing the most beautiful hat that had ever been seen in the Kingdom of Didd. It had a ruby larger than any the King himself had ever owned. It had ostrich plumes, and cockatoo plumes, and mockingbird plumes, and paradise plumes. Beside *such* a hat even the King's Crown seemed like nothing.

The Grand Duke Wilfred took a quick step forward. Bartholomew thought his end had come at last.

"Wait!" shouted the King. He could not take his eyes off the magnificent hat.

"I *won't* wait," the Grand Duke talked back to the King. "I'm going to push him off now! That new big hat makes me madder than ever." And he flung out his arms to push Bartholomew off.

But the King was quicker than Wilfred. He grabbed him by the back of his fine lace collar. "This is to teach you," His Majesty said sternly, "that Grand Dukes *never* talk back to their King." And he turned the Grand Duke Wilfred over his knee and spanked him soundly, right on the seat of his royal silk pants.

"And now," smiled the King, lifting Bartholomew down from the wall, "it would be nice if you'd sell me that wonderful hat!"

"... 498 ... 499 ..." broke in the tired voice of Sir Alaric, who had just arrived at the top of the steps, "and *that* ..." he pointed to the hat on Bartholomew's head, "makes exactly 500!"

"*Five Hundred!*" exclaimed the King. "Will you sell it for 500 pieces of gold?"

"Anything you say, Sire," answered Bartholomew. "You see ... I've never sold one before."

The King's hands trembled with joy as he reached for the hat.

Slowly, slowly, Bartholomew felt the weight of the great hat lifting from his head. He held his breath. . . . Then suddenly he felt the cool evening breezes blow through his hair. His face broke into a happy smile. The head of Bartholomew Cubbins was bare!

"Look, Your Majesty! *Look!*" he shouted to the King.

"No! *You* look at *me*," answered the King. And he put the great hat on right over his crown.

Arm in arm, the King and Bartholomew went down to the counting room to count out the gold. Then the King sent Bartholomew home to his parents ... no basket on his arm, no hat on his head, but with five hundred pieces of gold in a bag.

And the King commanded that the hat he had bought, and all the other hats, too, be kept forever in a great crystal case by the side of his throne.

But neither Bartholomew Cubbins, nor King Derwin himself, nor anyone else in the Kingdom of Didd could ever explain how the strange thing had happened. They only could say it just "happened to happen" and was not very likely to happen again.

Tom and Elizabeth Orton Jones

MINNIE THE MERMAID

ILLUSTRATED BY *Elizabeth Orton Jones*

ICK had had a busy morning. But now he was not busy at all. He was just standing, with his toes in the sand, looking out over the water to Sugar Lump Point.

It was a pretty long swim away. But Mick could see something sparkling on Sugar Lump Beach.

So he said, to no one, "Well, I think I'll just swim over there and see what it is. Yes, that's a very good idea."

So he started off.

When he was about halfway there, he stopped, all of a sudden, and said, "Say! Who's tickling me?" But then he felt a little foolish and swam right on.

Pretty soon he stopped again and said, "Say! Who *is* tickling me?" Then he felt still more foolish and swam on again. Then he began to wonder just how deep it was. So he held his nose and went straight down. It was very deep!

But Mick quickly forgot all about that, because—

whom do you suppose he saw right there, face to face with him? It was MINNIE THE MERMAID! Mick opened his mouth at once to say, "My goodness!" But as soon as he opened it, a great deal of water got in. Of course. So he had to go spluttering to the surface, as fast as he could.

Then he said, to no one, "Pooh! I must have been imagining!"

But even as he said it, somebody's head appeared, quite near to his own, and it said, "Hello!"

"My goodness!" said Mick, at last.

"Who are you?" said the head. It wore hair ribbons.

"I'm Mick," said Mick. "Who are you?"

"Minnie," said Minnie.

"Oh," said Mick. And then, "How do you do?"

"I do very well," said Minnie. "You don't do badly either. Would you like to have a little race to the point?"

"Yes!" said Mick.

So they had a race to Sugar Lump Point—and Minnie swam circles around Mick all the way! Mick was glad to see Sugar Lump Beach because, of course, he was still wondering what could have been sparkling there.

"Let's sit on the beach!" he said, rather out of breath.

"Let's!" said Minnie, not out of breath at all. So they did.

Mick had noticed, when he first saw Minnie, that she was not quite like other people. That is, she did not have any legs. But she did have a long—very like a fish's—tail!

"I—I see you are a Mermaid," said Mick, as politely as possible.

"Of course," said Minnie. "Why shouldn't I be?"

"It must be fun!" said Mick, who had only legs.

"It *is* fun!" said Minnie. She flipped her tail. "What would you like to play?"

Mick hadn't any idea.

"Shall it be Who's-Got-The-Barnacle?" asked Minnie.

"I'm afraid I don't know that game," said Mick.

Then Minnie said, "How about Follow-The-Lobster?"

"Whoever heard of following a lobster!" laughed Mick.

"Well!" said Minnie. "Have you ever played Drop-The-Halibut?"

"No, not the halibut!" said Mick.

"Well?" asked Minnie.

Then Mick said, in his most polite manner, "I'd like to play whatever *you* feel like playing."

So Minnie said, "I feel like playing a trick!"

"Oh!" said Mick, very much surprised.

And while he was wondering if the trick was going

to be on *him*, Minnie pulled something out from behind
a Sugar Lump rock and held it up.

"Oh! Oh!" cried Mick. "Is it yours?"

"It's my great-great-great-great-grandmother's," said
Minnie, proudly, "but I'm her namesake!"

It was—a great-great-great-great big golden comb!
Mick had never seen any comb like it. And there was a
diamond sparkling in the handle.

"So *that's* what I saw sparkling away over here!" said
Mick. "What do you use it for?"

"For playing tricks," said Minnie, "like this one!"

"This one? . . . Oh, yes . . . yes, of course," said Mick.
And then, "Is—is it a trick on me?"

Minnie just giggled.

Mick knew that it wasn't everybody could play a
trick on him. But he began to think that it might be a
very good idea to change the subject. So he did.

"What would happen if you played a tune on that
big golden comb?" he said.

"You'd probably turn right into a Merboy!" said
Minnie. "Then you could come and live with us!"

38

"Where do you live?" asked Mick, very quickly.

"Over there," said Minnie the Mermaid, pointing straight out to sea. "In a ship."

"I don't see any ship," said Mick, squinting hard.

"Of course you don't," said Minnie. "It's a sunken ship!"

"Oh!" said Mick, very much excited. "Is it upside down?"

"Well, yes! Very!"

"Carpets on the ceiling and lights on the floor?"

"Yes."

"Even the bunks upside down?"

"Of course."

"Then how do you sleep?"

"Oh, I just lie down and float up against the springs," said Minnie. "It's very comfortable!"

"I don't believe it," said Mick. "What's the name of the ship?"

"It's the LIZZIE CODFISH out of Boston," said Minnie.

"Really?" said Mick, very much surprised. "How

many of you mermaids live there?"

"Oh, just our family," said Minnie. "Let's see now . . ."

She counted on all her fingers, then she counted on Mick's. Then she counted on all of Mick's toes, and Mick said, "Say! That tickles!"

"I think we're about sixty-six," said Minnie, finally. "SIXTY–SIX?"

"Yes. There's my mother and my thirty-nine sisters and my eleven half-sisters and my old cousin fifteen-times-removed and my ten great aunts and my great-great-grandmother and my great-great-great-grand-mother and my great-great-great-great-grandmother and m—"

"Oh, my *Good*ness!" said Mick.

Minnie began to giggle again. She flashed the diamond in the big golden comb.

"I think I'll just swim over and see *Lizzie Codfish!*" said Mick, thinking that this was a good time to do so, before any trick might begin.

So he slid into the water and started off.

Minnie slid in, too.

After a while, Mick looked around and said, "Minnie!"
But Minnie was nowhere in sight!

After another while, he called "MINNIE!" very loudly.

Then he felt very foolish, for there was Minnie, right beside him, holding up the great-great-great-great big golden comb! Then Minnie began to play a tune on the comb. The tune had a good many trills up along the handle.

Mick gave a splash and swam round in a circle.

"Oh, Minnie!" he said. It was *such* a silly tune!
But Minnie wouldn't stop playing.

Mick swam around in another circle. The tune made him.

It made him swim in a fast circle.

It made him swim in a furious circle.

It even made him swim—in a circle *underneath*—without holding his nose!

Mick had never swum like this before!

"Oh, my Goodness!" he said, as he swam. "Perhaps I really am turning into a Merboy!"

He began to wonder if he had a *flippery tail!*

He wondered so hard that, before he knew it, he was turning a backwards somersault.

Well! When a backwards somersault is over, aren't you always just a bit surprised to find yourself where you are?

Mick was *very much* surprised, because—where do you suppose he was when *his* somersault was over?

He was just standing, with his toes in the sand, looking out over the water to Sugar Lump Point!

It *does* look pretty far, doesn't it?

Something was still sparkling away on Sugar Lump Beach.

"Well!" thought Mick. "It was all a trick! It was a great-great-great-great big trick!"

He chuckled to himself. And then he stopped.

"But it isn't everybody can play a trick on *me!*" said Mick, proudly, to no one.

No one?

"Hello, Mick!" said a deep voice, just behind him.

Mick gave a surprised little jump.

"Aren't you coming swimming with me?" said Mick's father, laughing.

"Why . . ." said Mick, "why . . . I already . . . well, you see, I . . . why, yes!"

Then he quickly pointed out over the water. "Look!"

42

he said. "There's something sparkling away on Sugar Lump Beach!"

Mick's father squinted hard. While he was squinting, Mick ran round him in a great-great-great-great big circle, singing the silliest, trilliest, chilliest tune that ever his father had heard.

And then—Mick splashed in!

THOUGHTS ABOUT GRASSHOPPERS

Florence Page Jaques

Grasshoppers certainly must have fun,
They hop so high in the summer sun.
They make queer noises in the grass
And fly on your hat whenever you pass.

But grasshoppers have such solemn faces.
Sad and thoughtful they sit in places.
If I were a grasshopper, how I'd shout
And sing and laugh as I hopped about.

A. A. *Milne*

THE KING'S BREAKFAST

ILLUSTRATED BY *Ernest H. Shepard*

The King asked
The Queen, and
The Queen asked
The Dairymaid:
"Could we have some butter for
The Royal slice of bread?"

The Queen asked
The Dairymaid,
The Dairymaid
Said, "Certainly,

Taken from *When We Were Very Young*, by A. A. Milne, illustrations by Ernest H. Shepard, published and copyright, 1924, by E. P. Dutton & Co., Inc., New York.

I'll go and tell
The cow
Now before she goes to bed."

The Dairymaid
She curtsied,
And went and told
The Alderney:
"Don't forget the butter for
The Royal slice of bread."

The Alderney said sleepily:
"You'd better tell His Majesty
That many people nowadays
Like marmalade
Instead."

The Dairymaid
Said, "Fancy!"
And went to
Her Majesty.
She curtsied to the Queen, and
She turned a little red:
"Excuse me,
Your Majesty,
For taking of
The liberty,
But marmalade is tasty, if
It's very
Thickly
Spread."

The Queen said
"Oh!"
And went to
His Majesty:
"Talking of the butter for
The Royal slice of bread,
Many people
Think that
Marmalade
Is nicer.
Would you like to try a little
Marmalade
Instead?"

The King said,
"Bother!"
And then he said,
"Oh, deary me!"
The King sobbed,
"Oh, deary me!"
And went back to bed.
"Nobody,"
He whimpered,
"Could call me
A fussy man:
I *only* want
A little bit
Of butter for
My bread!"

The Queen said,
"There, there!"

And went to
The Dairymaid.
The Dairymaid
Said, "There, there!"
And went to the shed.
The cow said,
"There, there!
I didn't really
Mean it;
Here's milk for
	his porringer
And butter for
	his bread."
The Queen took
The butter
And brought it to
His Majesty;

The King said,
"Butter, eh?"
And bounced out of bed.
"Nobody," he said
As he kissed her
Tenderly,
"Nobody," he said,
As he slid down
The banisters,
"Nobody,
My darling,
Could call me
A fussy man—BUT
I do like a little bit of
butter to my bread!"

Marjorie Flack

ANGUS
AND THE DUCKS

ILLUSTRATED BY *Ruth van Tellingen*

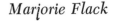

ONCE there was a very young little dog whose name was Angus, because his mother and his father came from Scotland.

Although the rest of Angus was quite small, his head was very large and so were his feet.

Angus was curious about many places and many things:

He was curious about what lived under the sofa and in dark corners and who was the little dog in the mirror.

He was curious about things-which-came-apart and those things-which-don't-come-apart, such as slippers and gentlemen's suspenders and things like that.

Angus was also curious about things-outdoors, but he could not find out much about them because of a leash.

The leash was fastened at one end to the collar around his neck and at the other end to somebody else.

But Angus was most curious of all about a noise which came from the other side of the large green hedge at the end of the garden. The noise usually

49

sounded like this: Quack! Quack! Quackety! Quack!!
But sometimes it sounded like this: Quackety! Quackety! Quackety! Quack!!

One day the door between outdoors and indoors was
left open by mistake; and out went Angus without the
leash or somebody else.

Down the little path he ran until he came to the
large green hedge at the end of the garden.

He tried to go around it but it was much too long. He
tried to go over it but it was much too high. So Angus
went under the large green hedge and came out on the
other side. There, directly in front of him were two
white ducks. They were marching forward, one-foot-
up and one-foot-down.

Quack! Quack! Quackety! Quack!!

Angus said:

Woo-oo-oof!!!

Away went the ducks all of a flutter.

Quackety! Quackety!

Quackety! Quackety! Quackety!!!

Angus followed after.

Soon the ducks stopped by a stone watering trough
under a mulberry tree.

Angus stopped, too. Each duck dipped a yellow bill
in the clear cool water. Angus watched. Each duck
took a long drink of the cool clear water. Still Angus
watched. Each duck took another long drink of cool
clear water.

Then Angus said:

Woo-oo-oof!!!

Away the ducks scuttled and Angus lapped the cool
clear water.

van Tellingen

Birds sang in the mulberry tree.

The sun made patterns through the leaves over the grass.

The ducks talked together:

Quack! Quack! Quack!

Then:

Hiss-s-s-s-s-s!!! Hiss-s-s-s-s-s!!!

The first duck nipped Angus' tail!

Hiss-s-s-s-s-s!!! Hiss-s-s-s-s-s!!!

The second duck flapped his wings!

Angus scrambled under the large green hedge, scurried up the little path, scampered into the house and crawled under the sofa.

For exactly *three* minutes by the clock, Angus was *not* curious about anything at all.

THE OLD GOOSE

Helen Wing

I'll tell you a story
   About an old goose
Who waddled so much
   All her feathers came loose.

"My gracious," she cried,
   As she looked all around,
"It's only July, and there's
   Snow on the ground!"

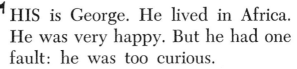

H. A. Rey

CURIOUS GEORGE

ILLUSTRATED BY THE AUTHOR

THIS is George. He lived in Africa. He was very happy. But he had one fault: he was too curious.

One day George saw a man. He had on a large yellow straw hat. The man saw George too.

"What a nice little monkey," he thought. "I would like to take him home with me."

He put his hat on the ground and, of course, George was curious. He came down from the tree to look at the large yellow hat.

The hat had been on the man's head. George thought it would be nice to have it on his own head. He picked it up and put it on. The hat covered George's head. He couldn't see. The man picked him up quickly and popped him into a bag. George was caught.

The man with the big yellow hat put George into a little boat, and a sailor rowed them both across the water to a big ship. George was sad, but he was still a little curious.

On the big ship, things began to happen. The man took off the bag. George sat on a little stool, and the man said, "George, I am going to take you to a big Zoo in a big city. You will like it there. Now run along and play, but don't get into trouble."

George promised to be good. But it is easy for little monkeys to forget.

On the deck he found some sea gulls. He wondered how they could fly. He was very curious. Finally he HAD to try. It looked easy. But—oh, what happened! First this—

and then this!

"WHERE IS GEORGE?"

The sailors looked and looked. At last they saw him struggling in the water and almost all tired out.

"Man overboard!" the sailors cried as they threw him a lifebelt. George caught it and held on. At last he was safe on board.

After that George was more careful to be a good monkey, until, at last, the long trip was over.

George said good-bye to the kind sailors, and he and the man with the yellow hat walked off the ship on to the shore and on into the city to the man's house.

After a good meal and a good pipe George felt very tired. He crawled into bed and fell asleep at once.

The next morning the man telephoned the Zoo. George watched him. He was fascinated. Then the man went away.

George was curious. He wanted to telephone, too. One, two, three, four, five, six, seven. What fun!

DING–A–LING–A–LING!

GEORGE HAD TELEPHONED THE FIRE STATION!

The firemen rushed to the telephone. "Hello! Hello!" they said. But there was no answer.

Then they looked for the signal on the big map that showed where the telephone call had come from. They didn't know it was GEORGE. They thought it was a real fire.

HURRY! HURRY! HURRY!

The firemen jumped on to the fire engines and on to the hook-and-ladders. Ding-dong-ding-dong. Everyone out of the way! Hurry! Hurry! Hurry!

The firemen rushed into the house. They opened the door.

NO FIRE! ONLY a naughty little monkey.

"Oh, catch him, catch him," they cried.

George tried to run away. He almost did, but he got caught in the telephone wire, and—a thin fireman caught one arm, and a fat fireman caught the other.

"You fooled the fire department," they said. "We will have to shut you up where you can't do any more harm."

They took him away and shut him in a prison. George wanted to get out. He climbed up to the window to try the bars. Just then the watchman came in. He got on the wooden bed to catch George. But he was too big and heavy. The bed tipped up, the watchman fell over, and, quick as lightning, George ran out through the open door.

He hurried through the building and out on to the roof. And then he was lucky to be a monkey: out he walked on to the telephone wires. Quickly and quietly over the guard's head, George walked away. He was free!

Down in the street outside the prison wall, stood a balloon man. A little girl bought a balloon for her brother. George watched. He was curious again. He felt he MUST have a bright red balloon. He reached over and tried to help himself, but—instead of one balloon, the whole bunch broke loose. In an instant the wind whisked them all away and, with them, went George, holding tight with both hands.

Up, up he sailed, higher and higher. The houses looked like toy houses and the people like dolls. George was frightened. He held on very tight.

At first the wind blew in great gusts. Then it quieted. Finally it stopped blowing altogether. George was very tired. Down, down he went—bump, on to the top of a traffic light. Everyone was surprised. The traffic got all mixed up. George didn't know what to do, and then he heard someone call, "GEORGE!"

He looked down and saw his friend, the man with the big yellow hat! George was very happy. The man was happy too. George slid down the post, and the man with the big yellow hat put him under his arm. Then he paid the balloon man for all the balloons. And then George and the man climbed into the car and at last, away they went to the ZOO!

What a nice place for George to live!

Johanna de Witt

THE LITTLEST REINDEER

ILLUSTRATED BY *Nora Unwin*

T HE littlest reindeer was unhappy. Flowers were blooming through the arctic snow. Birds were singing. All the other reindeer were prancing up and down, waving their antlers and making merry. Only the littlest reindeer stood alone and felt sad. He was ashamed to prance with the others because he had no antlers.

The biggest reindeer had antlers six feet high and six feet wide. The next biggest reindeer had antlers five feet high and five feet wide. Even the next to the littlest reindeer had antlers that were half a foot high and half a foot wide. Only the littlest reindeer had none at all. He stood alone and was ashamed.

The biggest reindeer called to him, "Come join the dance, little one. It is our last dance near the arctic circle this year."

But the littlest reindeer shook his head and stayed where he was.

The next day the biggest reindeer called all the reindeer to him. "Come with me," he said in a loud voice. "Winter is coming. Today we go south to the land of

58

the woods so we may eat when the snow is deep. Come!" he said and tossed his antlers.

All the reindeer lined up in single file behind the biggest reindeer and followed him. All but the littlest reindeer. He hid behind a large rock and cried and cried as he watched the others march away.

The air grew colder and the flowers stopped blooming. A snowbird lighted on a rock by the littlest reindeer and cocked his head in wonder.

"What's the matter here?" asked the snowbird. "Why didn't you go with the others, little reindeer?"

"I was ashamed to go because I have no antlers," cried the littlest reindeer.

"What nonsense!" said the snowbird. "You will have antlers in due time if you wait patiently."

"Not I," said the littlest reindeer. "I shall never have antlers."

"Go join the others and wait for spring," said the snowbird. "See then if you have antlers."

The littlest reindeer said nothing. The snowbird snapped his bill twice in disgust and shrugged. "All right, then," he said, and flew away.

Snow began to fall. First slowly and then faster and faster. But the littlest reindeer did not notice. Neither did he notice a great musk ox coming slowly from the north. But the musk ox saw the littlest reindeer and stopped beside him.

"What's the matter here?" rumbled the musk ox in a large voice. "Why didn't you go with the others, little reindeer?"

"I was ashamed to go because I have no antlers," cried the littlest reindeer.

"What nonsense!" roared the musk ox.

"You can say nonsense," said the littlest reindeer. "You *have* horns. You can walk with your kind and not be ashamed." The littlest reindeer looked up through his tears at the musk ox's horns curving down in two great curves.

"You will have antlers in due time if you wait patiently," said the musk ox. "Go join the others and wait for spring."

"Not I," said the littlest reindeer. "I shall never have antlers."

The musk ox snorted twice in disgust and walked off through the snow.

It grew colder and colder. The littlest reindeer cried and cried. All of a sudden one of his tears froze into a shining bead of ice. Very soon a long glittering chain of frozen tears hung from the littlest reindeer's eyes. He could cry no more.

"I must cry because I have no antlers," said the littlest reindeer. He snapped off his icicle tears and ran across the snow. "Perhaps if I go toward the south my tears will not freeze," he said. So he tried to go the same way the other reindeer had gone.

Nighttime came, and the littlest reindeer wondered if he would ever reach the south. Just then he took one step and there was no snow. His little hooves struck something hard and slippery.

"Am I south now?" he wondered. "I shall see if I can cry." But as soon as he squeezed out one tear it froze in the corner of his eye. He stamped his foot in anger, and at that moment the northern lights filled the sky with a thousand ribbons of light. The littlest rein-

deer saw that he was on a ledge of ice at the edge of the sea. Right beside him a sleepy walrus lifted his head.

"What's the matter here?" barked the walrus. "Why do you stamp your foot and wake me up?"

"I am angry because I cannot cry," said the littlest reindeer.

"And why must you cry?" asked the walrus.

"Because I have no antlers," said the littlest reindeer.

"What nonsense!" said the walrus.

"You can say nonsense," said the littlest reindeer. "You have tusks. You can swim with your kind and not be afraid." The littlest reindeer could see the walrus's great white tusks shining in the gleam of the northern lights.

"Now you think I have always had tusks?" asked the walrus. "No. I had to wait for them to grow. You must wait for antlers to grow. When it is time for you to have them, you will have them."

"Not I," said the littlest reindeer. "I shall never have antlers."

At that moment a great white shape moved out from behind a hill of ice. It was a polar bear, and his eyes shone red in the northern lights.

The littlest reindeer did not see him. He was saying to the walrus, "Just tell me which way is south so I can go there and cry. I must cry because I have no antlers."

The walrus snorted twice in disgust, turned from the ledge of ice, and splashed into the sea.

Then the littlest reindeer saw the polar bear.

"I like little reindeer that have no antlers," said the polar bear. "They are very tender eating indeed."

The littlest reindeer was so frightened that for a minute he could not move. The polar bear came nearer and nearer, padding on his great white paws.

The littlest reindeer picked up his hooves and ran. The polar bear ran after him.

"Don't be ashamed of not having antlers," called the polar bear. "I don't mind a bit."

Suddenly the northern lights went out. The ribbons of light were gone from the sky and the littlest reindeer was running in the dark.

"Ho, little reindeer!" called the polar bear. "Don't run off into the dark so I can't find you."

The littlest reindeer did not listen to the polar bear. He ran on and on into the dark. He ran until he could no longer hear the polar bear calling to him. He ran until the dark was gone and the sun peeked over the horizon.

The littlest reindeer ran faster. He did not know if he was running north or south. He knew only that he must run faster than the polar bear, who was getting closer and closer.

Then the littlest reindeer knew that he had been running south all night. He was in the land of the woods. There was no snow here. Instead the ground was covered with thick brown moss.

"Now I can cry," said the littlest reindeer. And so he did.

"What's the matter here?" asked a moose. "Why are you not with the other reindeer?"

"I am ashamed because I have no antlers," said the littlest reindeer.

"What nonsense!" said the moose.

"You have antlers," said the littlest reindeer. "You can run with your kind and not be ashamed."

"So you think I have always had antlers?" asked the moose. "No. I had to wait for them to grow. You must wait for them to grow. When it is time for you to have them, you will have them."

"Not I," said the littlest reindeer. "I shall never have antlers."

The moose snorted in disgust and went off through the woods. The littlest reindeer was all alone.

He looked around the quiet woods. He looked at the ground that was covered with thick brown moss. "Here I can rest and eat and cry," he said. And so he did, day after day, for a long time.

One morning his head began to itch. He rubbed his head against the rough bark of a tree and thought no more about it. Every day his head itched and, oddly enough, it itched right where his antlers should have been.

Then one day the littlest reindeer sniffed the air and knew that something was different. The sun crept up and up the sky until it poured sunshine down through the trees. Leaves popped out and birds began to sing. The littlest reindeer thought about the cool stretches of snow in the north. He thought of the biggest reindeer with his antlers six feet high and six feet wide.

Suddenly there was a thundering sound in the distance. It came closer and closer. The littlest reindeer peeked out from behind a tree and at that moment the whole herd of reindeer rushed past him, heading north. The biggest reindeer was leading, and he was waving his antlers. The others were pounding after him.

When they were out of sight the littlest reindeer crept out from behind the tree.

"Spring!" he said. "All the other reindeer are going north to dance up and down the arctic snow. All but me."

"Why not you?" asked a voice from somewhere.

The littlest reindeer was surprised. "Who's there?" he asked.

"It is I, the snowbird," said the voice.

"Where are you?" asked the littlest reindeer. The snowbird's voice seemed to come from above, but when the littlest reindeer looked up he could not see him.

"Look down," said the snowbird. "Look down into that pool of water beside you and see what you see."

The littlest reindeer went nearer to the pool and looked into the clear water. Then he gulped and looked again.

He saw the snowbird perched on the top of his own, his very own, foot-long antlers.

"Antlers!" shouted the littlest reindeer. "I have antlers!"

"Very fine antlers, too," said the snowbird.

"It was the antlers growing that made my head itch," said the littlest reindeer.

"Of course," said the snowbird. "But you wouldn't believe that sometimes you have to wait for something worth having." The snowbird snapped his bill shut and flew to a tree.

"Think of the tears you have wasted!" shouted the snowbird.

But the littlest reindeer did not hear him. He was running as fast as he could to join the other reindeer in the first dance of the year across the arctic snow.

Ruth Dixon

AUGUSTA GOOSE

ILLUSTRATED BY *Bianca*

ONCE there was an old white goose. Her name was Augusta. One day she woke up feeling very, very grumpy.

For breakfast that morning she wanted all the fattest, fuzziest caterpillars for herself. And bluebottles, too.

When Little Chick wanted one, Augusta said, "Honk!" very loudly, and flapped her wings.

Little Chick cried, "Peep! Peep! Peep!" and scuttled back to his Mother Hen.

Little Pig trotted over to the Big Pond. Here Augusta was taking a long, cool drink and looking at her beautiful white feathers.

"Honk!" said Augusta. "Go away!" And she stretched forth her long neck and snapped at his curly tail.

Little Pig squealed, "Eeek! Eeek! Eeek!" and scampered back to Mother Pig. Augusta had hurt his feelings —and his tail, too.

Mother Hen, Daddy Rooster, Uncle Percival Pig and the Duck Quintuplets came hurrying over.

Augusta was bowing and smiling at her other self in the water.

"Cut - cut ca - *da* - cut! Who do you think you are, you grumpy old goose?" clucked Mother Hen. "A king? A movie star?"

Augusta gave Mother Hen and her friends one look but didn't say a word. She just stuck out her tongue at them.

So Mother Hen and Daddy Rooster called Rover, the dog. And they all chased Augusta Goose out of the barnyard.

"We don't want grumpy creatures here," barked Rover.

Augusta waddled proudly down the dusty road. She didn't look back once.

Pretty soon she came to Bunny Long Ears hopping around a bush.

"Honk!" said Augusta. She flapped her wings and stretched her neck out at him.

She still felt grumpy and she wanted to keep in practice.

Bunny Long Ears hopped away into a forest very, very fast. His long ears quivered and so did his whiskers.

Augusta waddled into the forest, too.

"Perhaps I'll find some nice bugs for lunch here," she said.

But she couldn't catch one.

Pretty soon she came to a bush with red berries on it.

"I'll try these," she said greedily.

But they were sour, and she made a face.

A chipmunk and a squirrel and a porcupine went by. No one spoke to the old white goose.

Augusta felt lonely and ashamed.

"I guess I was grumpy—a little," she said to herself.

It began to thunder. Then the rain came down *hard*. Augusta hid beneath a tree. She felt wet in every feather. And she wanted to go back to the barnyard.

"I guess I was grumpy—quite a bit," she said to herself.

"Hooo! Hoooooo!" cried an owl up in a tree.

Augusta jumped.

A bat fluttered suddenly around her head.

Augusta jumped again.

Then she turned around and stumbled out of the

woods, looking behind her all the way.

"I *know* I was grumpy—awfully grumpy!" said Augusta Goose.

Mother Hen and her chickens, Daddy Rooster, Uncle Percival Pig and Little Pig, the Duck Quintuplets, and Rover, the dog, all stared very hard at Augusta as she came running into the barnyard.

Augusta hung her head. "I'm sorry I was grumpy," she said. "I'm happy now. Can't we be friends again?"

So then they were.

TEN LITTLE PUSSYCATS

Elizabeth Jones

Ten little pussycats marching in a line,
One stopped to chase a mouse and then there were
    nine.
Nine little pussycats fishing with their bait,
A big fish frightened one and then there were eight.
Eight little pussycats sat up till eleven,
One couldn't keep awake and then there were seven.
Seven little pussycats trying out new tricks,
One bumped his little nose and then there were six.
Six little pussycats going for a dive,
One lost his bathing suit and then there were five.
Five little pussycats sliding on the floor,
One got lost beneath the rug and then there were four.
Four little pussycats drinking catnip tea,
One drank a sip too much and then there were three.
Three little pussycats trying something new,
One blew a puff too many and then there were two.
Two little pussycats purring while they played,
"Squirt" went the garden hose, and only one stayed.
One little pussycat, his lonely heart was sore,
Went to seek some other friends, so there would be
    more.

Helen and Alf Evers

THIS LITTLE PIG

ILLUSTRATED BY *Helen Evers*

THIS little pig had a curly tail
But he wished that it were straight!
All his little sisters had curly tails—
All his little brothers had curly tails, too.
His father and mother liked his curly tail.
The farmer's little girl liked his curly tail.
The cow liked it.
The rooster, the hen, and the cat liked it.
But the little pig hated his curly tail,
So he went to town to get it straightened.
The blacksmith couldn't help him.
The carpenter couldn't help him.
And the doctor couldn't either.
When he asked a sailor the sailor laughed at him.
Then he asked a tailor and he laughed too.

72

He asked a policeman who sent him to the mayor.
The mayor couldn't help—the judge couldn't either.
The aldermen couldn't—nobody could!
So the poor little pig went home.
Then his whole family;
the cow, the horse, and
all the other animals; the
carpenter, the sailor, the
mayor, the judge, and
everybody else tied a
rope to his tail and—

pulled and pulled
and pulled *and pulled*
and pulled his tail *straight!*
His mother and father didn't like it.
Nobody liked it—
Everybody hated it.
But the little pig
just *loved* it!

GOOSIE GRAY

Leroy F. Jackson

What a busy, busy mother
Is Missus Goosie Gray,
With all her little goslings
To look after every day!
She gets them up at sunrise
And tucks them in at night
And tries her best to train them so
That they will grow up right.
She has to teach them how to squawk
And how to catch a frog
And how to hit the water
When they're diving off a log.
She shows them how to peck the grass
And not stand pigeon-toed,
And how they can look dignified
When walking down the road.
And every night at suppertime
She stands them in a row
And feeds them fuzzy dandelions
To make their feathers grow.

74

Lucy Fitch Perkins

KIT AND KAT GO FISHING

ILLUSTRATED BY THE AUTHOR

ONE summer morning, very early, Vrouw Vedder opened the door of her little Dutch kitchen and stepped out.

She looked across the road which ran by the house, across the canal on the other side, across the level green fields that lay beyond, clear to the blue rim of the world, where the sky touches the earth. The sky was very blue; and the great, round, shining face of the sun was just peering over the tops of the trees as she looked out.

Vrouw Vedder listened. The roosters in the barnyard were crowing, the ducks in the canal were quacking, and all the little birds in the fields were singing for joy. Vrouw Vedder hummed a slow little tune of her own as she went back into her kitchen.

Kit and Kat were still asleep in their little cupboard bed. She gave them each a kiss. The Twins opened their eyes and sat up.

"O Kit and Kat," said Vrouw Vedder, "the sun is up, the birds are all awake and singing, and Grandfather is going fishing today. If you will hurry, you may go with him! He is coming at six o'clock; so pop out of bed and get dressed. I will put some lunch for you in the yellow basket, and you may dig worms for bait in the garden. Only be sure not to step on the young cabbages that Father planted."

Kit and Kat bounced out of bed in a minute. Their mother helped them put on their clothes and new wooden shoes. Then she gave them each a bowl of bread and milk for their breakfast. They ate it sitting on the kitchen doorstep.

They did just as their mother said, and did not step on the young cabbages. They sat on them, instead. But that was an accident.

Kit dug the worms, and Kat put them into a basket with some earth in it to make them feel at home.

When Grandfather came, he brought a large fishing-rod for himself and two little ones for the Twins. There was a little hook on the end of each line.

Vrouw Vedder kissed Kit and Kat good-bye.

"Mind Grandfather, and don't fall into the water," she said.

Grandfather and the Twins started off together down the long road beside the canal.

The house where the Twins lived was right beside the canal. Their father was a gardener, and his beautiful rows of cabbages and beets and onions stretched in long lines across the level fields by the roadside.

Grandfather lived in a large town, a little way beyond the farm where the Twins lived. He did not often have a holiday, because he carried milk to the doors of the people in the town, every morning early. Sometime I will tell you how he did it; but I must not tell you now, because if I do, I can't tell you about their going fishing.

This morning, Grandfather carried his rod and the lunch-basket. Kit and Kat carried the basket of worms between them, and their rods over their shoulders, and they were all three very happy.

They walked along ever so far, beside the canal. Then they turned to the left and walked along a path that ran from the canal across the green fields to what looked like a hill.

But it wasn't a hill at all, really, because there aren't any hills in Holland. It was a long, long wall of earth, very high—oh, as high as a house, or even higher! And it had sloping sides.

There is such a wall of earth all around the country of Holland, where the Twins live. There has to be a wall, because the sea is higher than the land. If there were no walls to shut out the sea, the whole country would be covered with water; and if that were so, then there wouldn't be any Holland, or any Holland Twins, or any story. So you see it was very lucky for the Twins that the wall was there. They called it a dyke.

Grandfather and Kit and Kat climbed the dyke. When they reached the top, they sat down a few minutes to rest and look at the great blue sea. Grandfather sat in the middle, with Kit on one side, and Kat on the other; and the basket of worms and the basket of lunch were there, too.

They saw a great ship sail slowly by, making a cloud of smoke.

"Where do the ships go, Grandfather?" asked Kit.

"To America, and England, and China, and all over the world," said Grandfather.

"Why?" asked Kat. Kat almost always said "Why?" and when she didn't, Kit did.

"To take flax and linen from the mills of Holland to make dresses for little girls in other countries," said Grandfather.

"Is that all?" asked Kit.

"They take cheese and herring, bulbs and butter, and lots of other things besides, and bring back to us wheat and meat and all sorts of good things from the lands across the sea."

"I think I'll be a sea captain when I'm big," said Kit.

"So will I," said Kat.

"Girls can't," said Kit.

But Grandfather shook his head and said, "You can't tell what a girl may be by the time she's four feet and a half high and is called Katrina. There's no telling what girls will do anyway. But, children, if we stay here we shall not catch any fish."

So they went down the other side of the dyke and out onto a little pier that ran from the sandy beach into the water.

Grandfather showed them how to bait their hooks. Kit baited Kat's for her, because Kat said it made her all wriggly inside to do it. She did not like it. Neither did the worm!

They all sat down on the end of the pier. Grandfather sat on the very end and let his wooden shoes

LUCY FITCH PERKINS

hang down over the water; but he made Kit and Kat
sit with their feet stuck straight out in front of them,
so they just reached to the edge—"So you can't fall in,"
said Grandfather.

They dropped their hooks into the water and sat
very still, waiting for a bite. The sun climbed higher
and higher in the sky, and it grew hotter and hotter on
the pier. The flies tickled Kat's nose and made her
sneeze.

"Keep still, can't you?" said Kit crossly. "You'll scare
the fish. Girls don't know how to fish, anyway."

Pretty soon Kat felt a queer little jerk on her line.
She was perfectly sure she did.

Kat squealed and jerked her rod. She jerked it so hard that one foot flew right up in the air, and one of her new wooden shoes went—splash—right into the water!

But that wasn't the worst of it! Before you could say Jack Robinson, Kat's hook flew around and caught in Kit's clothes and pricked him.

Kit jumped and said "Ow!" And then—no one could ever tell how it happened—there was Kit in the water, too, splashing like a young whale, with Kat's hook still holding fast to his clothes in the back!

Grandfather jumped then, too, you may be sure. He caught hold of Kat's rod and pulled hard and called out, "Steady there, steady!"

And in one minute there was Kit in the shallow water beside the pier, puffing and blowing like a grampus!

Grandfather reached down and pulled him up.

When Kit was safely on the pier, Kat threw her arms around his neck, though the water was running down in streams from his hair and eyes and ears.

"O Kit," she said, "I truly thought it was a fish on my line when I jumped!"

"Just like a g-g-girl," said Kit. "They don't know how to f-f-fish." You see his teeth were chattering because the water was cold.

"Well, anyway," said Kat, "I caught more than you did. I caught you!"

Then Kat thought of something else. She shook her finger at Kit.

"O Kit," she said, "Mother told you *not* to fall into the water!"

" 'T-t-twas all your fault," roared Kit. "Y-y-you began it! Anyway, where is your new wooden shoe?"

"Where are both of yours?" screamed Kat.

Sure enough, where were they? No one had thought about shoes, because they were thinking so hard about Kit.

They ran to the end of the pier and looked. There was Kat's shoe sailing away toward America like a little boat! Kit's were still bobbing about in the water near the pier.

"Oh! Oh! Oh!" shrieked Kat; but the tide was going out and carrying her shoe farther away every minute. They could not get it; but Grandfather reached down with his rod and fished out both of Kit's shoes. Then Kat took off her other one and her stockings, and they all three went back to the beach.

Grandfather and Kat covered Kit up with sand to keep him warm while his clothes were drying. Then

81

Grandfather stuck the Twins' fish-poles up in the sand and tied the lines together for a clothesline, and hung Kit's clothes up on it, and Kat put their three wooden shoes in a row beside Kit.

Then they ate their luncheon of bread and butter, cheese, and milk, with some radishes from Father's garden. It tasted very good, even if it was sandy. After lunch Grandfather said, "It will never do to go home without any fish at all."

So by and by he went back to the pier and caught one while the Twins played in the sand. He put it in the lunch-basket to carry home.

Kat brought shells and pebbles to Kit, because he had to stay covered up in the sand, and Kit built a play dyke all around himself with them, and Kat dug a canal outside the dyke. Then she made sand-pies in clamshells and set them in a row in the sun to bake.

They played until the shadow of the dyke grew very long across the sandy beach, and then Grandfather said it was time to go home.

He helped Kit dress, but Kit's clothes were still a little wet in the thick parts. And Kat had to go barefooted and carry her one wooden shoe.

They climbed the dyke, and crossed the fields, and walked along the road by the canal. The road shone like a strip of yellow ribbon across the green field. They walked quite slowly, for they were tired and sleepy.

By and by Kit said, "I see our house"; and Kat said, "I see Mother at the gate."

Grandfather gave the fish he caught to Kit and Kat, and Vrouw Vedder cooked it for their supper; and though it was not a very big fish, they all had some.

Grandfather must have told Vrouw Vedder something about what had happened; for that night, when she put Kit to bed, she felt of his clothes carefully—but she didn't say a word about their being damp. And she said to Kat, "Tomorrow we will see the shoemaker and have him make you another shoe."

Then Kit and Kat hugged her and said good night, and popped off to sleep before you could wink your eyes.

WHIZZ!

Clara E. Randall

The airplane has a buzzing nose
Which whirrs around from start to stop;
But the helicopter always goes
With a whizzy hat stuck on its top!

Inez Hogan

TWIN SEALS

ILLUSTRATED BY THE AUTHOR

W AY up North in the ice and snow, there lived a mother seal. She had two baby seals. They were twins.

When the twin seals were very young, their mother tucked them under the snow.

And she said, "Don't move about or try to peek out." Then she made a smooth mound of snow over the top, so no one could find her baby pups.

And she dove into the water. She went swimming to catch fish for food.

And the twin seals always lay still. They didn't move about or try to peek out, while their mother caught fish for herself.

She fed milk to her babies when they were little. And they grew bigger and bigger, until . . . they were

84

big enough to learn to swim. Then the mother seal pushed the twins into the water.

At first, their heads went down and their tails went up. They scrambled out, snuggled against Mother, and cried. But the mother seal just pushed them in again, until they learned to float and then to paddle around. After that the twins played in the water all day.

They played games with other seal pups. They would dive for shells and toss them in the air and grab at jellyfish. They learned to catch fish for themselves.

When they were tired, they scrambled up on the ice. And just for fun, one twin pushed the other off into the water.

"Don't push," said the mother.

"We can't help it," said the twins. "We slip and we slide. We slip on the ice and slide into the water."

After that everyone called them Slip and Slide, the twin seals.

Slip and Slide were never still a minute. They played leapfrog with the other seal pups.

One day the mother seal dug a hole in the ice for the pups. She covered them with snow and made a hole in the top, like a little chimney, so they could breathe.

And she said, "Don't move about or try to peek out." Then Mother went fishing and while she was gone . . . a big white bear came and sniffed around the hole. But the twin seals didn't move about or try to peek out. So the big bear went away.

One day Slip and Slide were out chasing fish. Slide swam 'way out to sea after a big fish, and he saw a huge whale. Slide was frightened.

The whale spouted water into the air, and Slide began to bark. He reached up out of the water as far as he could and barked and barked. He barked so loud that . . . Mother Seal heard her pup. She swam out to him and cried, "Dive under the ice!"

Slide dove. He came up under the ice and bumped his head. Mother Seal dove too. And they stayed under the ice until the huge whale had gone. Then Slide rode home on his mother's back, because he was so tired.

Slide told his twin brother all about the whale. He said, "Never swim off by yourself, or the huge whale will get you." So Slip didn't swim off by himself.

But one day not long after, he crawled off by himself, over the ice and snow. And he saw something he had never seen before. 'Way off in the distance an Eskimo boy was coming. He had a sled drawn by a big dog. Slip scrambled over the ice, to get a better look.

The Eskimo boy was named Matka. He saw the baby seal and ran over the snow. "You'll make a good pet," he shouted.

Matka picked Slip up in his arms and stroked his back. Slip didn't try to get away. He snuggled into Matka's fur coat. Slip liked being stroked.

"I'll take you home with me," said Matka.

He put Slip into his sled and drove over the ice and snow. And they came to the Eskimo village where Matka lived.

"See what I found," shouted Matka.

All the Eskimo boys and girls came running out.

"A seal pup!" said Matka. "I'm going to keep him for a pet."

The children all gathered around and Slip crawled

up and nudged one after the other with his nose. The Eskimo children laughed.

Matka took good care of his new pet. Every day he threw fish for Slip to catch in his mouth. And he taught the seal pup to do tricks. Slip learned to balance a snowball on his nose.

Slip liked his new friend. He followed Matka around. But after a while, the seal pup got lonesome. He wanted to go back to his twin brother.

Days and days passed, and the winter came. The sun didn't shine any more. It was night all the time.

Slip waited until no one was looking and crept quietly out of the Eskimo village. He traveled a long way without seeing anything but the stars in the sky. Everything was frozen solid.

Slip was hungry, and there was nothing to eat but snow. He dug a hole for himself in the ice and went to sleep. The wind began to shriek and whistle.

The little seal woke up. The snow was falling. Slip was frightened, but he hurried on his way over the ice and snow as fast as he could travel. And at last . . . he came to the place where he had left his twin brother and the other seals. But they were gone.

Slip looked everywhere, but not a seal could be found. Then he began to bark, he barked as loud as he could. And out came a head from a hole in the ice.

"My twin brother!" shouted Slip, and he scrambled over the ice.

"Where are all the others?" he cried. "Where have they gone?"

"They swam away to warmer waters," said Slide, "but I stayed here, to wait for you to come back."

Slip put his flippers around his twin brother and hugged him. "I'm glad you didn't go," he said, "I'll take you back to the Eskimo village with me."

So the twin seals traveled over the ice and snow. And they came to the Eskimo village. Matka was surprised . . . he saw two little seals instead of one.

They looked so much alike that Matka couldn't tell which one was his pet.

So he said, "Now I have two pets." And he built an igloo, a little snow house, for Slip and Slide to live in during the cold winter.

And the twin seals were very happy in their new home.

Wanda Gág

THE FUNNY THING

ILLUSTRATED BY THE AUTHOR

IT WAS a beautiful day in the mountains. The sun was playing hide-and-seek among the fluffy, floating clouds, and the air was soft and warm.

Bobo, the good little man of the mountains, was waiting for the birds and animals to come. To come for what do you suppose? To come for food—because at the door of his mountain cave, Bobo had many good things for them to eat.

He had nut cakes for the fuzzy-tailed squirrels.

He had seed puddings for the pretty fluttering birds.

He had cabbage salads for the long-eared rabbits.

He had tiny cheeses—no bigger than cherries—and these were for the little mice.

90

Now on this beautiful sunny day, there came a Funny Thing which Bobo had never seen before. It looked something like a dog and also a little like a giraffe, and from the top of its head to the tip of its curled tail, there was a row of beautiful blue points.

"Good morning," said Bobo. "And what kind of an animal are you?"

"I'm not an animal," said the Funny Thing. "I'm an *aminal!*"

Bobo was about to say that there was no such word as *aminal*, when the Funny Thing looked around fiercely and cried, "And what have you for a hungry *aminal* to eat?"

"Oh," said Bobo, "here are some lovely nut cakes."

"I also have some fine seed puddings."

"This cabbage salad is very nice—"

"—and I'm sure you'd like these little cheeses."

But the Funny Thing turned away and said, "I never heard of such silly food! No *aminal* would eat those things. Haven't you any dolls today?"

"Dolls!" cried Bobo in surprise.

"Certainly," said the Funny Thing. "And very good they are—dolls."

"To eat?" cried Bobo, opening his eyes very wide at such an idea.

"To eat, of course," said the Funny Thing smacking his lips. "And very good they are—dolls."

"But it is not kind to eat up little children's dolls," said Bobo, "I should think it would make them very unhappy."

"So it does," said the Funny Thing, smiling pleasantly, "but very good they are—dolls."

91

"And don't the children cry when you take away their dolls?" asked Bobo.

"Don't they though!" said the Funny Thing with a cheerful grin, "but very good they are—dolls."

Tears rolled down Bobo's face as he thought of the Funny Thing going around eating up dear little children's dolls.

"But perhaps you take only naughty children's dolls," he said, brightening up.

"No, I take them specially from good children," said the Funny Thing gleefully, "and *very* good they are—good children's dolls!"

"Oh, what shall I do?" thought Bobo, as he walked back and forth. He was trying to think of a plan to make this naughty *aminal* forget to eat dolls.

At last he had an idea!

So he said to the Funny Thing, "What a lovely tail you have!"

The Funny Thing smiled and wriggled his tail with a pleased motion.

"And those pretty black eyebrows," Bobo continued.

The Funny Thing looked down modestly and smiled even more.

"But most wonderful of all is that row of blue points down your back," said Bobo.

The Funny Thing was so pleased at this that he rolled foolishly on the ground and smiled very hard.

Then Bobo, who was really a wise old man, said to the Funny Thing, "I suppose you are so beautiful because you eat a great many jum-jills?"

The Funny Thing had never heard of them.

"Jum-jills?" he asked eagerly. "What is a jum-jill— is it a kind of doll?"

"Oh, no," said Bobo. "Jum-jills are funny little cakes which make blue points more beautiful, and little tails grow into big ones."

Now the Funny Thing was very vain, and there was nothing he would rather have had than a very long tail and bigger and more beautiful blue points. So he cried, "Oh, please, dear kind man, give me many jum-jills!"

"Very well," said Bobo. "Sit down under this tree and wait for me."

The Funny Thing was all smiles and did as he was told, while Bobo went into his cozy little home, which was like a sort of tunnel under the mountain.

First he had to go through his little bedroom. Next he came to his study and finally he reached the kitchen, where he usually made up the food for the birds and animals.

Now he took a big bowl, into which he put:

> seven nut cakes,
> five seed puddings,
> two cabbage salads,
> and fifteen little cheeses.

He mixed them with a spoon and rolled them into little round balls.

These little balls were jum-jills.

He put them all on a plate and carried them out to the Funny Thing, who was still waiting under the tree.

"Here are your jum-jills," said Bobo, as he handed the plate to the Funny Thing.

The Funny Thing ate one and said, "And very good they are—jum-jills."

Then he ate another and said, "And very good they are—jum-jills."

And so on until he had eaten them all up. "And *very* good they are—jum-jills," he said with a smack of his lips, after they were all gone.

Then the Funny Thing went home, but the next day he came back for more jum-jills. His tail was already a little longer, his blue points were beginning to grow, and he looked very happy indeed.

Every day the Funny Thing came back for more jum-jills. He came for a long, long time, and each day his tail was a little longer. But on the twentieth day

his tail had grown so long that he couldn't move about much.

So he chose a nice big mountain and sat on the very top of it. Every day Bobo sent birds to carry jum-jills to the Funny Thing, and as the Funny Thing's tail grew longer and longer, he curled it contentedly around his mountain.

His one joy in life was his beautiful blue-pointed tail, and by and by the only words he ever said were:

"And very good they are—jum-jills!"

So of course he ate no more dolls, and we have kind old Bobo to thank for that.

MR. RABBIT

Dixie Willson

Mr. Rabbit has a habit
That is very cute to see.

He wrinkles up and crinkles up
His little nose at me.

I like my little rabbit
And I like his little brother,

And we have a lot of fun
Making faces at each other.

Helen and Alf Evers

A LITTLE LAMB

ILLUSTRATED BY *Helen Evers*

"Mary had a little lamb,
Its fleece was white as snow;
And everywhere that Mary went
The lamb was sure to go.
He followed her to school one day—
That was against the rule;
It made the children laugh and play,
To see the *lamb* at school."

AND so the teacher turned him out—
but the lamb didn't go home.

His father and mother, his uncles and his aunts were
all such solemn sheep. They never played, they never
jumped. They just looked sad all the time. The little
lamb wanted to go where everyone was happy.

He trotted down the road to the store and walked
in. There were three old men sitting inside. One of
them was telling a long story of how he had plowed
twelve acres in one day. All the men looked just as
solemn as the lamb's father and mother and uncles and
aunts. So the lamb said "Ba-a-aa" as loud as he could,
and ran out.

97

Then he saw a family of hounds playing across the road. But when he went close to them, they looked even sadder than his father and mother and uncles and aunts. They had the saddest faces in the world. So the lamb said "Ba-a-aa" and ran away.

As he ran down the road, the lamb saw a flock of ducks jumping, running, and quacking. They looked happy to *him*. But they *weren't!* They were being chased out of a garden and were only trying to get away as fast as they could. So the little lamb went on.

He came to a pool. There was a frog sitting on a lily pad. He looked solemnly at the little lamb. Then he said, "Gl-u-mp" and dove under the water. He looked and sounded so sad that the lamb almost cried as he went away.

He came to a field where the sad oxen and the farmer were plowing. He said, "Ba-a-aa" very nicely. But they didn't even look at him.

And then he came to a farmhouse. He heard voices inside, so he pushed open the door and walked in. The ladies of the village were having a quilting bee. They were very busy, but they looked just as sad as the lamb's father and mother and uncles and aunts. The lamb wanted to make them play and look happy. So he jumped up on the quilting frame.

His feet went right through it. He was caught! So he wriggled and kicked and tore the quilt to pieces, trying to get out.

First the ladies screamed and jumped! Then they took out their handkerchiefs and cried. And the poor lamb was so sorry that he cried, too.

He walked home and cried all the way. But when his father and mother and uncles and aunts saw him coming home crying—they jumped and played to make him happy again. And when the lamb stopped crying, and jumped happily around the field—they were all so glad that they never, never looked sad again as long as they lived.

But *sometimes* the lamb was just a little sad—when he thought of the ladies' quilt, which he had spoiled.

Jean de Brunhoff

THE STORY
OF BABAR

ILLUSTRATED BY
THE AUTHOR

IN THE great forest a little elephant is born. His name is Babar. His mother loves him very much. She rocks him to sleep with her trunk while singing softly to him.

Babar has grown bigger. He now plays with the other little elephants. He is a very good little elephant.

Babar is riding happily on his mother's back, when a wicked hunter, hidden behind some bushes, shoots at them.

The hunter has killed Babar's mother! The monkeys hide, the birds fly away, Babar cries.

The hunter runs up to catch poor Babar.

Babar runs away because he is afraid of the hunter.

After several days, very tired indeed, he comes to a town. . . .

He hardly knows what to make of it because this is the first time that he has seen so many houses.

So many things are new to him! The broad streets! The automobiles and buses! However, he is especially interested in two gentlemen he notices on the street.

He says to himself: "Really they are very well dressed. I would like to have some fine clothes, too! I wonder how I can get them?"

Luckily, a very rich Old Lady who has always been

fond of little elephants understands right away that he is longing for a fine suit.

As she likes to make people happy, she gives him her purse.

Babar says to her politely: "Thank you, Madam." Without wasting any time, Babar goes into a big store.

He enters the elevator. It is such fun to ride up and down in this funny box, that he rides all the way up ten times and all the way down ten times. He did not want to stop but the elevator boy finally said to him: "This is not a toy, Mr. Elephant. You must get out and do your shopping. Look, here is the floorwalker."

Babar then buys himself: a shirt with a collar and tie, a suit of a becoming shade, then a handsome derby hat, and also shoes with spats.

Well satisfied with his purchases and feeling very elegant indeed, Babar now goes to the photographer to have his picture taken.

Babar dines with his friend the Old Lady. She thinks he looks very smart in his new clothes.

After dinner, because he is tired, he goes to bed and falls asleep very quickly.

Babar now lives at the Old Lady's house. In the mornings, he does setting-up exercises with her and then he takes his bath.

He goes out for an automobile ride every day.

The Old Lady has given him the car. She gives him whatever he wants.

A learned professor gives him lessons. Babar pays attention and does well in his work. He is a good pupil and makes rapid progress.

In the evening, after dinner, he tells the Old Lady's friends all about his life in the great forest.

However, Babar is not quite happy, for he misses playing in the great forest with his little cousins and his friends, the monkeys.

He often stands at the window, thinking sadly of his childhood and cries when he remembers his mother.

Two years have passed. One day during his walk he sees two little elephants coming toward him. They have no clothes on.

"Why," he says in astonishment to the Old Lady, "it's Arthur and Celeste, my little cousins!"

Babar kisses them affectionately and hurries off with them to buy them some fine clothes.

He takes them to a pastry shop to eat some good cakes.

Meanwhile, in the forest, the elephants are calling and hunting high and low for Arthur and Celeste, and their mothers are very worried.

Fortunately, in flying over the town, an old marabou bird has seen them and comes back quickly to tell the news.

The mothers of Arthur and Celeste have come to the town to fetch them. They are very happy to have them back, but they scold them just the same because they ran away.

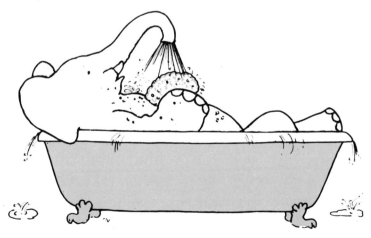

Babar makes up his mind to go back with Arthur and Celeste and their mothers to see the great forest again. The Old Lady helps him to pack his trunk.

They are all ready to start.

Babar kisses the Old Lady good-bye. He would be quite happy to go if it were not for leaving her. He promises to come back some day. He will never forget her.

They have gone. . . . There is no room in the car for the mothers, so they run behind, and lift up their trunks to avoid breathing the dust. The Old Lady is left alone. Sadly she wonders: "When shall I see my little Babar again?"

Alas, that very day, the King of the elephants had eaten a bad mushroom.

It poisoned him and he became ill, so ill that he died. This was a great calamity.

After the funeral the three oldest elephants were holding a meeting to choose a new King.

Just then they hear a noise, they turn around. Guess what they see! Babar arriving in his car and all the elephants running and shouting: "Here they are! Here they are! Hello Babar! Hello Arthur! Hello Celeste! What beautiful clothes! What a beautiful car!"

Then Cornelius, the oldest of all the elephants, spoke in his quavering voice: "My good friends, we are seeking a King, why not choose Babar? He has just returned from the big city, he has learned so much living among men, let us crown him King." All the other elephants thought that Cornelius had spoken wisely—and eagerly they await Babar's reply.

"I want to thank you one and all," said Babar, "but before accepting your proposal, I must explain to you that, while we were traveling in the car, Celeste and I became engaged. If I become your King,—she will be your Queen."

"Long live Queen Celeste! Long live King Babar!!!" cry all the elephants without a moment's hesitation. And thus it was that Babar became King.

"You have good ideas," said Babar to Cornelius, "I will therefore make you a general, and when I get my crown, I will give you my hat. In a week I shall marry Celeste. We will then have a splendid party in honor of our marriage and our coronation."

Then, turning to the birds, Babar asks them to go and invite all the animals to the festivities, and he tells the dromedary to go to the town and buy some beautiful wedding clothes.

The wedding guests begin to arrive. The dromedary returns with the bridal costumes just in the nick of time for the ceremony.

After the wedding and the coronation everybody dances merrily.

The festivities are over, night has fallen, the stars have risen in the sky. King Babar and Queen Celeste are indeed very happy.

Now the world is asleep. The guests have gone home, happy, though tired from too much dancing. They will long remember this great celebration.

And now King Babar and Queen Celeste, both eager for further adventures, set out on their honeymoon in a gorgeous yellow balloon.

POLITELY

Dixie Willson

When Goldilocks went calling
  On the Little Baby Bear
And spoiled his bowl of porridge
  And sat holes into his chair—

I hope she hurried home again
  For others nice and new
And took them back politely
  To the Baby Bear. Don't you?

Ellis Credle

DOWN
DOWN
THE MOUNTAIN

ILLUSTRATED BY THE AUTHOR

NCE upon a time, in a little log cabin away up in the Blue Ridge Mountains, there lived a little girl named Hetty and her brother Hank.

Although their home was a small one, it was a cozy place to live. There was a big stone fireplace at one end. That was where Mammy cooked beans and corn-meal mush and fried pork in a big, black, frying pan.

There was a big bed in one corner and a little bed in the other corner, and in the middle of the room there was a long table made of planks. That was where Mammy and Pappy and Hetty and Hank ate their dinner every day.

All kinds of things hung from the rafters, strings of shucky beans, bunches of bright red peppers, ears of popcorn all tied together, hams, and sausages, and baskets full of this and that.

Never in all their lives had Hetty or Hank had a pair of shoes. In the summer it was fun to run around barefoot, but when winter came, and the snow lay on the mountains like a chilly white blanket, their little feet were blue with cold and they longed for a pair of shoes.

They each wanted a beautiful shining pair that sang, "Creaky—squeaky—squeaky," every time they walked.

They begged their Mammy to buy them some shoes, but she said, "You can't find shoes like that in these hills! Such shining shoes come from the town, away down down at the foot of the mountain."

So they asked their Pappy, but he said, "There's not a cent of money in this household. We've everything we need right here in these hills."

Hetty and Hank felt very sad, but they did not give up.

"Let's ask our Granny," said Hetty. And they did.

"Some shining shoes?" chirped Granny. "I'll tell you how you can get them yourselves."

"How? How?" cried Hetty and Hank.

"Plant some turnip seeds," said Granny, "and when they have grown into fine big turnips, you can take them all the way down to town and trade them off for some shining, creaky, squeaky shoes."

"Thanky Ma'am, that's what we'll do," cried Hetty and Hank.

They raced away and planted some turnip seeds in a tilted field right next to Pappy's corn patch.

Home they went singing,

> *"Our fields are high up in the air,*
> *We wouldn't dare plant pumpkins there,*
> *For pumpkins grow so big and round,*
> *They'd break right off and tumble down.*

> *"But turnips grow on hills or vales,*
> *Because they twist their little tails*
> *Around the rocks and hold on tight*
> *And don't let go for day or night!"*

109

When Hetty and Hank got home it was dark. The whippoorwills were calling sadly from the deep woods, "Whip-poor-will! Whip-poor-will!" and a little owl was asking "Who? Who-o-o?"

Mammy was waiting for them. She gave them a nice supper of corn bread and butter and yellow honey. Then she tucked them snugly into bed. They dreamed all night about shining shoes that played a creaky, squeaky tune, just like Pappy's fiddle.

The next day they climbed up the steep, steep mountainside to see if the turnip seeds had come up. But they had not, and Hetty and Hank had to wait and wait and wait, before they spied the baby turnip leaves peeping out of the ground.

Then there was plenty of work for Hetty and Hank! They had to chop away the weeds each day, and chase away the worms and the bugs and the grasshoppers that come for a taste of nice green turnip leaves.

When there was no rain and the little turnips felt dry and thirsty, Hetty and Hank had to bring big buckets of water to make them fresh and green again.

The little turnips were very grateful. They grew and grew until they were the finest and the biggest turnips to be found anywhere in the hill country.

Then Hetty and Hank brought Granny and Mammy and Pappy up to see them.

"Sakes alive!" cried Mammy, "I never saw such big turnips!"

"Yes siree!" smiled Granny. "These are mighty juicy turnips."

"And they'll fetch a fine price in the town," said Pappy. "Hetty and Hank shall have the old gray horse to take them down the mountain."

So Hank quickly brought the gray horse. Then they pulled up all the beautiful turnips and packed them into a big bag.

Pappy laid the bag proudly across the gray horse's back, then he gave Hetty and Hank a boost and settled them safely right behind the turnips. Now they were ready to go.

"It's no trouble to find the town," said Granny. "Just you keep to the road, and it will lead you down. Sometimes it's steep—just like a stair. Sometimes it's narrow —like a hair. It turns and twists and winds around, but at the end you'll find the town!"

"We'll keep to the road," promised Hetty and Hank.

Hank pulled on the reins. Hetty gave the gray horse a slap on the side, and they were off.

"Good-bye!" cried Granny and Mammy and Pappy.

"Good-bye!" waved Hetty and Hank. And away they went, clippity, cloppity, down the road to town.

They had not gone very far before they came to an old man cutting sugar cane in a field beside the road.

"Howdy young ones!" he called. "What have you in that big bag?"

"Some turnips we're taking to sell in the town," said Hank proudly.

"Oh, my! Turnips!" cried the old man. "How I'd love some nice juicy turnips for my dinner. Couldn't you spare me just a few?"

"I suppose we wouldn't miss just a few," said Hetty, and she gave him some.

On they jogged between great bushes of pink mountain laurel, and after awhile they came to an old woman who was making soap in a big black kettle.

"Howdy, children!" she called. "What have you in that big bag?"

"Some turnips we're taking down to town," said Hank.

"Turnips!" cried the old woman. "Mercy me! How I'd love just a taste of turnip for my dinner. Couldn't you spare me just two, one for my old man and one for me?"

"I suppose we wouldn't miss just two," said Hetty, and she gave her two big ones.

Down, down, down they went between the rows of tall blue mountains, down, down, down until they came to a little stream flowing over the rocks. There the little road ended. They looked here, they looked there, they

looked everywhere, but it was nowhere to be seen.

But just then along came a woman on horseback, splishing and splashing right down the middle of the stream.

"What's the matter, young ones?" she called.

"We've lost the little road to town," said Hank.

"Follow the creek," said the woman. "That's all the road there is in these parts."

So Hetty and Hank went splashing along and along, and pretty soon they spied the little road leading up from the water.

They said good-bye to the kind woman and gave her a bunch of turnips for her dinner.

On they went along the little road beneath the tall pine trees. After awhile they overtook a man who was driving a flock of turkeys down to town. "Howdy,"

greeted the man. "What have you in that big bag?"

"Some turnips we're taking to sell in the town," said Hank.

"Oh my stars!" said the man. "Turnips! and I've had nary a bit to eat since break of dawn. A nice, juicy turnip would taste mighty good now, for I've been running after these turkeys 'til I'm nigh worn out."

"We'll have to give him a handful of turnips," said Hetty. And she did.

"Thanky, thanky," said the man, "you're kind and generous young ones!"

Now they were very near to town. They could look down and see the rooftops in the valley.

The little road became so smooth and straight that the gray horse broke into a gallop.

"Here's the town!" cried Hank.

Along they went, clippity clop, clippity clop, past the schoolhouse, past the church, past the courthouse, and suddenly there was the little red store.

"Whoa!" cried Hank, pulling on the reins. "Here's the place to trade our turnips off for some shining shoes!"

They climbed down and lifted off the sack. Somehow it felt very light and very, very empty. Had they given all their turnips away?

Hetty put her hand into the bag and brought out one large, fat, lonesome turnip. It was the only one left.

And there—shining through the store window—were those beautiful, creaky, squeaky, shining shoes!

Hetty and Hank gazed at them longingly. But one turnip would not buy a pair of shoes.

Two big tears began to roll down Hetty's cheeks.

"There! There!" said Hank. "No use crying. We'll just walk around and see the sights. Come on."

So they walked along the little road looking this way and that way. They saw the big covered wagons, all loaded with apples, come rumbling down from the hills. They saw the men trading horses in the courthouse square. Then a train went thundering past and they watched it with round eyes.

Along and along they went and after awhile they came to a field where there were many, many people. A big sign over the gate said "COUNTY FAIR."

Hetty and Hank went hustling and bustling about in the crowd. Pretty soon they came to a long row of tables, each one groaning with a different kind of vegetable. There were tomatoes on this one, and beans on that one, and pumpkins on the other one.

"Oh, here are some turnips!" cried Hetty.

"Are they as big as ours?" asked Hank.

Hetty held up her turnip. It seemed larger and juicier than the rest.

"Howdy, young ones," said the old man who was looking at the turnips. "Do you want to enter that turnip in the contest?"

"What contest?" asked Hank.

"Why there's a prize offered for the finest turnip at the fair," replied the old man.

"Mercy me!" said Hetty. "Let's try it."

"You bet your life!" said Hank.

So the old man wrote their names on a tag and tied it to the fat turnip. Then he laid it carefully among all the other turnips.

"You are just in the nick of time," he said, "for I was just a-getting ready to do the judging."

He began to examine the turnips. He weighed each one to see how heavy it was. He felt each one to see how firm it was. And when he had tried them all he held one large turnip high above his head.

"Folks!" he cried. "Here's the finest turnip at the fair. It belongs to a little girl and a little boy!"

Hetty and Hank listened with all their ears.

"Come forward, young ones, and receive the prize!"

Hetty held out her hand and there shining up at her was a bright five-dollar gold piece.

"Oh, thank you, sir!" cried Hetty and Hank. "Now we can buy our shining shoes!"

They dashed along past the beans and tomatoes. They ran past the squash and skipped past the potatoes. They dodged through the hustle and the bustle on the fair grounds. They raced along the street until they came to the little red store.

The storekeeper was standing behind the counter.

"We want to buy some beautiful, creaky, squeaky, shoes!" said Hank all out of breath.

The storekeeper got down his brightest shoes, and Hetty and Hank each chose a pair that played a creaky, squeaky tune.

Then they bought some gifts to take home with them. A yellow hat for Pappy, a bright sash for Mammy, and a big red handkerchief and a package of needles for Granny.

And off they started on the long trip home. Up, up, up they wound, round and round the mountain, past the pink laurel flowers, along the little stream and underneath the tall pine trees.

After a long, long climb they reached their own little cabin. There sat Mammy and Pappy and Granny waiting on the porch. How pleased they were to see Hetty and Hank and all the new things they had brought!

The next day was Sunday, so they put on their beautiful things and went to preaching.

Hetty and Hank walked proudly into the meeting-house. Their shoes were playing such a creaky, squeaky tune that all the people craned their necks to see who could be wearing such beautiful shoes.

GREGORY GRIGGS

Laura E. Richards

Gregory Griggs, Gregory Griggs,
Had forty-seven different wigs;
He wore them up, and he wore them down,
To please the people of Boston town.
He wore them east, and he wore them west,
But he never could tell which he liked the best.

Hugh Lofting

THE STORY
OF MRS. TUBBS

ILLUSTRATED BY THE AUTHOR

ONCE upon a time, many, many years ago, there lived a very old woman, and her name was Mrs. Tubbs. She lived on a little farm, way off in the country. Her little house stood on the edge of the woods, not very far from a village with a little church, and a little river with a little bridge over it flowed close by the house. There was a barn, too, for cows and horses, only the woman hadn't any cows or horses; she lived all alone with a dog and a duck and a pig. The dog's name was Peter Punk, the duck's name was Polly Ponk, and the pig's name was Patrick Pink. The old woman called them Punk, Ponk, and Pink for short.

Punk and Ponk had known one another for many years and were very good friends. The pig they treated as a baby because they said he was very young and hadn't much sense.

The old woman did not own the farm although she had lived on it so long. The farm belonged to a man up in London who never came there at all. This man, one fine day at the end of summer when the leaves were beginning to fall in the woods, sent his nephew,

119

a very silly young man with a red face, down from London to live in the farmhouse instead of Mrs. Tubbs.

Punk, Ponk, and Pink and the old woman were all dreadfully sad at having to leave the home where they had been so happy together for so many years.

As the sun was going down behind the little church one evening at the end of Summer when the leaves were beginning to fall in the woods, they all left the farm together, Punk in front, then Pink, then Ponk and Mrs. Tubbs behind.

They walked a long, long way along the edge of the woods, and at last when they saw a seat under a tree they all sat down to rest.

"Oh, dear, oh, dear," Mrs. Tubbs kept saying, "now I have no home, no place to sleep. And me an old woman. To be turned off the farm after all these years! What shall I do, where shall I go? Oh, dear, oh, dear!"

Then she stopped talking. Peter Punk and Polly Ponk both understood what she said because they had lived with her so long. Pink couldn't understand because he was only a baby, and he kept saying in animal language,—"Let's go on. I don't like this place. There's nothing to eat here."

"I do think it's a shame," Polly Ponk said to Punk, "that the old woman should be turned out. Did you see the way that stupid man slammed the door after we had gone? I'd like to see him turn *me* out of *my* house that way. I'd give him such a peck on his red nose he wouldn't try it again! But of course she is old, very old. I often wonder how old she really is."

"She is over a hundred, I know," said Punk. "Yes, it is a shame she should have to go for that stupid booby.

'Beefsteak-and-Onions' I call him. But it isn't altogether his fault. He's only sent here from London by his uncle who owns the farm."

"Well, what are we going to do with the old lady?" asked Ponk. "She can't stay here."

"We will wait till she falls asleep," said Punk. "Then we'll go into the woods and find a cave for her to spend the night in and cook something to eat."

"Isn't she asleep now?" asked Ponk. "Her eyes are shut."

"No," said the dog, "she's crying. Can't you feel the seat shaking? She always shuts her eyes and shakes when she cries."

Presently the old lady and the pig began to snore together. So they waked poor Pink up and all three went into the woods. They set Pink digging truffles and Polly Ponk went off to the river and caught a fine trout while Punk got sticks together and made a fire.

"Now who's going to do the cooking?" asked Punk.

"Oh, I'll do that," said Ponk.

"Can you cook?" asked the dog.

"Indeed I can," said Polly Ponk. "My Aunt Deborah used to cook at a hotel and she showed me how. You get the fire burning, and I'll soon have the fish fried."

So very soon they had a nice meal ready of fried trout and truffles for the old lady.

"Now," said Punk, "we must go into the cave and get a bed ready for Mrs. Tubbs."

So they went into the cave and made a fine, soft bed of leaves.

"What shall we do for a pillow," said Punk. "Shall we use the pig, he would be nice and soft?"

"No," said Ponk, "I'm going to use him as a hot water bottle. It's very important to keep the old lady's feet warm. But I have some feathers back home which will make a fine pillow. They are some of my own which I kept last moulting season."

"What did you do that for?" asked Punk.

"Well," said the duck, standing first on one foot then on the other, "the fact is I'm not getting any younger myself and I thought that if, when I am very old, I should get bald, I could have them stuck on with glue or something. I'll fly over to the farm and fetch them. I know just where I put them: they're in the left-hand drawer of my bureau under my lavender bonnet."

With a flap of her wings she flew over the treetops to the farm and in a minute was back again with the feathers in a bag.

When they had everything ready they went and fetched Mrs. Tubbs and showed her the supper they had prepared. But the old woman would not eat anything but kept saying, "Oh dear, oh dear! What shall I do? I am turned out of house and home, and me an old woman!"

So they put her to bed in the cave, covered her over with leaves and placed Pink at her feet as a hot-water bottle. And presently she cried herself to sleep.

Punk and Ponk now began to worry over what they should do with the old woman next.

"She can't stay here," said Ponk. "That's certain. You see, Punk, she isn't eating anything. She is so upset and she is so old. What we've got to do is to find some way to turn that booby out of the farm so she can go back and live there."

"Well, what shall we do?" said the dog.

"I don't just know yet," Polly Ponk answered. "But in the morning before she wakes up, we must go back to the farm and see what can be done."

So next morning, while the old woman was still asleep, off they all went as the sun was getting up behind the woods. Just before they got to the farm as they were crossing the bridge over the stream, they saw Tommy Squeak, the King of the Water Rats coming down for his morning bath in the river.

"Catch him!" said Ponk. "Perhaps he'll be able to help." And they all started running as hard as they could after the water rat. Poor Tommy Squeak was dreadfully frightened at seeing a dog and a pig and a duck coming after him, and he made off for the river as fast as his legs would carry him. When he came to the river he jumped in with a splash and disappeared. Punk and Pink sat down on the grass and said, "We've lost him!"

But Polly Ponk, running up behind, never stopped but dived into the river, swam under the water and just caught poor Mr. Squeak as he was popping into a hole way down at the bottom of the river. She pulled him up by his tail, carried him to the shore, and put him on the grass. Then they all gathered round him so he couldn't run away.

"Now," said the duck, "don't be frightened. Stay where you are and do as you are told, and we won't hurt you. Listen. Do you remember, last summer, when you were stealing cheese from the pantry up at the farm, and you fell into a bucket of water and Mrs. Tubbs came and caught you? Do you remember?"

"Yes," said Tommy Squeak, shaking the water off his whiskers, still very frightened.

"And she didn't hurt you or give you to the cat. Do you remember?"

"Yes," said Tommy Squeak.

"She let you go and told you never to come back again. Did she not?"

"Yes," said Tommy Squeak.

"You know that she is the kindest woman to animals in all the world, don't you?"

"Yes," said Tommy Squeak.

"All right," said Polly. "Now listen. A red-faced booby from London Town has been sent down here to turn Mrs. Tubbs out of her house. She is terribly old, as you know; we have taken her up into the woods. But she won't eat her food, she is so sad, and we can't do a thing with her. The winter is coming on, and we must get her back into the farm somehow. Now you are the king of the water rats, and this is what you must do: Call all the rats of the river together—every one of them, thousands of them—and take them to the farm. Then worry the booby every way you can think of. Rattle the pans in the kitchen at night so he can't sleep. Pull the stuffing out of the chairs. Eat holes in his best hat. Do everything you can to drive him out. Then, if he goes back to London Town, we can put Mrs. Tubbs back on the farm."

"All right," said Tommy Squeak. "I'll do my best for the old woman. She certainly ought to be put back on the farm."

Then he stood up on his hind legs by the riverbank and facing up the stream, he gave a long, loud, wonder-

ful squeak. Then he turned and facing down the stream he gave another.

And presently there was a rustling sound in the grasses all around and a whispering sound in the bushes and a splashing sound from the water. And everywhere rats appeared, hopping and jumping towards him—big ones and little ones, black ones, gray ones, brown ones, piebald ones—families of them, hundreds of them—thousands—millions. And they gathered round Tommy Squeak the King-Rat in a great, great big circle. Their beady, black eyes looked very frightened when they saw a dog there but they didn't run away because the king had called them.

Then Tommy Squeak stood up to speak to them and they all stopped cleaning their whiskers to listen.

"Rats," he said, "we have a job of work to do. Follow me." And waving his paw to Punk, Ponk, and Pink, he led the way to the farm.

For a whole day and a night the rats worked very hard, trying to turn the man out. They rattled the pans in the kitchen at night. They pulled the stuffing out of his chair. They ate holes in his new, green hat. They stopped the clock. They pulled the curtains down upon the floor. But the man sent to London Town and got three wagon-loads of cats, and the rats were all driven back to the river. Tommy Squeak came to Punk, Pink, and Ponk on the second day and said, "I am sorry. We did our best, but we couldn't move him."

So Ponk said to Punk, "Well, we must try something else." And they left the old woman in the woods and started off again.

As they were crossing the river this time before they got to the farm, they saw Tilly Twitter, the Queen of the Swallows, sitting on the corner of the bridge.

"Good morning!" said Tilly. "You all look very sad."

"Oh, Tilly," said Punk, with tears in his eyes, "Mrs. Tubbs has been turned out of house and home."

"Good gracious!" cried Tilly. "You don't say! Who turned her out?"

"A man from London," said Punk. "I call him 'Beef-steak-and-Onions.' Do you think you can do anything to help us get her back to the farm?"

"Certainly I'll do my best," said Tilly, pushing her crown further back on her head. "I have built my nest over the old woman's door for three springs now. I would hate to have her leave the farm for good. I'll see what I can do."

Then she flew up into the air going round and round in circles. Higher and higher she flew, and all the time she sang a beautiful song at the top of her voice.

126

And this is the song she sang:

"The leaves are falling in the woods.
Go get your traveling rugs and hoods.
The Summer's gone; the snow'll soon be here.
It's time to fly; but we'll come back next year."

Now every year when all the swallows heard Tilly
Twitter sing this song they knew it was time for them
to get together to fly to Africa because they don't like
the winter's cold in England. So now when they heard
it they got their children together and snatching up
their bags and bundles, they all flew towards Mrs.
Tubb's farm. So many of them came that the sky grew
dark, and people thought the night was come. And the
farm boys in the country around stopped their plow-
horses and said, "There go the swallows, getting ready
to fly to Africa. The frost will soon be here."

For five hours they kept coming, more and more and
more of them. They gathered around Tilly, sitting on
the house, on the barn and the railings, on the gates,
on the bridge, and on the stones. But never on the trees.
Swallows never sit on trees. So many of them came that
the whole land seemed covered with the blue of their
wings and the white of their breasts.

And when they had all arrived Tilly got up and
spoke.

"Swallows," she said, "many years ago, when I first
built my mud nest under the eaves of this farm, I had
five children in my nest. They were my first family, and
I was very proud of them. That was before I became
the Queen of the Swallows. And being a very inexperi-
enced mother I built the nest too small. When my chil-

dren grew up there was not proper room for them. Philip—a very strong child—was always twisting and turning in the nest, and one day he fell out. He bumped his nose badly on the ground, but it was not far to fall and he was not much hurt. I was just going to fly down and try to pick him up when I saw a large weasel coming across the farmyard and get him. My feathers stood up on the top of my head with fright. I flew to the farmhouse window and beat upon the glass with my wings. An old woman came out. When she saw Philip on the ground and the weasel coming to get him, she threw her porridge-spoon at the weasel, picked Philip up, and put him back in my nest. That old woman's name was Mrs. Tubbs. She has now been turned out of her house and a very stupid red-faced man is living on the farm in her place. We have got to do our best to turn him out and put Mrs. Tubbs back in her house, the same as she put my child back in his nest. So I have called you all together a week earlier than usual this year for our long journey to Africa, and before we leave England we have got to see what we can do. The first thing we'll do is to stop up his chimney so his fire won't burn. Then put mud all over the windows so the light will not come in. Bring all the straw from the barn and fill his bedroom with it. Take his best necktie and drop it in the river. And do everything you can to drive him out."

So the swallows set to work and Punk, Ponk, and Pink went back to the old woman in the woods.

But after two days Tilly came to them and said, "I am very sorry, but I have not succeeded. The cats have driven my swallows away. He has a thousand cats in

128

the place. What can one do?"

So Punk said to Ponk, "We must go out and try something else."

But Polly Ponk answered, "No, you go alone this time. The old woman is getting a cold, and I must stay and look after her."

So Peter Punk went off with his tail dragging on the ground. He hung about the farm and was very sad and wondered what he could do to drive Beefsteak-and-Onions out of the house.

Presently, feeling hungry, he remembered he had hidden a ham-bone in the trunk of a tree behind the house some weeks ago and he went off to see if it was still there. When he got to the tree he stood up on his hind legs and looked into the hole. A wasp flew out and stung him on the nose. He sat down on the grass and watched the tree for a minute and saw many wasps coming in and going out through the hole. Then he understood what had happened. Thousands of wasps had made a nest in the hollow tree.

So he thought of a plan. He went and got a big stick and threw it into the hole in the tree. Then all the wasps came flying out and tried to sting him. He went running towards the house with the wasps after him and ran in through the back door of the house. The wasps kept following him—though a few stopped to sting some of the cats that were hanging about the back door. Then he ran up the stairs by the front staircase, into the bedrooms and down by the backstairs. In the hall he found Beefsteak-and-Onions, who had just come in from digging potatoes, with a spade in his hand. Punk ran between his legs and out through the front door.

When the wasps could not find Punk any more they thought the man had hidden him somewhere so they set upon him and stung him. And the rest of them stung all the cats they could find in the house and drove them away across the fields.

Poor Beefsteak-and-Onions ran out into the yard and shut himself up in the barn to get away from the wasps. Then he laid down his spade and put on his coat and said, "I'll leave this house today. My uncle can come and live here himself if he wants to. But I'm going back to London Town. I didn't want to turn the old lady out anyway. I do not believe my uncle knew anyone was living here at all. I am going today."

Punk was listening outside the door and heard him, so he ran off at once back to the woods. When he got to Ponk and Pink he started dancing on his hind legs.

"What's the matter?" asked Ponk. "Have you gone crazy?"

But all he answered was:

"Hooray, Hooray!
He's going away,
Old Beefsteak-and-Onions
Is going today."

Then he told them how he had at last succeeded, and they both thought he was a very clever dog.

It was now getting late in the evening, so they went and got Mrs. Tubbs and they all walked back to the farm by moonlight.

And the old woman was so happy to get back to her little house that she made them all a very fine supper. And Pink said, "I am glad to get back. There is something to eat here."

And so when the leaves were all fallen in the woods, and the trees stood bare waiting for the snow, they used to sit round the warm fire in the evenings toasting chestnuts and telling stories while the kettles steamed upon the hob and the wind howled in the chimney above. And they never had to leave the farm again and they all lived happily ever after.

William Donahey

THE TEENIE WEENIE PICNIC

ILLUSTRATED BY THE AUTHOR

IT HAD been a very rainy spring. For almost a week the rain had come down hard, and everything was soaking wet beneath the rosebush under which the Teenie Weenie village stands. It would stop for a time, but then it would start again and rain even harder. The tiny houses in the village were dry and comfortable, however, and for a few days the little people were contented, for they kept themselves busy doing odd jobs.

The Old Soldier with a wooden leg whittled a chair rung out of a safety match and fitted it neatly into one of the dining-room chairs, which had been broken.

The Turk and Gogo made a new set of mouse harness from some strong frog leather which the Teenie Weenies had tanned the fall before. The Lady of Fashion knit a pair of stockings from spider web, and the other Teenie Weenie women spent their time mending tiny garments. The Cowboy worked hard at making a new mouse saddle, for he loves nothing so much as mounting a spirited mouse and riding through the woods.

The little people played games and the Cook prepared some wonderful meals, but nevertheless they all became restless from being cooped up for so long, for

132

they all love to wander about outdoors. It is really dangerous for such little folks, who are no taller than a match, to go out in the rain, for one big raindrop would soak them to the skin.

"*Ah shucks!*" exclaimed the Dunce as he stared through the sitting-room windows of the shoehouse. "It's been coming down by the thimbleful all day. You'd think it would run out of rain after a while."

"It looks as though it might clear up by tomorrow," said the Doctor as he joined the Dunce at the window.

"Well, I hope so," said the Dunce. "I want to go to the woods and see the spring flowers. They ought to be up and in bloom now."

"I'd like to go, too, Dunce," said the Lady of Fashion. "I'm sure the trilliums and violets are in bloom by this time."

"It will do us all good to get out," put in the General. "As soon as it clears up we'll have a picnic and spend the day in the woods."

"*Hooray!*" shouted the Dunce, and the rest of the Teenie Weenies joined him, for the little people all loved a picnic in the woods.

It stopped raining during the night, and the next morning was full of bright sunshine. The Lady of Fashion and the Cook set to work packing acorn baskets with lunch. The Lady of Fashion packed a basket full of smoked frog ham sandwiches, while the Cook filled another acorn with doughnuts and cookies. There was a three-drop cherry seed jar of pickles, too, and half a thimbleful of sassafras tea.

"Where will we go?" asked the Policeman when everything was ready.

"Oh, to the big woods, of course," said the Lady of
Fashion.

"That's a long way from here," said the Policeman.

"But that's where the prettiest wild flowers grow,"
said the Lady of Fashion.

"Sure!" exclaimed the Dunce. "There are jack-in-the-
pulpits, trilliums, and every kind of wild flower there
is, over there."

"All right," said the Policeman, and he and Gogo set
off, carrying the thimble of sassafras tea, followed by
the rest of the Teenie Weenies.

After a long tramp the little folks finally arrived at
the big woods. They chose a pretty, mossy spot near
a fallen tree for their picnic place, hid the food under
some wild strawberry vines, and then scattered about,
looking at the wild flowers. They found great white and
red trilliums, lady's slippers, star flowers, and great
bunches of violets, purple, white, and yellow.

"Say, I'm hungry," said the Dunce after the little
people had wandered about the woods for a time.
"Can't we eat now?"

"It's too early to eat now," said the Cook. "If you're hungry you can go and get a couple of doughnuts out of the basket. But that doesn't mean the whole basket. Just two, that's all."

The Dunce set off on a run for the place where the lunch had been left, and as he came in sight of the spot he saw a chipmunk going off with the acorn basket of doughnuts and cookies. The chipmunk carried the basket in his mouth, and he was skipping away at top speed.

"*Hey!*" bellowed the Dunce. "You can't do that!" and then he let out a special yell which is a signal to the Teenie Weenies when trouble threatens them. Instantly Teenie Weenies came running from all directions and the chipmunk, who no doubt had never seen a Teenie Weenie before, ran up on a log and stopped in wide-eyed astonishment, still holding the acorn basket.

"You've taken our lunch," said the General when the Teenie Weenies had surrounded the log on which the chipmunk sat. "If you take it we won't have anything to eat. However, we would be very glad to share some of it with you."

The Teenie Weenies have a way of making themselves understood by the animals, especially the Chinaman, who understands most of what the birds and small animals say. It was plain that the General was not making the chipmunk understand, and so he called on the Chinaman to see what he could do. The Chinaman soon had the chipmunk making some sounds, and these he translated to the Teenie Weenies.

"He say," began the Chinaman, "that he smell something and he find our lunch under the strawberry. He say he no know it belong to us and he take. He say he sorry."

"Tell him to join us in our lunch," said the General. "He'll be very welcome."

The Chinaman repeated the General's invitation and the chipmunk showed plainly that he was much pleased. He brought back the doughnuts and cookies at once and put them where he had found them.

The Cook and the Lady of Fashion spread out the lunch, and the Teenie Weenies all sat about on the moss and heartily enjoyed the feast. The chipmunk ate seven doughnuts and five cookies. He refused the frog sandwiches, telling the Chinaman that he never ate meat.

The little people had a fine time and they became very friendly with the chipmunk. He took the Dunce for a ride on his back and promised to visit the Teenie Weenie village sometime.

William Donahey

UPPITY ORIOLES

ILLUSTRATED BY THE AUTHOR

GOGO squatted on the kitchen porch of the shoehouse with a Teenie Weenie chopping bowl held tightly between his tiny knees. The bowl had been made from half a hickory-nut shell. The little chap hacked at some pieces of boiled frog ham which would soon appear on the Teenie Weenie dinner table in a heap of delicious brown hash. Gogo began to nod his head with the even clop of the tiny hash knife and presently broke into an old Teenie Weenie song.

"De fish is in de watah, a-paddlin' wid his fin;
De cat is sittin' on de sho'e, wishin' he could swim.
De mouse is in de bottle, a-wrinklin' up his nose;
De cat is nearly frantic, as yo' can well suppose.
De bird is in de treetop, way up in de sky;
De cat is sittin' on de ground, a-wishin' he could fly."

The Cook came to the kitchen door carrying a cherry-seed bowl in which he was rapidly beating a sauce for the baked raisin he had just taken out of the Teenie Weenie stove.

"That song you were singing reminds me that we are going to have a new neighbor," said the Cook.

"How dat?" asked Gogo.

137

"A bird is building a nest over in that old tree," answered the Cook, pointing with his Teenie Weenie fork toward a tall tree that stands along the lane near Teenie Weenie Town.

"What kind of bird buildin' dat nest?" asked Gogo.

"Baltimore oriole," said the Cook.

Gogo wiped the chopping knife on the side of the bowl and set the hickory-nut shell on the porch floor. "Oriole mighty pretty bird," he said, "and dey make a fine nest. Maybe we-all can help wid de nest. Birds all time lookin' fo' string and horsehairs. We ought to find some, and dat would save de bird a heap of flyin'."

The Teenie Weenies are always interested when birds build their nests in the neighborhood of Teenie Weenie Town. They were particularly interested in this nest, for Baltimore orioles build very neat and unusual nests. The little people gathered strings and bits of thread. They found some long horsehairs and laid them out where the bird could easily find them. The Teenie Weenies tried to make friends with the orioles, but neither the highly colored bird nor his not-so-gayly dressed wife would have anything to do with them.

138

At first the little people thought nothing of their behavior because they knew the birds were very busy building their nest and had little time for visiting. When the long pouchlike nest had been finished, the mother bird was constantly sitting on her eggs, and her husband spent most of his time gathering food for his wife. When the young birds were hatched out, the parent birds were busy bringing bugs and worms to their hungry children.

As the summer came on, the Teenie Weenies often captured caterpillars or grubworms and gave them to the birds, who received them with a mere nod of the head in thanks.

"Say!" growled the Dunce one morning. "Those orioles are uppity. They think they are too good to have anything to do with us. I'm not going to break my back luggin' caterpillars to such uppity neighbors."

"I don't think they are uppity," put in the Cowboy. "They are just quiet birds and they are too busy taking care of their young ones to have time for visiting."

"Well, I think they are uppity," said the Dunce, "and

I'm not going to have anything to do with them."

All through the summer the orioles went about their affairs without paying much attention to the Teenie Weenies, and so the Teenie Weenies paid little attention to the orioles, for the little folks were busier than usual.

Some of the vegetables had done well in the Teenie Weenie garden, but the corn had turned out badly. The little people had planted three stalks of corn. One stalk had been eaten off by a strange rabbit and the other two had died, for the weather had been very dry. The Teenie Weenies had carried hundreds of thimblefuls of water from the creek, but even this tremendous amount of work had not been enough to save the corn.

Corn is a very important crop to the Teenie Weenies. It is really the Teenie Weenie staff of life, for they make most of their bread from corn. A grain of corn, parched and hammered into flour, will make a loaf of Teenie Weenie bread. One grain, when soaked in lye water, swells up into a white fluffy grain of hominy which is then cut into slices and fried crisply in hickory-nut oil. The little people always like to store away more corn than they would use, for they often feed the hungry birds during the winter when the snow covers the ground.

For days the Teenie Weenies talked of nothing but the loss of their corn. It would be a lean winter without corn, so the little people began hunting seeds. They had some wheat left over from the year before, and of course they would have some vegetables from their garden to put away in their storehouse. They found a

number of sunflower seeds, and the Teenie Weenie
Indian discovered some wild rice, but the mallard
ducks had eaten most of it, and the little folks were
able to gather only a few grains.

"We could probably get some corn from that farm
down the road," suggested the Cowboy.

"That's too dangerous," said the Old Soldier with a
wooden leg. "I'd have to be mighty hungry before I'd
go there."

Most of the little people nodded their tiny heads in
agreement. To reach the farm the Teenie Weenies
would have to travel through strange country where
they were not known to the cats and dogs along the
way. The little folks had many friends among the dogs
and cats in their neighborhood, but strange animals
wouldn't know the Teenie Weenies were friendly people. They might pounce suddenly on a Teenie Weenie,
thinking he was a mouse. It had been reported that
several weasels lived near the cornfield, and a weasel
is the last animal a Teenie Weenie would care to meet.

One day late in September, while several of the
Teenie Weenies were salting frog hams near the tomato
can that the little folks used for a smokehouse, the
oriole flew down and settled on the lower branch of a
bush near by. The bird held a grain of corn in his beak

141

and looked inquiringly at the Teenie Weenies.

"It's that uppity bird!" said the Dunce. "Don't pay any attention to him."

"Allie same he want to say somethings," said the Chinaman, and the little chap ran over to hear what the oriole had to tell.

The bird hopped out of the bush and dropped the grain of corn on the ground. Then he made motions with his head and wings which the Chinaman understood to be an invitation to climb on the bird's back. The little chap climbed on, and the bird spread his wings, flew over the treetops, and landed in the lane that passes near Teenie Weenie Town. There, right in the middle of the road, lay two large ears of yellow corn. There were fresh wagon tracks along the lane, and it was plain to see that the corn had fallen off the farmer's wagon as he had driven by.

"Jimminy Clismas! Muchie much clorn!" shouted the delighted Chinaman. Thanking the bird, he set off for the shoehouse as fast as his short legs could carry him.

The Teenie Weenies were greatly excited with the news. They hurried to the lane, where they shouted with joy over the sight of the two big ears of corn.

"That corn must be moved out of the road as soon as possible," said the Old Soldier with a wooden leg. "If an automobile should drive along here and run over that corn, it would be ruined."

"That's right," agreed the General. "We must drag the ears off the road. It will take too long to shell the corn there, and a car may come along at any moment."

The Teenie Weenie men ran back to the town and began carrying up boards, Teenie Weenie jacks, Teenie

Weenie tools, and a number of lead pencils on which the big ears of corn could be rolled out of the road. First the little men worked a stout Teenie Weenie plank under one of the ears of corn, and then they dug down into the ground and set a Teenie Weenie jack under each end of the plank. The same thing was repeated on the other end of the ear and then four of the Teenie Weenies screwed up the jacks until the corn was lifted off the ground. When the corn was raised high enough other planks and several pencils were placed under the ear. Next the Teenie Weenies fixed a stout string to the cradle on which the corn lay, and the other end of the string was fastened to a Teenie Weenie windlass. When everything was ready the Old Soldier gave the word and two of the stoutest Teenie Weenies began turning the cranks of the windlass. As the corn was slowly moved along, some of the Teenie Weenie men laid boards in front of it for a track, while others kept placing pencils in front of the corn as fast as they rolled out at the back. Little by little, they moved the corn out of the lane and left it in a little cleared spot near some asters.

While the men were working, the oriole flew down and settled on a stick that lay near by. The General thanked the bird for his kindness in telling them about the corn, but it was plain to see the bird did not understand what he said.

"Me tell 'im," said the Chinaman, and the little chap began making motions and queer chirping sounds. The bird seemed to understand the Chinaman. He chirped back at a great rate and then, bowing to the Teenie Weenies, he flew away.

"Well, drown me in a thimbleful of molasses if that don't beat you!" exclaimed the Dunce. "I thought that was an uppity bird, and now he turns out to be most unuppity."

"That's just what I've been telling you all summer," said the Cowboy. "Just because a bird doesn't want to loaf around you is no sign he's uppity."

Several unprincipled mice had been hanging around the neighborhood of Teenie Weenie Town, so the General thought it might be best to place a guard over the two ears of corn during the night.

The next morning the little people began carrying the grain to their storehouse. Some Teenie Weenies pried the big grains from the cob with some small finishing nails that had been made into crowbars, while others carried the corn in sacks to the Teenie Weenie storehouse. Now the little people would have plenty of food to last them through the winter, for which they could thank an uppity neighbor who wasn't really uppity.

Dorothy and Marguerite Bryan

THERE WAS TAMMIE!

ILLUSTRATED BY *Marguerite Bryan*

WHO is ready to go on a picnic?" Mother called, one fine morning.

It was exactly the sort of day for a surprise—a pleasant surprise, like a picnic.

"I am."

"I am."

"Bow-wow."

"I am."

Sally, Peter, Tammie, and little George all ran to Mother, who was waiting beside their automobile.

Mother lifted little George onto the front seat.

"George and I will ride here," she said.

"And Fuzzy, too?" he asked.

"And Fuzzy, too," Mother agreed.

"Sally and Peter, you hop in the back. But watch out for the chocolate cake on the seat."

So Sally and Peter climbed into the rumble seat most carefully and sat one on either side of the cake.

"Now," said Mother, "have we forgotten anything? Chocolate cake, big umbrella, red-striped cushion, and my new book. Picnic basket, thermos bottle, old fringed rug, and Fuzzy. Little George, Sally, Peter—"

"And Tammie," shouted all the children together.

"Oh, no!" Mother objected. "I do not see how we can possibly fit Tammie in, too. We will have to leave him at home this time. You stay home, like a good dog, Tammie."

145

So, a little sadly, they all drove off for the picnic and left poor Tammie standing alone.

They had turned at the gate and started down the street when little George's hat blew off.

Mother stopped the car and waited while Peter climbed out and ran back to get it.

Sitting beside the hat and looking very pleased with himself—there was Tammie!

Peter picked up the hat and ordered, *quite* firmly, "Go home, Tammie, old boy."

Tammie started home. Every few steps he turned around and *looked* at Peter.

Peter walked slowly back to the car, put little George's hat on his head again, and climbed in beside the chocolate cake.

They drove on to the grocery store. Mother stopped the car across the street. She wanted to buy some animal crackers for little George.

"We will save some of them for Tammie," she promised as she started away to the store.

146

"I will save a whole elephant for Tammie," called little George.

When Mother came out with the crackers—there, wagging his tail and looking hopefully up at her, THERE WAS TAMMIE!

Mother shook her finger at him and spoke very firmly. "You can *not* come with us. GO HOME TAMMIE!"

Tammie turned towards home.

Mother drove on to the gas station on the next corner.

After the serviceman had filled the tank of their automobile with gasoline and put air in the back tires, he came around to Mother.

"Is this your dog, lady?" he asked. "He was on the step of your car." The man held out his arms and— THERE WAS TAMMIE!

"Yes, thank you," Mother answered. "That is our Tammas. He is a very bad dog."

Being a Scotch dog, his real name is Tammas, but Mother only calls him so when she is *very* stern.

The gas-station man put Tammas down and Mother said, *very* sternly, "GO HOME TAMMAS!"

The poor little fellow turned towards home—l-o-o-k-i-n-g back at every step.

Mother, Sally, Peter, and little George drove out into the country. So many of the things that they passed made the children think of Tammie.

They passed a sparkling brook. Tammie would have loved to splash there with those three ducks who were marching down for a swim.

They passed Tammie's special dog friends, Michael and Patsy, trotting back from having fun. Tammie liked to go places, too.

They passed three saucy squirrels sitting by the roadside, their cheeks round with nuts. Tammie would have chased them quickly up a tree.

They passed a boy on a bicycle, with two dogs running gaily along beside him. Tammie would have barked at him, if only he had been there.

And Tammie would have barked, too, at all the honking horns on the automobiles that passed by—if only *he* had come on the picnic instead of the chocolate cake! Tammie loved to bark at honking horns.

They turned down a little lane where it was very quiet until HONK! HONK! sounded behind them. Then Honk! Honk! Honk! HONK! nearer and louder.

HONK!

HONK!

The car passed them.

A large man was driving it and sitting beside him, looking at them out of the window—THERE WAS TAMMIE!

The large man was Mr. Beam, their next door neighbor.

"I guess that you forgot your Tammie," he said. "I found him back at the gas station. We have had a chase to catch you."

Tammas looked at Mother.

Mother looked at Tammas.

"Well," said Mother. "Here he is!"

"Well," said Mother again—"Thank you, Mr. Beam. Jump in, Tammie."

Happily, they drove on for the picnic. The chocolate cake was on the floor and tucked in between Sally and Peter on the rumble seat—THERE WAS TAMMIE!

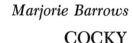

Marjorie Barrows

COCKY

ILLUSTRATED BY *Clarence Biers*

ONCE there was a little helicopter named Cocky. He was smarter than an airplane. He could spin his rotor blades like a giant hummingbird, *whirrrrrr!* He could zip straight up in the air. He could fly straight down into a front yard. He could hover over one spot for ever so long. He could fly sideways. And he could *fly backward!*

No airplane could do these things. But Cocky could. And he liked to hear people say, "Oh!" when they watched him.

But Cocky really did not care much for flying. It was too much work. Even when he felt lazy he had to keep his engine going and his rotors spinning fast.

Once he was so lazy he dropped down and took a ride on the top of a bus. The people inside poked their heads out to see what had happened. And Cocky's pilot had to tickle his controls to coax him up again.

Cocky liked to rest cozily in his nice hangar. He liked that better than flying.

And best of all he liked to have people look at him there and say, "Oh, see that new kind of flying machine! That cute little helicopter! So safe and useful! *That's* the one I like best."

150

Cocky agreed with them.

He liked himself very much.

One day Cocky said right out loud, "Bless my rotors! I know what I'll do! Next time my pilot takes me up in the air, I *won't mind him*. I'll have the jitters. I won't fly safely, the way all helicopters fly. I'll turn somersaults and loop the loop *backward*. After *that*, my pilot will let me stay in my nice cozy home. *Wheeeee!*"

Cocky was so pleased with himself that he bounced up and down on his landing gear.

"My cockpit!" said Zip, the airplane next to him. "Flying is your job. Be a good little helicopter and always fly well. It's fun!"

Cocky made a face at Zip. Then he whirled sideways and gave another bounce.

"I shall do as I please!" he muttered. "I don't care *what* you say. It's *cold* up in the sky. And my rotor blades get *tired*. Next time I go 'way up there, you just *watch me!*"

Next morning a man came and gave Cocky a nice bath. *Splash-splash! Scrub-scrub-scrub!*

"*Ka-chew!*" sneezed Cocky. "Watch out what you're doing! You got some water in my nose. Yes, sir, right in my *nose!* KA–CHEW!"

But the man did not hear him at all.

Pretty soon another man came and gave Cocky his breakfast. He put a hose in the helicopter's tank and pumped him a nice drink of gasoline.

Cocky drank and drank. *Gurgle-gurgle! Gurgle-gurgle!*

"My g-g-g-gears, but I was thirsty!" gulped Cocky. "How about another pint? Just a wee drop, eh?"

But the man did not hear him at all.

Pretty soon another man came. He tested Cocky's machinery. He tried his engine and his rotor blades. He jiggled Cocky's pedals and his throttle and his clutch to make sure they worked.

"Ouch! Stop! You're tickling me!" giggled Cocky, lashing his tail rotors around and around.

But the man did not hear him at all.

By and by the calm pilot came and sat up in front at Cocky's controls. He was right behind lots of buttons and handles and levers that made Cocky go.

"My throttle!" said Cocky, making a face at him. "Just you wait and see how I'm going to fly *this* time!"

But the pilot did not hear him at all.

Two important people came to take a ride in Cocky that day. They thought it would be fun to fly in one of those new helicopters.

One was the mayor of the town. He was a tall thin man, and he had long black hair. He wore a high hat, drooping mustaches, and his Sunday clothes. The other was the mayor's wife. She was a very fat lady, and she clutched an umbrella and a bag full of striped peppermint candies.

"All right! Contact! Let's take off! Let's go!" shouted Cocky, whirling his rotor blades around and around.

But nobody heard him at all.

Whirrrrrrrrrrrr! The pilot started the helicopter and Cocky soared straight up, up, up into the sky. The houses and people down below grew smaller and smaller and smaller.

"Now for some fun!" shouted Cocky. "I *won't* fly safely as all helicopters fly!" His rotors and his engine were just making a whispery sound, but he shouted, anyway.

FLIP-FLOP-FLIP-FLOP-FLIP-FLOP!

Cocky backed up *very* suddenly. And the mayor and his wife bumped each other. After that Cocky began to play hide-and-seek with a cloud.

"Yoo-hoo!" shouted Cocky. "Now for some *more* fun!" WHIRRRRRRRRRRRRR! growled the rotors.

Cocky began to loop the loop high up there in the air. Then he did it backward.

The pilot, the mayor, and the fat lady were all standing on their heads.

"Stop somersaulting!" shouted the mayor to the pilot. "Help!"

"Ha-ha-ha-ha-ha-ha-ha-ha-ha-ha-ha-ha!" laughed the fat lady. She was enjoying herself.

Cocky roared with laughter.

"Now for still more fun!" he shouted. "Now I'll do something no helicopter *ever* does!"

WHANG!

Cocky stuck his nose straight toward the earth, whirled his tail, and took a dive

DOWN!

DOWN!

DOWN!

"Lost control!" shouted the pilot. "Take your parachutes and JUMP."

Out jumped the fat lady, still laughing. *Zip.* Out

came her parachute, billowing in the breeze. All her striped peppermints and her umbrella, too, scattered through the sky.

Out jumped the mayor. *Zip-zip.* Out came his parachute. His long mustaches stood straight up in the air. His high hat floated down. His black wig fell off, and his bald head looked cold.

Out jumped the calm pilot with his parachute. *Zip-zip-zip.*

The mayor and the fat lady and the pilot all floated gently in the air. And they all landed safely on the ground.

"Ha! Ha!" laughed Cocky. "Now I'm rid of you people, I guess I'll go up again and coast along the clouds all by myself."

But oh, my goodness sakes! Cocky couldn't turn *up* again. He had jammed his control stick. He had sprained his rotors. He was falling *down* fast.

BANG! WHAM! THUMP!

Crash!

Poor little Cocky fell into a treetop. He stopped smiling. *Ouch!* His blades were sprained. His tail rotor was bruised. His engine was broken. He ached all over.

And he felt very, very sorry for himself.

The helicopter doctors came. They mended Cocky's engine with bolts and screws. They fixed his control stick. They pounded his rotor blades and his tail rotors with a hammer. *Rat-a-tat-tat.*

Oh, how it hurt! But Cocky just closed his eyes. He didn't say *Ouch* once.

And pretty soon he was all well again.

And Zip never said, "I told you so!"

He simply stuck his nose up in the air and flapped his wings very, very fast.

After that Cocky, with the foolishness knocked out of him, minded his pilot as all helicopters do. And so he always flew well. For he had found out that flying was his job, and it was *fun*.

Every day he flew backward and forward and sideways. And he flew straight up and straight down. And he stood perfectly still right up in the air!

And everybody *loved* to ride with him.

Almost any day now if you look up in the sky, perhaps you can see a small shiny helicopter flying, *wheeeeee-eeee!*

It is a little helicopter that is still quite pleased with itself.

That's Cocky.

Margery Clark

THE PICNIC BASKET

ILLUSTRATED BY *Ruth van Tellingen*

ONE cool summer morning Andrewshek's Auntie Katushka said, "Andrewshek, I think I will put some sandwiches and some cottage cheese and some poppy-seed cakes and two eggs in our picnic basket. Then we will go to the park and eat our lunch there, near the water."

"May I go with you, Auntie Katushka?" said Andrewshek.

"Of course you may go to the park with me," said Auntie Katushka. "But first we have a great many things to do before we can start to the park. I must go into the garden and catch the white goat. I will tie her up so she will not run away. Please find the kitten, Andrewshek, and put her in the cellar, so she will not worry the chickens while we are gone."

But all Andrewshek really did was to lift up the red and white napkin which Auntie Katushka had laid over the picnic basket and look at the eggs and the poppy-seed cakes and touch the sandwiches and taste the cottage cheese.

The goat was not easy to catch. The goat wanted to go to the park, too. She galloped round and round the garden.

At last Auntie Katushka caught her and tied her firmly to a post.

Then Auntie Katushka went into the house to get

158

Andrewshek and the lunch basket. She saw Andrewshek peeping under the red and white napkin and tasting the cottage cheese. He had forgotten all about the kitten.

The kitten was nowhere to be found. "I think she must be paying a visit to the mouse family," said Auntie Katushka.

Then Auntie Katushka put on her bright shawl and took her umbrella with the long, crooked handle under one arm. Then she picked up the lunch basket with the red and white napkin on top and she and Andrewshek started for the park.

They went down the hill and across the tracks and past the market and down a long street until they came to the park by the water.

Andrewshek sat down on the grass beside a little stream. Andrewshek's Auntie Katushka laid her umbrella with the long crooked handle and the basket of lunch on the grass beside Andrewshek.

"Andrewshek," said Auntie Katushka, "I must go to the spring and get some water for us to drink. Please watch the basket with the eggs and the sandwiches and poppy-seed cakes and cottage cheese while I am gone."

"Yes, indeed, I will watch the basket of lunch," said Andrewshek.

But what Andrewshek really did was to say to himself, "I would like to take off my shoes and my stockings and wade in the little stream. I believe I will!"

Andrewshek took off his shoes and his stockings and went wading in the little stream.

A big white swan came floating calmly down the stream. He saw the picnic basket lying on the grass. He stopped and stretched and stretched his long neck, till he could touch the basket. "Honk! honk! honk!" said he. "I wonder what is under the red and white napkin."

The big white swan lifted the napkin with his red bill and looked in the basket. "Oh, oh, oh! Won't Mother Swan be pleased with this nice lunch!" said he. "Sandwich bread makes fine food for baby swans."

He picked up the basket in his strong red bill and floated it ahead of him down the stream.

Andrewshek could not wade after the big white swan. The water was too deep.

"Stop! stop! White Swan!" cried Andrewshek. "That is my Auntie Katushka's picnic basket and it has our lunch in it. Please put it back on the grass."

"No, indeed! I will not put the basket back," honked the big white swan. "Sandwich bread makes fine food for baby swans, and I have ten baby swans to feed."

The big white swan gave the picnic basket a little push with his red bill. The basket floated on down the little stream. The big white swan floated calmly behind it.

Just then Andrewshek's Auntie Katushka came hurrying up with the spring water. She saw the big white swan floating down the stream, with the lunch basket floating ahead of him.

Andrewshek stood in the middle of the stream, crying.

Auntie Katushka picked up her umbrella with the long, crooked handle. Auntie Katushka ran along the shore until she overtook the big white swan, with the lunch basket floating ahead of him.

She caught the handle of the picnic basket in the

crook of her long-handled umbrella. She drew the basket safely to shore.

"Well! well!" said Auntie Katushka, as she spread the red and white napkin on the grass and laid the sandwiches and the poppy-seed cakes and the cottage cheese and the eggs upon it. "It always pays to carry an umbrella to a picnic."

IN THE GARDEN

Helen Coale Crew

There is a murmur
All night in the garden;
There is a murmur
All day, all day;
No, not the pigeons;
No, not the honey bees;
Only the silver
Fountain at play!

161

Helen and Alf Evers

THE HAPPY HEN

ILLUSTRATED BY *Helen Evers*

Here is a happy brown hen. She hasn't any teeth like the dog—or hands like the farmer; or whiskers like the cat. And yet, she is happy.

She doesn't want to moo like the cow or to swim like the ducks. She is just a happy stay-at-home hen.

But the *other* chickens wanted to travel. And so one day when their gate blew open they rushed and scrambled and flew away. But the little brown hen was too happy at home to go traveling.

Then everyone said, "Look at the brown hen. *She* is staying at home. She didn't want to go away with the rest. She must be ill! Perhaps she has a headache or a cold or a fever."

So the farmer put the hen to bed, near the stove, and gave her pink pills, white pills, and brown pills. He mixed the poor hen a hot mustard plaster. His wife made her gargle, the baby gave her rhubarb and soda, they wrapped her in blankets, with a hot-water bottle—until her head drooped—her eyes half-closed—and she ached *all* over!

So the farmer said, "There's no hope!" and he put the hen back in the chicken yard.

Then she ran and jumped—she clucked and cackled. And looked healthier and happier than ever. And everyone said, "We've cured her!"

But she *knew* why she was healthy and happy—nobody bothered her and she was *home!*

Dinah Maria Mulock

ADVENTURES OF A BROWNIE

ADAPTED BY *Mathilda Schirmer*
ILLUSTRATED BY *Ruth van Tellingen*

ONCE upon a time there was a wee little man called Brownie. His face and hands were brown. His clothes, too, were brown, from the top of his peaked cap to the tips of his pointed shoes.

Brownie lived in the coal cellar of an old house, which is a curious place to live, but Brownie liked it.

Only the children who lived upstairs in the house ever saw Brownie. They said he was more fun than anybody, even though he was years and years old. He was full of mischief and up to all sorts of tricks.

Every night Cook put a bowl of milk behind the cellar door for Brownie's supper. And every morning it was empty. But no one ever saw Brownie at his supper.

Gardener said to Cook one night, "Put sour milk in the bowl, instead of sweet. Brownie wouldn't know the difference."

"Yes," said Gardener's wife. "It's more important that we should have everything you can spare for our ducklings, and pigs, and cows."

"Fiddlesticks," said Cook, and she went right ahead and poured sweet milk into the bowl.

Brownie hid under his coal. "Dear me, I must teach these mortals better manners," he said.

The next morning Gardener and his wife went into

163

the farmyard, but they could not find the ducklings anywhere.

"Oh, who can have carried off my ducklings?" cried Gardener's wife. "They have wandered away because you did not make the pond for them as you promised," she said to Gardener.

"Cluck, cluck," mourned the big Brahma hen who had hatched them. If she had been able to speak she might have told how a large white duck had waddled out, coaxing them after him. But even the hen didn't know that the large, white duck was Brownie!

Just then the six boys and girls who lived upstairs came running into the farmyard. Sometimes, when they had been very, very good, they were allowed to go with Gardener. Each would carry his own mug and Gardener would give them a rich, creamy drink of milk, warm from the cow. But this day Gardener sent them back to the kitchen with their mugs.

"You may come to the field," said Gardener, "but I haven't a drop of milk to spare, and Cook is wanting more."

The children walked back to the kitchen.

Then they followed Gardener to the field. It was such a beautiful morning that soon they were scampering and playing and laughing.

Several rabbits darted past, and one very large brown rabbit dodged in and out. Once he nearly threw Gardener down, pail and all, by running across his feet.

They came to a large oak tree where Dolly the cow lay chewing her cud. It was great fun to stir her up, and she let them do it; for Dolly was the gentlest cow in the world.

164

But then something strange seemed to happen to her. She stood switching her tail and looking as savage as so mild an animal possibly could look. She refused to be milked.

"Shh, Dolly! Good Dolly!" said Gardener. But Dolly was anything but good.

"Look," said the biggest boy. He pointed to a large wasp.

"Oho, that's the reason," said Gardener. Dolly was so frightened that with one wild bound she darted away to the farther end of the field.

"I'll get a rope, and tie her legs together," cried Gardener.

"Ha, ha, ha!" laughed somebody. Gardener thought it was the children, but they knew it was somebody

else. The minute Gardener walked away Dolly came back quietly, led by a little brown man who was no taller than Dolly's knees. He guided her by a string as thin as a spider web, floating from one of her horns.

"Whoa, Dolly! Good Dolly!" said Brownie. "Now who wants breakfast?"

"We do!" cried the children together.

"So do I," said Brownie.

Brownie climbed up on the milking stool and sat on the edge, his little legs dangling halfway down. Dolly stood as still as could be while he milked, till he had filled the whole pail with delicious milk—frothing and yellow.

The children's mouths watered for it, but they didn't say a word even when Brownie put his mouth to the pail. He drank and drank until it seemed as if there wouldn't be any milk left. But when he popped his head up again, the pail was as full as ever!

"Now, boys and girls, now's your turn. Where are your mugs?"

"We haven't any," they said. "Gardener made us take them back again."

166

"Never mind. Gather six of the biggest buttercups you can find."

"What nonsense!" thought the children; but they did it. Brownie laid the flowers in a row upon the eldest girl's lap—blew upon them one by one, and each turned into the most beautiful golden cup that ever was seen! Then he filled each cup and gave them to the children. When they were empty he filled them up again.

"Good, Dolly! Thank you, Dolly!" he said again, mimicking Gardener's voice. As he spoke the real voice was heard behind the hedge. The children snatched up their mugs, but they had all turned into buttercups again.

Gardener jumped over the stile, with an old rope in his hand.

"Bother, bother!" he said. "Breakfast ready, and no milk yet. And such a to-do over those lost ducklings. Hello, Dolly. Quiet! Quiet!"

Dolly was quiet, but not a drop of milk was in the pail.

"The creature's bewitched," cried Gardener. "Or else

167

somebody has milked her dry already!"

"Look in your pail again," cried a voice from the other side of Dolly. Gardener looked, and there in the pail was the usual quantity of milk.

"It must be the Brownie!" exclaimed Gardener. He took off his hat. "Thank you, sir," he said.

Gardener started back to the farmyard with the children following after him. "You children had better tell your mother all about it. I left her in the farmyard worrying about her ducklings," he said.

Now Brownie heard this and was sorry because he liked the children's mother, who had always been kind to him. So instead of going to bed in the coal cellar he went to the farmyard. He hid behind the hen-coop.

"What can have become of those poor ducklings," said the children's mother.

Suddenly a handsome guinea hen ran in front of

the children and across the farmyard, screaming.

"Oh, what a beautiful bird!" cried the children, and they ran after it.

They followed it through the gate and out into the lane. It turned a corner. When they ran around the corner, there was Brownie. He was sitting on the top of a big thistle. His legs were crossed, and his arms, too. His little brown cap was cocked on one side, and he was laughing.

"How do you do? How do you do?" he said. "I'll help you find your ducklings."

They crossed the field to a wood, and to a green path in it. It led to a beautiful, sky-blue pond, as clear as crystal.

"Shut your eyes and you'll see the ducklings," said Brownie. They all laughed, but they did it. When they opened their eyes again there in front of them were all the ducklings, fat and content, swimming easily across the pond.

"There they are, all of them. Count them!"

"One-two-three-four-five-six-seven-eight," counted the eldest boy.

"Now try and catch them—if you can!" laughed Brownie.

It was not easy. They coaxed them. They shouted at

them. They threw little sticks at them. But as soon as they wanted them to go one way the ducks turned round and sailed another way.

Brownie watched them from a branch of the willow tree. He dangled his legs down to the surface of the pond, kicking at water spiders, and grinning with all his might.

After a while the children grew tired and asked him to help them.

"Turn around three times and see what you can find," he said.

They turned around and around and around, and then each little boy found in his arms, and each little girl found in her apron, a fine fat duckling. And the two elder children had two each.

The children hugged them and ran home as fast as they could, only turning to wave "thank you" to Brownie.

When they got to the farmyard their mother was as happy as they.

The ducklings ran to the old hen as soon as they were on the ground. "Cluck, cluck, cluck," she greeted each one.

"Where did you find them?" asked the children's mother.

They told her all about Brownie and about the beautiful pond. They never tired talking about it, but they never saw it again.

Gardener put a pond in the farmyard, and the ducklings were happy waddling and paddling in the water. They grew up into eight fat ducks, three gray ones, and five white ones, and never wandered away again, which made the mother hen very happy.

THE PEACEFUL PIRATE

Leroy F. Jackson

The Peaceful Pirate met my aunt
In front of Fuller's restaurant.
He asked her in and ordered up
The Bay of Biscay in a cup,
With satyr soup and dragon steak
And half a ton of ginger cake,
A barrel of mustard, half a whale,
A pickled salmon in a pail,
And salad made of Spanish moss,
With half a dozen kinds of sauce.
He was, as far as he could see,
As sweet and gracious as could be,
And even started in to bawl
Because she could not eat it all.

172

Phyllis McGinley

THE HORSE
WHO LIVED UPSTAIRS

ILLUSTRATED BY *Frances Eckart*

THERE was once a horse named Joey who was discontented. He was discontented because he didn't live in a red barn with a weathervane on top, and he didn't live in a green meadow where he could run about and kick up his heels.

Instead, he lived upstairs in a big brick building in New York. Joey worked for Mr. Polaski who sold fruits and vegetables to city people. Joey pulled the vegetable wagon through the city streets. And in New York, there isn't room for barns or meadows.

So every night when Joey came home, he stepped out from the shafts of the wagon, and into an elevator, and up he went to his stall on the fourth floor of the big brick building. It was a fine stall and Joey was very comfortable there. He had plenty of oats to eat and plenty of fresh straw to lie on.

He even had a window to look out of. But still Joey was discontented.

"How I long to sip fresh water from a babbling brook!" he often exclaimed.

And then he would sniff discontentedly at the old bathtub near the elevator which served him as a watering trough.

173

It wasn't that he had to work hard. Mr. Polaski was kind to him and brought him home at five o'clock every day.

In the winter Joey had a blanket to wear on his back to keep him warm.

And in the summertime Mr. Polaski got him a hat to wear on his head to keep him cool.

And every day he had many interesting adventures. Sometimes he met a Policeman who gave him sugar.

Sometimes ladies patted him on the nose and fed him carrots.

He was introduced to the highbred horses who drew the hansom cabs along the Plaza.

He saw the children playing in the playgrounds and the parks. But it made no difference to Joey.

"This is no life for a horse," he used to say to the Percheron who lived in the next stall to him. "We city horses don't know what real living is. I want to move to the country and sleep in a red barn with a weathervane on top, and kick up my heels in a green meadow."

So how happy he was when one day Mr. Polaski said to him, "Joey, I think I could sell more vegetables if I drove a truck. I will miss you, Joey, but you will like it on the farm where I am going to send you."

The next morning a big motor van rolled up. Joey got inside, and away he went to the country. Of course he said good-bye to the Percheron.

"Good-bye, Joey," called his friend. "I hope you will be contented on the farm."

When Joey reached the country, sure enough, there was the barn with its weathervane, and there was the meadow.

"This is the life!" cried Joey to himself.

But poor Joey! The barn was cold in winter and hot in summer. He didn't have a blanket and he didn't have a hat. And he had very little time to kick up his heels in the green meadow, for all day long he pulled a plow through the earth.

A plow is harder to pull than a wagon, and besides, the farmer worked from sunrise to sundown instead of the eight hours Joey was used to.

Sometimes they forgot to put fresh straw in his stall, and nobody thought to give him sugar or carrots.

There were plenty of children, but they climbed on his back and teased him when he wanted to eat. And instead of the Percheron, there was a cross old gray horse next door to him, who looked down his nose at Joey because Joey knew so little about farm life.

One day, when he wasn't pulling a plow, because it was Sunday, Joey saw several people picnicking in the meadow. He decided to join them, for they looked as if they came from the city, and he thought they might have a lump of sugar in one of their pockets.

When he reached the spot they had gone for a walk, so he ate up their lunch.

When they came back, they were very angry, and Joey was shut up in his stall for the rest of the day. He didn't even have a window to look out of.

He was lonely for his friends, the Policeman, and the ladies who patted him on the nose.

He was lonely for the highbred horses, and all the interesting sights of the city.

176

"I don't think I belong in the country after all," sighed Joey. "I am now more discontented than ever."

Next day he heard the honk of a horn. He looked from the door of the barn, and whom should he see but Mr. Polaski, getting out of the truck!

"I have come for Joey," Mr. Polaski told the farmer. "I think I'll sell fruit and vegetables from my wagon again."

My goodness, but Joey was happy!

He went back to the city with Mr. Polaski and got into the elevator and up he went to the fourth floor of the big brick building. There was his stall, and there was the window for him to look out of.

And there was the friendly Percheron. "Welcome back, Joey," exclaimed the Percheron. "I have missed you. The Policeman has missed you. The lady customers have missed you, and so have the children in the playgrounds and parks. Tell me, did you like the country?"

"The country is all right for country animals," Joey said, "but I guess I am just a city horse at heart."

And he was never discontented again.

Anne Stoddard

A GOOD LITTLE DOG

ILLUSTRATED BY *Miriam Hurford*

MY NAME is Bingo. I am a good little dog. Betty says so, and she ought to know.

I live at Our House. Betty and Bob live there, too. Bob teaches me to do tricks.

There is a garden at Our House. It is a fine place to bury bones. We play there. Tag is a good game and so is hide-and-seek. But I do not see why anybody wants to play dolls.

Everything would be lovely at Our House if it were not for Lisa. Lisa is a rag doll. She is no friend of mine, but Betty loves her. Sometimes I think Betty loves Lisa as much as me. It hurts my feelings.

Betty has a little red wagon. She gives Lisa a ride in it every morning. I run behind it and I pull Lisa out of the wagon. Then I chew her a little.

One day there were painters at Our House. They put a ladder up to the playroom window. "Here, Bingo!" said Bob. "I will teach you to climb this ladder." It looked hard. I did not know whether I wanted to climb or not.

Then I saw smoke coming out of Our House. It came out under the roof. Somebody shouted, "FIRE!" It was John, our gardener.

"Lisa is in the playroom!" cried Betty. "She will be burned up!"

I did not want Lisa to be burned, so I went up the ladder. The smoke was thick. It made tears run down my nose. A spark fell down, almost on my head. But I went on.

There was lots of smoke in the playroom. I could not see the dolls' bed where Lisa slept. At last I found it. I took Lisa in my teeth and went down the ladder.

Then the firemen came and put out the fire.

Betty said I was a good little dog, and Bob said I was a hero. I am, too.

I like Lisa now. And I do not tease her any more. If you save a doll's life, you just have to be kind to her.

Otto is a giant dog from France who, because of his size, is very helpful. In this adventure he comes over the sea to make a good-will tour of America.

William Pène du Bois

OTTO AT SEA

ILLUSTRATED BY THE AUTHOR

AFTER Otto had received a medal for extraordinary courage in Africa, the President of France invited Duke and Otto to Paris in order to give Otto a decoration.

Duke went to see the President and Otto waited outside.

The President looked beyond Duke, to the right of Duke, to the left of Duke, and all around, and then asked but one word: "Otto?"

"Otto, sir," said Duke, "is outside awaiting your slightest request. But as he is fully two stories high, I am sure that he might even apply his nose to this third-story window by standing on his hind legs, if you should so wish to see him."

"Let us go out on the balcony," said the President. Then, seeing Otto, he exclaimed, "His size is only comparable to his astounding feats of strength!"

And he decorated him.

"I should advise," said the President, "a good-will trip to America."

"Excellent," said Duke.

So Duke and Otto went to Le Havre to see the captain of the good ship *Caesar*.

They found the captain seated at his garden table in back of his house.

"We are passengers," said Duke.

"Passengers," said the captain, "and also most distinguished guests." And he jumped from his seat and ran into his house, yelling, "Otto, I cannot believe it —OTTO!"

He then came running out with his first mate, muttering: "Otto, such a dog—OTTO. I am honored!"

Then he started to talk to the first mate.

And after a while he said, "The first mate says there is room for Otto."

The *Caesar* sailed for New York the next day. Otto sat in the hold and Duke found the captain again seated at his garden table forward.

"I always bring my table," said the captain. "I am never without it—never."

"Let me introduce you to the only other two passengers," said the captain. "Emissaries of good will from the Tyrolean Mountains, and Olympic mountain-climbing champions."

The ocean was quite calm for the first few days, but after that it became extraordinarily rough. Otto leaned first to one side and then to the other and by so shifting his weight managed to keep the good ship *Caesar* as steady as if she were in calm waters.

"Remarkable," said the captain to the first mate. "Without Otto I fear *Caesar* would have long before been shaken and battered to pieces."

But as the waves became larger and heavier, Otto became worried. Some bothered him particularly, so, shifting his weight and lashing his tail to keep the

182

boat steady, he leaned way over one side and blew the enormous waves so hard that they completely disappeared. Unfortunately, as he was leaning over to smooth off the last small ripples, a gigantic wave came

from the other side and swept completely over the decks of the *Caesar*. This wave was followed by another bigger one, and two more still bigger, and they all landed amidships with a wallop, filling the *Caesar* well with water and ripping large holes in her sides.

Otto jumped overboard to make the ship lighter and stop it from sinking too fast.

The captain was at the back of the ship shouting orders to the first mate, and telling him to take care of the crew. He also asked the ambassadors of good will if they could possibly save his table.

Everybody was excited, shouting commands and scrambling off the ship as fast as they could. But after hours of terrifically rough seas all was calm.

And they traveled on to New York.

"There was no way to save *Caesar*," said the captain. "She would have gone down long before if Otto hadn't steadied her."

In New York they were greeted with cheers, and people threw papers and ticker tape out of the windows. and they all were very happy and proud—except Otto.

"These papers tickle me," he said, "and I cannot see the big buildings very well."

"Blow," said Duke.

So Otto blew and the streets were cleared.

"This is much better now," said Otto, "and I like this city very much."

So they marched down to the mayor's house. The mayor was waiting for them with a medal for Otto.

However, when Otto arrived, the mayor had trouble giving him his medal.

"I cannot quite reach the proper spot on Otto's chest," said the mayor. "What would you suggest, Duke, that I do?"

"We will take care of that," said the emissaries of good will. "We are mountain climbers."

So one emissary climbed on the other's shoulders, and for distinguished services at sea and extraordinary feats of lifesaving, Otto was presented with a most handsome medal.

EEYORE the Donkey, Pooh Bear, and Piglet are toys of a little boy named Christopher Robin. They are toys that talk and have many funny adventures. This time the storyteller tells Christopher Robin of what happened when Eeyore the Donkey had a birthday.

A. A. Milne

IN WHICH
EEYORE HAS A BIRTHDAY
AND GETS TWO PRESENTS

ILLUSTRATED BY *Ernest H. Shepard*

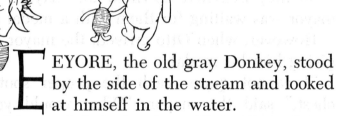

EYORE, the old gray Donkey, stood by the side of the stream and looked at himself in the water.

"Pathetic," he said. "That's what it is. Pathetic."

He turned and walked slowly down the stream for twenty yards, splashed across it, and walked slowly back on the other side. Then he looked at himself in the water again.

"As I thought," he said. "No better from *this* side. But nobody minds. Nobody cares. Pathetic, that's what it is."

There was a crackling noise in the bracken behind him and out came Pooh.

"Good morning, Eeyore," said Pooh.

"Good morning, Pooh Bear," said Eeyore gloomily. "If it *is* a good morning," he said. "Which I doubt," said he.

"Why, what's the matter?"

"Nothing, Pooh Bear, nothing. We can't all, and some of us don't. That's all there is to it."

"Can't all *what?*" said Pooh, rubbing his nose.

"Gaiety. Song-and-dance. Here we go round the mulberry bush."

"Oh!" said Pooh. He thought for a long time, and then asked, "What mulberry bush is that?"

"Bon-hommy," went on Eeyore gloomily. "French word meaning bonhommy," he explained. "I'm not complaining, but There It Is."

Pooh sat down on a large stone and tried to think this out. It sounded to him like a riddle, and he was never much good at riddles, being a Bear of Very Little Brain. So he sang *Cottleston Pie* instead:

> "Cottleston, Cottleston, Cottleston Pie,
> A fly can't bird, but a bird can fly.
> Ask me a riddle and I reply:
> '*Cottleston, Cottleston, Cottleston Pie.*'"

That was the first verse. When he had finished it, Eeyore didn't actually say that he didn't like it, so Pooh very kindly sang the second verse to him:

> "Cottleston, Cottleston, Cottleston Pie,
> A fish can't whistle and neither can I.
> Ask me a riddle and I reply:
> '*Cottleston, Cottleston, Cottleston Pie.*'"

Eeyore still said nothing at all, so Pooh hummed the third verse quietly to himself:

"Cottleston, Cottleston, Cottleston Pie,
Why does a chicken, I don't know why.
Ask me a riddle and I reply:
"Cottleston, Cottleston, Cottleston Pie,

"That's right," said Eeyore. "Sing. Umty-tiddly, umty-too. Here we go gathering Nuts in May. Enjoy yourself."

"I am," said Pooh.

"Some can," said Eeyore.

"Why, what's the matter?"

"*Is* anything the matter?"

"You seem so sad, Eeyore."

"Sad? Why should I be sad? It's my birthday. The happiest day of the year."

"Your birthday?" said Pooh in great surprise.

"Of course it is. Can't you see? Look at all the presents I have had." He waved a foot from side to side. "Look at the birthday cake. Candles and pink sugar."

Pooh looked—first to the right and then to the left.

"Presents?" said Pooh. "Birthday cake?" said Pooh. "*Where?*"

"Can't you see them?"

"No," said Pooh.

"Neither can I," said Eeyore. "Joke," he explained. "Ha ha!"

Pooh scratched his head, being a little puzzled by all this.

"But is it really your birthday?" he asked.

"It is."

"Oh! Well, many happy returns of the day, Eeyore."

"And many happy returns to you, Pooh Bear."

"But it isn't *my* birthday."

"No, it's mine."

"But you said 'Many happy returns'——"

"Well, why not? You don't always want to be miserable on my birthday, do you?"

"Oh, I see," said Pooh.

"It's bad enough," said Eeyore, almost breaking down, "being miserable myself, what with no presents and no cake and no candles, and no proper notice taken of me at all, but if everybody else is going to be miserable too——"

This was too much for Pooh. "Stay there!" he called to Eeyore, as he turned and hurried back home as quick as he could; for he felt that he must get poor Eeyore a present of *some* sort at once, and he could always think of a proper one afterwards.

Outside his house he found Piglet, jumping up and down trying to reach the knocker.

"Hello, Piglet," he said.

"Hello, Pooh," said Piglet.

"What are *you* trying to do?"

"I was trying to reach the knocker," said Piglet. "I just came round——"

"Let me do it for you," said Pooh kindly. So he reached up and knocked at the door. "I have just seen Eeyore," he began, "and poor Eeyore is in a Very Sad Condition, because it's his birthday, and nobody has taken any notice of it, and he's very Gloomy—you know what Eeyore is—and there he was, and—— What a long

190

time whoever lives here is answering this door." And he knocked again.

"But Pooh," said Piglet, "it's your own house!"

"Oh!" said Pooh. "So it is," he said. "Well, let's go in."

So in they went. The first thing Pooh did was to go to the cupboard to see if he had quite a small jar of honey left; and he had, so he took it down.

"I'm giving this to Eeyore," he explained, "as a present. What are *you* going to give?"

"Couldn't I give it too?" said Piglet. "From both of us?"

"No," said Pooh. "That would *not* be a good plan."

"All right, then, I'll give him a balloon. I've got one left from my party. I'll go and get it now, shall I?"

"That, Piglet, is a *very* good idea. It is just what Eeyore wants to cheer him up. Nobody can be uncheered with a balloon."

So off Piglet trotted; and in the other direction went Pooh, with his jar of honey.

It was a warm day, and he had a long way to go. He hadn't gone more than halfway when a sort of funny feeling began to creep all over him. It began at the tip of his nose and trickled all through him and out at the soles of his feet. It was just as if somebody inside him were saying, "Now then, Pooh, time for a little something."

"Dear, dear," said Pooh, "I didn't know it was as late as that." So he sat down and took the top off his jar of honey. "Lucky I brought this with me," he thought. "Many a bear going out on a warm day like this would never have thought of bringing a little something with him." And he began to eat.

"Now let me see," he thought, as he took his last lick of the inside of the jar, "where was I going? Ah, yes, Eeyore." He got up slowly.

And then, suddenly, he remembered. He had eaten Eeyore's birthday present!

"*Bother!*" said Pooh. "What *shall* I do? I *must* give him *something.*"

For a little while he couldn't think of anything. Then he thought: "Well, it's a very nice pot, even if there's no honey in it, and if I washed it clean, and got somebody to write 'A *Happy Birthday*' on it, Eeyore could keep things in it, which might be Useful." So, as he was just passing the Hundred Acre Wood, he went inside to call on Owl, who lived there.

"Good morning, Owl," he said.

"Good morning, Pooh," said Owl.

"Many happy returns of Eeyore's birthday," said Pooh.

"Oh, is that what it is?"

"What are you giving him, Owl?"

"What are *you* giving him, Pooh?"

"I'm giving him a Useful Pot to Keep Things In, and I wanted to ask you——"

"Is this it?" said Owl, taking it out of Pooh's paw.

"Yes, and I wanted to ask you——"

"Somebody has been keeping honey in it," said Owl.

"You can keep *anything* in it," said Pooh earnestly. "It's Very Useful like that. And I wanted to ask you——"

"You ought to write 'A *Happy Birthday*' on it."

"*That* was what I wanted to ask you," said Pooh. "Because my spelling is Wobbly. It's good spelling but it Wobbles, and the letters get in the wrong places. Would *you* write 'A Happy Birthday' on it for me?"

"It's a nice pot," said Owl, looking at it all around. "Couldn't I give it too? From both of us?"

"No," said Pooh. "That would *not* be a good plan. Now I'll just wash it first, and then you can write on it."

Well, he washed the pot out and dried it, while Owl licked the end of his pencil and wondered how to spell "birthday."

"Can you read, Pooh?" he asked a little anxiously. "There's a notice about knocking and ringing outside my door, which Christopher Robin wrote. Could you read it?"

"Christopher Robin told me what it said, and *then* I could."

"Well, I'll tell you what *this* says, and then you'll be able to."

So Owl wrote . . . and this is what he wrote:

HIPY PAPY BTHUTHDTH THUTHDA BTHUTHDY.

Pooh looked on admiringly.

"I'm just saying 'A Happy Birthday,'" said Owl carelessly.

"It's a nice long one," said Pooh, very much impressed by it.

"Well, *actually*, of course, I'm saying 'A Very Happy Birthday with love from Pooh.' Naturally it takes a good deal of pencil to say a long thing like that."

"Oh, I see," said Pooh.

While all this was happening, Piglet had gone back to his own house to get Eeyore's balloon. He held it very tightly against himself, so that it shouldn't blow away, and he ran as fast as he could so as to get to Eeyore before Pooh did; for he thought that he would like to be the first one to give a present, just as if he had thought of it without being told by anybody. And running along, and thinking how pleased Eeyore would be, he didn't look where he was going . . . and suddenly he put his foot in a rabbit hole and fell down flat on his face.

BANG!!!???***!!!

Piglet lay there, wondering what had happened. At first he thought that the whole world had blown up; and then he thought that perhaps only the Forest part of it had; and then he thought that perhaps only *he* had, and he was now alone in the moon or somewhere, and would never see Christopher Robin or Pooh or Eeyore again. And then he thought, "Well, even if I'm in the moon, I needn't be face downwards all the time," so he got cautiously up and looked about him.

He was still in the Forest!

"Well, that's funny," he thought. "I wonder what that bang was. I couldn't have made such a noise just falling down. And where's my balloon? And what's that small piece of damp rag doing?"

It was the balloon!

"Oh, dear," said Piglet. "Oh, dear, oh, dearie, dearie, dear! Well, it's too late now. I can't go·back, and I haven't another balloon, and perhaps Eeyore doesn't *like* balloons so *very* much."

So he trotted on, rather sadly now, and down he came to the side of the stream where Eeyore was and called out to him.

"Good morning, Eeyore," shouted Piglet.

"Good morning, Little Piglet," said Eeyore. "If it *is* a good morning," he said. "Which I doubt," said he. "Not that it matters," he said.

"Many happy returns of the day," said Piglet, having now got closer.

Eeyore stopped looking at himself in the stream and turned to stare at Piglet.

"Just say that again," he said.

"Many hap——"

"Wait a moment."

Balancing on three legs, he began to bring his fourth leg very cautiously up to his ear. "I did this yesterday," he explained, as he fell down for the third time. "It's quite easy. It's so as I can hear better. . . . There, that's done it! Now then, what were you saying?" He pushed his ear forward with his hoof.

"Many happy returns of the day," said Piglet again.

"Meaning me?"

"Of course, Eeyore."

"My birthday?"

"Yes."

"Me having a real birthday?"

"Yes, Eeyore, and I've brought you a present."

Eeyore took down his right hoof from his right ear, turned round, and with great difficulty put up his left hoof.

"I must have that in the other ear," he said. "Now then."

"A present," said Piglet very loudly.

"Meaning me again?"

"Yes."

"My birthday still?"

"Of course, Eeyore."

"Me going on having a real birthday?"

"Yes, Eeyore, and I brought you a balloon."

"*Balloon?*" said Eeyore. "You did say balloon? One of those big colored things you blow up? Gaiety, song-and-dance, here we are and there we are?"

"Yes, but I'm afraid—I'm very sorry, Eeyore—but when I was running along to bring it you, I fell down."

"Dear, dear, how unlucky! You ran too fast, I expect. You didn't hurt yourself, Little Piglet?"

"No, but I—I—oh, Eeyore, I burst the balloon!"

There was a very long silence.

"My balloon?" said Eeyore at last.

Piglet nodded.

"My birthday balloon?"

"Yes, Eeyore," said Piglet sniffing a little. "Here it is. With—with many happy returns of the day." And he gave Eeyore the small piece of damp rag.

"Is this it?" said Eeyore, a little surprised.

Piglet nodded.

"My present?"

Piglet nodded again.

"The balloon?"

"Yes."

"Thank you, Piglet," said Eeyore. "You don't mind my asking," he went on, "but what color was this balloon when it—when it *was* a balloon?"

"Red."

"I just wondered. . . . Red," he murmured to himself. "My favorite color. . . . How big was it?"

"About as big as me."

"I just wondered. . . . About as big as Piglet," he said to himself sadly. "My favorite size. Well, well."

Piglet felt very miserable and didn't know what to say. He was still opening his mouth to begin something, and then deciding that it wasn't any good saying *that*, when he heard a shout from the other side of the river, and there was Pooh.

"Many happy returns of the day," called out Pooh, forgetting that he had said it already.

"Thank you, Pooh, I'm having them," said Eeyore gloomily.

"I've brought you a little present," said Pooh excitedly.

"I've had it," said Eeyore.

Pooh had now splashed across the stream to Eeyore, and Piglet was sitting a little way off, his head in his paws, snuffling to himself.

"It's a Useful Pot," said Pooh. "Here it is. And it's got 'A Very Happy Birthday with love from Pooh' written on it. That's what all that writing is. And it's for putting things in. There!"

When Eeyore saw the pot, he became quite excited.

"Why!" he said. "I believe my Balloon will just go into that Pot!"

"Oh, no, Eeyore," said Pooh. "Balloons are much too big to go into Pots. What you do with a balloon is, you hold the balloon——"

"Not mine," said Eeyore proudly. "Look, Piglet!" And as Piglet looked sorrowfully round, Eeyore picked the balloon up with his teeth and placed it carefully in the pot; picked it out and put it on the ground; and then picked it up again and put it carefully back.

"So it does!" said Pooh. "It goes in!"

"So it does!" said Piglet. "And it comes out!"

"Doesn't it?" said Eeyore. "It goes in and out like anything."

"I'm very glad," said Pooh happily, "that I thought of giving you a Useful Pot to put things in."

"I'm very glad," said Piglet happily, "that I thought of giving you Something to put in a Useful Pot."

But Eeyore wasn't listening. He was taking the balloon out, and putting it back again, as happy as could be. . . .

. . . . .

"And didn't *I* give him anything?" asked Christopher Robin sadly.

"Of course you did," I said. "You gave him—don't you remember—a little—a little——"

"I gave him a box of paints to paint things with."

"That was it."

"Why didn't I give it to him in the morning?"

"You were so busy getting his party ready for him. He had a cake with icing on the top, and three candles, and his name in pink sugar, and——"

"Yes, *I* remember," said Christopher Robin.

Hardie Gramatky

HERCULES

ILLUSTRATED BY
THE AUTHOR

THIS is the story of Hercules, a famous fire engine. When *your* grandfather was young, he and his friends thought that Hercules was one of the finest fire engines ever built. Then nobody had ever heard of a fire truck.

It wasn't so long ago, either.

Today Hercules is in a museum. Had it not been for a wonderful act of courage—and a little luck—he never would have won such a fine place.

This is how it happened. The day Hercules came from the factory the whole town turned out; and the Mayor made a long speech and proudly referred to Hercules as "the most modern, the most up-to-date fire engine in the world."

It was a proud day for Hercules. His brass gleamed, his safety valve danced, and the quivering needle on the steam gauge showed how strong he was.

Hercules was drawn by three horses—one black, one white, and one dapple-gray. And the people of the town presented him with a mascot, a spotted coach dog to run with him to the fires.

Hercules had a crew of three—Hokey, Pokey, and Smokey. Hokey was the fireman. He kept steam up in the big boiler.

Pokey was engineer. He watched the gauges and connected the hose to hydrants.

And Smokey sat on the front seat and drove the horses.

They made a great team. People used to hang around the firehouse for hours on end, on the chance an alarm might ring.

It was exciting to see the horses leap toward their harness when the gong struck.

It was even more exciting to see them in full flight through the town.

And it was most exciting of all to see how quickly they put out a fire. One blast of water from Hercules' hose and it was all over.

Anyhow, that's how it was in the beginning. The trouble was that time was passing, and new things were being invented.

There was a strange, noisy vehicle—the automobile. People called it a "horseless carriage."

It was almost too much for the horses. . . .

Hokey didn't like the looks of this at all. "First thing you know," he said, "they'll be puttin' motors in fire engines. And when they do that Hercules and all of us are done for."

But Smokey and Pokey said he was plumb crazy. Smokey jeered, "We'll stick by Hercules and our horses. At least with them we'll always get to the fire."

This was true. But Smokey, in his pride and affection, had overlooked the simple fact that with a fire engine what counts above everything else is getting to a fire *first*.

For there came a day . . . when Hercules, though

he rolled as fast as ever, arrived too late.

The fire was out.

It had been put out by a new kind of fire engine—
an engine that wasn't pulled by horses at all.

This new-fangled machine chugged under its own

power. Already one of these monsters was coming back from the fire and at the top of the hill Hercules met him face to face.

The upstart blasted his exhaust in Hercules' face and nearly choked him to death.

HARDIE GRAMATKY

Life was unbearable after that. The Aldermen and the Mayor solemnly decided that Hercules was "obsolete." He was too old—too slow. So they retired him.

From then on nothing seemed to happen. The alarm never sounded.

The horses were sold—the black one to a riding academy, the dapple-gray to a junk dealer, and the white one to the police force.

And Hercules grew old like a soldier pining for the smell of gunpowder.

But Hokey, Pokey, and Smokey, because they loved the firehouse, stayed on.

"Wait and see," said Smokey, "someday there's goin' to be a fire—the worst fire this city ever saw. An' we'll be there—with Hercules. There's things that Hercules and horses can do that those trucks can't do."

That day came sooner than even Smokey had dared to hope. Their own alarm suddenly sounded. The cobwebs flew in all directions.

"It's a general alarm," yelled Smokey. "The City Hall. We've got to do something." However, there were no horses to pull Hercules.

But he knew what to do—he began to ring his big brass bell.

When the old black horse heard that familiar clang, he shot like a bolt from under his gentleman rider and tore to the firehouse.

The dapple-gray abandoned his junk wagon.

And the white horse just brought his new master right in with him.

"Here they come," yelled Pokey.

"We can use that hose," yelled Hokey. They stopped

only long enough to pick it up.

Then they overtook Hook and Ladder No. 1. No. 1 had blown a tire, then the spare, and the crew were sweating to pump it up.

"Never mind that," Smokey bellowed. "Get aboard with the ladder."

Emergency Truck No. 3 was hopelessly stuck in a muddy ditch.

"Get aboard," Pokey yelled to the dumfounded crew, "and bring your life net."

On the steep hill near the City Hall they heaved past Chemical No. 2. It just didn't have the power to get up the slope.

Hercules could do things that no fire truck could *ever* hope to do. . . .

The bridge was out, but . . .

Hercules never stopped. . . .

This was the worst fire he had ever seen. The heat was so scorching that Pokey had to unharness the horses and lead them away.

If they were to save the City Hall, Hercules had to pump water as he had never pumped before. While Hokey fed coal under the boiler, Pokey threw himself on the safety valve, and Hercules pumped until he was *blue* in the face.

Everyone was saved, including the Mayor and the Aldermen, with no hurt except to their dignity.

And that was how Hercules got into the Museum.

Dorothy and Marguerite Bryan

PIXIE, DIXIE, TRIXIE, AND NIXIE

ILLUSTRATED BY
Marguerite Bryan

FOUR small Cocker Spaniel puppies lived in a big box in a dog store.

Their names were Pixie, Dixie, Trixie, and Nixie.

Pixie was black. Dixie was black, too. Trixie was white, with odd black patches that made him look very comical indeed.

Nixie was soft brown and the smallest puppy of all. His legs were too short, and his ears were not as fine and long as those of his three handsome brothers.

Pixie, Dixie, Trixie, and Nixie were for sale, but no one came for a Cocker Spaniel puppy for a long time.

So Pixie grew to be a strong, steady black dog.

And Dixie grew to be a very proud black dog.

And Trixie grew to be a funny, silly, spotted dog.

While little Nixie—well, little Nixie grew to be just a *nice* soft brown dog.

Now although Pixie, Dixie, Trixie, and Nixie were not unhappy living together in the dog store, still each one did wish that someone would buy him and take him to a special home.

One day a kind-looking lady came into the store and spoke to the man there.

206

"I want a small, strong dog that would be good to a baby," she said.

The dog-store keeper led her over to where Pixie, Dixie, Trixie, and Nixie sat, all in a row. She looked them over carefully. She stopped a long time before Nixie, and Nixie looked longingly back at her. "This one looks *nice* enough for a baby, but he is really *too* small to take care of a baby. I will buy *this* one," she ended, patting Pixie on the head.

So then only Dixie, Trixie, and Nixie were left in the dog store, wishing for a home.

One day a proud-looking young lady came into the store and ordered, "I want a small, handsome dog that will ride with me in my automobile."

The dog-store keeper led her over to where Dixie, Trixie, and Nixie sat, three in a row. She looked them over briskly. When she turned towards Dixie, he put his nose high in the air and looked prouder than ever.

"I will buy *this* one," the young lady decided.

So then only Trixie and Nixie were left in the dog store, wishing for a home.

One day a jolly-looking man came into the store and called, "I want a small, lively dog that can act in my circus and make the children laugh."

The dog-store keeper led him over to where Trixie and Nixie sat, just two of them.

The jolly-looking man looked at Trixie and laughed. "Here is the silly circus dog I want to buy," he declared. He tweaked Nixie's ear, but it was Trixie that he tucked under his arm and carried away.

So then only little Nixie was left, *wishing* for a home.

The dog-store man moved Nixie into a cage in the

window, and there he sat all day, watching for someone to come along and want him.

One day Nixie saw Pixie trotting by, looking very
important. And no wonder, for Pixie was taking care
of, not one baby—but *two* babies in a carriage!

And Nixie wished *he* had somebody to take care of.

Another day Nixie saw Dixie go whizzing by, seated
very proudly on the back of a shining automobile, with
his ears flying out behind him.

And little Nixie wished hard that *he* had somebody
to take *him* riding.

Another sunny day Nixie heard a loud burst of music
and a circus parade marched right by the window
where he sat. There were brightly-dressed ladies on
prancing ponies and tumbling clowns riding in a
donkey cart, and all sorts of animals—lions, tigers, a
giraffe, monkeys in a gold cage, and walking at the end
of the circus parade, there was a line of big elephants.
Last of all trudged a baby elephant, with Trixie riding
gaily on his back, making all the children laugh.

And little Nixie wished *so* hard that *he* could ride
in a circus parade.

Many days went by and still little Nixie sat in the dog store, *wishing* for a home.

One morning a nice-looking lady came into the store with a little girl and said to the man, "I want to buy a dog for my little girl."

So the lady and the little girl started looking at all the dogs in the store—the big dogs and the small ones, the black dogs and the white ones and the brown ones, too. Finally they came to Nixie.

"This is just little Nixie," the dog-store man said, starting to move by. But the little girl stood still.

"I like *him* best," she said.

"But he is not a very good Cocker Spaniel," the dog-store man argued. "His legs are too short and his ears are too short, too."

The little girl knelt down on the floor and took Nixie in her arms. "I don't care. He is the *nicest* dog. I like little Nixie better than any dog in the store—better than any dog in the world."

So Pixie, Dixie, Trixie, and Nixie each found the special home that he had wished for—but little Nixie was sure that his was the very *nicest* home of all.

209

Maud Lindsay

MRS. TABBY GRAY

ILLUSTRATED BY *Esther Friend*

MRS. Tabby Gray, with her three little kittens, lived out in the barn where the hay was stored. One of the kittens was white, one was black, and one, gray, just like her mother, who was called Tabby Gray from the color of her coat.

These three little kittens opened their eyes when they grew old enough, and thought there was nothing so nice in all this wonderful world as their own dear mother, although she told them of a great many nice things, like milk and bread, which they should have when they go up to the big house where she had her breakfast, dinner, and supper.

Every time Mother Tabby came from the big house she had something pleasant to tell. "Bones for dinner today, my dears," she would say, or "I had a fine romp with a ball and the baby," until the kittens longed for the time when they could go, too.

One day, however, Mother Cat walked in with joyful news.

"I have found an elegant new home for you," she said, "in a very large trunk where some old clothes are kept; and I think I had better move at once."

Then she picked up the small black kitten, without any more words and walked right out of the barn with him.

The black kitten was astonished, but he blinked his eyes at the bright sunshine and tried to see everything.

Out in the barnyard there was a great noise, for the white hen had laid an egg and wanted everybody to know it; but Mother Cat hurried on, without stopping to inquire about it, and soon dropped the kitten into the large trunk. The clothes made such a soft, comfortable bed, and the kitten was so tired after his exciting trip, that he fell asleep, and Mrs. Tabby trotted off for another baby.

While she was away, the lady who owned the trunk came out into the hall; and when she saw that the trunk was open, she shut it, locked it, and put the key in her pocket, for she did not dream that there was anything so precious as a kitten inside.

As soon as the lady had gone upstairs, Mrs. Tabby Gray came back, with the little white kitten; and when she found the trunk closed, she was terribly frightened. She put the white kitten down and sprang on top of the

ESTHER
FRIEND

211

trunk and scratched with all her might, but scratching did no good. Then she jumped down and reached up to the keyhole, but that was too small for even a mouse to pass through, and the poor mother mewed pitifully.

What was she to do? She picked up the white kitten and ran to the barn with it. Then she made haste to the house again and went upstairs to the lady's room. The lady was playing with her baby, and, when Mother Cat saw this, she rubbed against her skirts and cried, "Mee-ow, mee-ow! You have your baby, and I want mine! Mee-ow, mee-ow!"

By and by the lady said, "Poor Kitty! she must be hungry," and she went down to the kitchen and poured sweet milk in a saucer, but the cat did not want milk. She wanted her baby kitten out of the big black trunk!

The kind lady decided that she must be thirsty. "Poor Kitty, I will give you water," but when she set the bowl of water down, Mrs. Tabby Gray mewed more sorrowfully than before. She wanted no water,— she only wanted her dear baby kitten; and she ran to and fro crying, until, at last, the lady followed her; and she led the way to the trunk.

"What can be the matter with this cat?" said the lady; and she took the trunk key out of her pocket, put it in the lock, unlocked the trunk, raised the top—and in jumped Mother Cat with such a bound that the little black kitten waked up with a start.

"Purr, purr, my darling child," said Mrs. Tabby Gray, in great excitement; and before the black kitten could ask one question she picked him up and started for the barn.

The sun was bright in the barnyard, and the hens were still chattering there; but the black kitten was glad to get back to the barn. His mother was glad, too; for, as she nestled down in the hay with her three little kittens, she told them that a barn was the best place after all to raise children.

And she never afterwards changed her mind.

THE GIRAFFE

Arthur Kramer

The giraffe from his head to his toes
Is the longest beast that grows.
He can stand on a knoll,
With his feet in a hole,
And be touching a star with his nose.

Alice Crew Gall and Fleming Crew

THE SONG OF THE LITTLE DONKEY

ILLUSTRATED BY *Ruth van Tellingen*

COLUMBUS, a small gray donkey, was being made ready for a journey. He stood very still while his master put his bridle on him and hitched him to the shafts of the cart, but when at last his little bell was fastened to his bridle he shook his head, so that the bell sent forth a series of tinkling notes. Columbus liked this sound: it made him feel cheerful.

"Just a minute now and we'll be off," his master said to him. "But first I have to load the cart." Columbus moved his ears back and forth to show he understood, and then shut his eyes while he waited.

But though his eyes were shut, he knew just what was happening. His master was carrying chairs from the house and putting them onto the cart. They were fine, dark chairs, so beautifully polished that they looked like satin, and Columbus knew that when the word to start was given he must walk very carefully,

214

so that these chairs would not joggle against each other and get marred and scratched.

Several times each year the little donkey and his master made a journey from the small house by the side of the road to a great city not far away. The cart was always filled with chairs when they started and always empty when they returned, for Columbus' master was such a fine cabinet-maker that he never had any trouble at all in selling the things he made.

And chairs were the things he liked best to make. "They are so friendly," he told Columbus, "for they are always inviting us to sit down and rest. And they provide a seat at the table when mealtime comes. The world would be a dreary place without chairs."

The old cabinet-maker often talked like this to his donkey, because he lived alone and had no one else to talk to. And Columbus always listened politely. The cabinet-maker and his donkey were good friends and got along well together, but there was one thing about which they could *not* agree and that was—roads. Each time they started to the city, the old cabinet-maker wanted to go straight along and get there as soon as possible. But Columbus wanted to explore, and always tried to turn in at the lanes and byways, because he felt sure he would find something there that was new and interesting.

Whenever he did this his master would give the lines a jerk and say: "No, no, Columbus. We have no time now to discover new places. We must get to town so that I can sell my chairs." And Columbus would have to give up the lanes and byways and go straight along.

Today, when the cart was loaded, the old cabinet-

215

maker climbed into the driver's seat and picked up the lines as he always did. "Giddap!" he said, making a little clucking noise, and Columbus opened his eyes, shook a few tinkles from his bell and trotted off.

The old cabinet-maker turned his head for a last look at his house. "It's a funny thing," he told his little donkey, "the way I feel today. I love my home better than any place on earth. I love the hills around it; I love Butterfly Brook that runs just behind it; and I love the trees and flowers that grow beside it. I don't like cities and never did—they are too crowded. But today I am glad to be going to the city. I am lonesome for the sound of children's voices. I want to hear them laugh and watch them play. Maybe it's because it's spring that I feel like this. Maybe the spring has got into my blood."

Columbus put his ears back and listened. There was a glad note in his master's voice that he had never heard before, and it made the little donkey so happy that he opened his mouth and sang. At least he *meant* it for singing, though really it was not so very musical.

"You understand how I feel, don't you, old fellow?" laughed the cabinet-maker. "Well, I'll tell you something else. Today, after I sell my chairs, I am going to find some place where children are playing, and we are going to stop and watch them, you and I. We are going to watch them even though it makes us late in getting back to Butterfly Brook."

Columbus tried to pay attention to what his master was saying, but his mind wandered. For just ahead he saw a shady lane running off from the highway. It was an inviting lane, and the little donkey hastened his steps. He would turn in there, he thought, and have a look at it. Surely on a day like this, when the air smelled so good and the grass was so green, his master would not mind stopping for a little while.

But when he turned toward the entrance to the lane his master gave the usual jerk on the lines. "Not today, Columbus," he said. "Someday when we have more time I'll let you explore all you want to; but not now." And so, once again, the little donkey had to go straight along.

"Here's the place we'll stop first," the old cabinet-maker said, when they had reached the city and traveled along one of its wide streets until they came to a handsome house. Columbus stopped obediently and looked around him.

The house stood well back on a beautiful lawn, and was surrounded by great trees and beds of blooming flowers. It looked even more inviting than the shady lane, he thought, and he wished he could go in and nibble some grass. But around this lawn was a high iron fence and there seemed to be no way of getting through it.

"Stand still, Columbus," the cabinet-maker told him, "and I'll go and ring the bell, there by the gate. I hope there's someone at home."

Climbing down from the cart, he pushed the bell, and at once a tall servant hurried forward.

"Good morning," said the old cabinet-maker. "If your master is at home, I should like to show him some chairs."

The tall servant looked at the cabinet-maker, and then at Columbus, and then at the cart. "My master is

217

at home," he said, "but I don't believe you had better try to sell him anything today. He's not in a very good humor."

"Oh, that doesn't matter," the cabinet-maker answered. "He will be in a good humor when he sees my chairs."

The tall servant opened the gate. "Very well," he said. "You may drive your little donkey up to the house. You'll find my master on the front porch, but don't blame *me* if he's cross with you."

Columbus could scarcely believe it when the cabinet-maker took him by the bridle and led him through the gate. He was going into the beautiful yard after all, he thought, and at once he started for the flower beds.

"Keep your donkey off the grass!" shouted the tall servant. And he sounded so stern that Columbus knew it was no use; he would have to go straight along.

"Good morning," said Columbus' master to the man who was sitting on the porch. "I am the cabinet-maker of Butterfly Brook, and I should like to show you my chairs."

"I don't want to see them," growled the man on the porch. "I have no use for any more chairs, because I live alone."

"I live alone, too," the cabinet-maker told him, "but I like to have lots of chairs around me. Chairs are good friends."

"Humph!" growled the man again. "I don't care for friends."

"That's too bad," said the cabinet-maker, shaking his head and looking off across the wide lawn to where a fountain sparkled in the sunshine. "I should think you'd

218

want to have someone to enjoy all this beauty with you. This yard would be a fine place for children to play in."

"Children!" shouted the man, jumping to his feet. "They would trample my grass and pick my flowers and throw stones in my fountain! They're a nuisance, children are. Look there," he went on, pointing across the lawn to the side fence. "See those children? They come here every day and stare at me and my lawn, but I never let them in."

The old cabinet-maker looked at the children pressing their faces against the fence. "Dear, dear," he said sadly. "I don't see how you have the heart to keep them out. One reason I came to town today was to see children. I wanted to watch them play and to hear them shout and laugh."

The cabinet-maker's voice was so sad that Columbus stopped admiring the soft green grass and shook his little bell as hard as he could, to make things sound more cheerful. And when he did this, the children outside the yard broke into peals of laughter.

"Do it again, little donkey. Shake your bell again!" they cried.

Columbus not only shook his bell again for them, but he moved his ears back and forth and, after a moment, he lifted his head and sang as he had done that morning on the road.

At this, the children laughed so hard that their voices were like hundreds of silver bells all being rung at the same time.

The man on the porch leaned forward and listened. "Well, I declare," he said. "That sounds pretty, doesn't it?"

"Children's laughter is the prettiest sound in the world," the old cabinet-maker told him. "Why won't you let them come into your yard and play for a while? They won't hurt anything, and it will make them so happy that they will laugh a great deal. You'd like that, wouldn't you?"

"I believe I would," the man on the porch said slowly. "Somehow it sounds like spring and makes me happier than I have been in years."

As he finished speaking he touched a bell on the table beside him. "Open the gates and invite the children in," he said when the tall servant appeared. "And then go and tell the cook to prepare a great deal of food —cookies and other things that children like. We'll have lunch out here on the lawn. And don't forget to fetch some food for the little donkey."

The old cabinet-maker tried to tell the man on the porch how fine he thought this was, but his words were drowned by the shouts and laughter of the children as they came trooping through the gate.

"Thank you for letting us in," they called. "We think you have the loveliest house and lawn in the world!"

"Do you?" said the man, smiling in spite of himself. "Well, make yourselves at home. There's a little stream at the back of the lawn that you might like to wade in."

"A stream! A stream!" cried the children, dashing away. "We're going to wade in a stream!"

When they had gone, the man on the porch turned to the old cabinet-maker. "I have changed my mind about your chairs," he said. "I am going to buy all of them— for the children to sit on when they eat their lunch. Unload them, and turn your little donkey loose to graze

220

on my lawn. He ought to have some pleasure, too."

Columbus could scarcely wait until his master un-hitched him. And when this was done he walked off across the lawn, nibbling as he went. Nothing like this had ever happened to him before, and he was so happy that he kicked his heels to show how glad he was to be alive on this fine spring morning.

And a fine spring morning it was for everyone. The children played leap frog and tag and blindman's buff, while the two men sat on the porch and watched them. They rode Columbus up and down the garden paths and, at last, they all sat down to such a luncheon as they had never eaten before.

When they had eaten all they could hold, they gathered round the master of the house to thank him and say good-bye. "I'm glad you have had a good time," he told them. "But don't thank *me* for it. The thanks belong partly to the cabinet-maker of Butterfly Brook, and partly to the springtime. But mostly they belong to the little donkey, Columbus. He made you laugh, and your laughter made me happy. And so I let you in."

"Thank you, Columbus!" shouted the children, patting the little donkey. "Thank you ever so much."

"Listen," said the master of the house, holding up his hand for quiet. "I have just had a wonderful idea. Each day, from now on, I shall leave my gate open so that you can come into the yard and play. And whenever the cabinet-maker and his little donkey come to town, we will have lunch on the lawn as we did today."

At this, the children jumped up and down and clapped their hands and the old cabinet-maker went over and put his arms about Columbus' neck and gave him a big hug.

When the last child had scampered out through the great iron gates, Columbus' master hitched him to the donkey cart, said good-bye to the man on the porch, and started home, feeling happier than he ever had before.

The little donkey was happy too. It had been a wonderful day for him, and he shook his bell gaily as he trotted along over the country roads. But after a while he slackened his pace. And then he came to a full stop. He had reached the shady lane that he had so long wanted to explore. What if he went in there now? he wondered. Would his master stop him?

"All right, Columbus," the old cabinet-maker said with a laugh. "You deserve a little treat as a reward for the way you behaved today. You made a good many people happy because you sang at just the right time.

So go ahead and enjoy yourself. Butterfly Brook will be there when we get back."

Without waiting a moment, Columbus crossed the road and turned in at the shady lane. And this time there was no jerk on the lines to stop him!

GOODY O'GRUMPITY

Carol Ryrie Brink

When Goody O'Grumpity baked a cake
The tall reeds danced by the mournful lake,
The pigs came nuzzling out of their pens,
The dogs ran sniffing and so did the hens,
And the children flocked by dozens and tens.
They came from the north, the east, and the south
With wishful eyes and watering mouth,
And stood in a crowd about Goody's door,
Their muddy feet on her sanded floor.
And what do you s'pose they came to do!
Why, to lick the dish when Goody was through!
And throughout the land went such a smell
Of citron and spice—no words can tell
How cinnamon bark and lemon rind,
And round, brown nutmegs grated fine
A wonderful haunting perfume wove,
Together with allspice, ginger, and clove,
When Goody but opened the door of her stove.
The children moved close in a narrowing ring,
They were hungry—as hungry as bears in the spring;
They said not a word, just breathed in the spice,
And at last when the cake was all golden and nice,
Goody took a great knife and cut each a slice.

Catherine Woolley

LITTLE BEAR TAKES HIS NAP

ILLUSTRATED BY *Ruth van Tellingen*

ONE morning when Little Bear went out to play in the woods, he found the air chilly. The ground was covered with something wet and white.

The something-wet on the ground sparkled in the sun like white fire.

Just then Little Bear heard his mother calling.

"Come, Little Bear," called Mother Bear. "There is white frost on the ground. Winter is coming. Time for little bears to come in for their long winter nap."

Little Bear was wiggling his little black nose around in the cold white frost. He was having fun. He didn't want to take his long winter nap.

He pretended not to hear Mother Bear.

Pretty soon Little Bear heard a rustling noise. He looked up in the trees. The autumn leaves were turn-

224

ing brown and dry and whirling down to the ground.

"Come, Little Bear," called Mother Bear. "The leaves are falling. Winter is coming. Time for little bears to come in for their long winter nap."

Little Bear was scuffling in the crackly red leaves. He was turning somersaults in the crisp gold leaves. The dusty leaves tickled Little Bear's nose and made him sneeze. That was funny! He didn't want to take his long winter nap.

"No," said Little Bear to Mother Bear.

After a while Little Bear felt something wet on his little black nose. He looked up in astonishment. Pretty white flakes were drifting and floating in the cold gray air.

"Come, Little Bear!" Mother Bear called. "The snow is falling. Winter is coming. Come in this minute for your long winter nap."

Little Bear was reaching up with his paws, trying to catch the snowflakes. Every time he caught a snowflake it melted right away on his warm fur. Little Bear couldn't understand it. But he was having fun. He didn't want to take his long winter nap.

"Pretty soon," said Little Bear to Mother Bear.

After a while Little Bear heard Mother Bear calling again.

"Good-bye," Mother Bear called. "I'm going home for my long winter nap. You stay and play in the snow."

Little Bear stopped playing and looked around.

He watched Mother Bear go lumbering off toward home.

Little Bear didn't want to stay out in the woods alone.

Suddenly he thought how funny it would be to fool Mother Bear.

He turned softly around. He tiptoed after her, very quietly, so she wouldn't know he was following.

Mother Bear got to the door of the bearhouse.

Little Bear heard her talking to herself.

"I'm going in the house," said Mother Bear. "I'm going to shut the door. If Little Bear comes home he won't be able to get in. That will teach him a lesson!"

Little Bear put his paw over his mouth to keep from giggling. He was right behind Mother Bear. He slipped in the door.

Mother Bear closed the door.

"There!" said Mother Bear to herself. "Now that Little Bear can just stay out all winter!

"Now," said Mother Bear, "I'll get in my warm bed. I'll just bet Little Bear wishes he could get in his warm bed!"

She climbed into bed.

Little Bear climbed in very softly next to Mother Bear's back.

"What is tickling my back?" said Mother Bear. "Must be a mosquito in here!"

She flapped her paw at the mosquito.

Little Bear was just bursting to laugh.

He wiggled closer to Mother Bear.

"There is some animal in bed with me!" said Mother Bear. "I'm going to find out what!"

She reached her paw back and felt of Little Bear's ears. Little Bear was still as a mouse.

"Hmm," said Mother Bear.

She felt of Little Bear's snout.

226

"My goodness!" said Mother Bear.

She felt of Little Bear's little fat tummy. And she tickled!

The giggles burst right out of Little Bear!

He doubled up his little feet and he waved his little paws and he squealed and laughed and giggled at the top of his lungs.

Mother Bear was so astonished she nearly fell out of bed.

"For goodness, gracious sake!" gasped Mother Bear. "How in the world did you get here?"

"I fooled you!" squealed Little Bear, laughing till the tears almost rolled down his cheeks.

"You certainly did!" said Mother Bear.

Little Bear gave a deep sigh of joy to think he had fooled Mother Bear.

Then he gave a yawn.

He snuggled a little closer.

He went to sleep for his long winter nap.

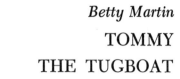

Betty Martin

TOMMY
THE TUGBOAT

ILLUSTRATED BY *Clarence Biers*

TOMMY the Tugboat was born at exactly two and a half minutes past three P.M. on a Thursday just one year ago. He was born to *Robert Fulton* and his wife *Susy Q* at the Anderson Shipyards near Pier 67. And everyone who knows *anything* at *all* knows that *Robert Fulton* and *Susy Q* are pretty fine boats.

Tommy *thought* he was a pretty fine boat himself. But nobody else did. For poor Tommy was afraid of everything—even boats. He did not do a bit of work. He did not do any of the hard things tugs do. He never pushed big ships into the docks to be unloaded. And he never pulled them out to sea when they needed help at the beginning of a trip.

That is, he never did until one day when he overheard three tugs talking about him.

"I think Tommy is a dreadful sissy!" said one tug, giving a great big snort. "He's no good at all. He just clutters up the harbor!"

"I think Tommy is a loafer!" said another, giving two snorts. "Why do his important parents spoil him

228

so? They should see that he learned his tug trade, that's what!"

"I think Tommy is a fraidy cat!" said still another tug, giving three snorts. "He *talks* a lot, and I guess he *thinks* a lot, but he never *does* anything—just cruises around the pier and then, when there's work to do he just hides behind the largest liner he can find. What a pity!"

The three tugs chugged away in disgust. And Tommy's boiler blushed as he sidled up to the giant liner *The Queen Mary*. But she was talking to another boat about him, too!

"I was saying just last week to *Elizabeth*, what's the matter with young *Tom Fulton?* One would think he had everything—good looks, fine parents, and a perfectly lovely voice."

The other boat nodded. "Yes," she said, "I heard him vocalizing the other day. And he *is* good looking with his chinese red smokestack, his neat black trim and his name in red letters on his spotless white hull. Why *is* he content to do nothing?"

"And don't forget his toot," said *The Queen Mary*. "It's so cheery and gay. And when it comes to making smoke there isn't a tug that can touch him!"

Tommy was so pleased with the nice things the big liners said about him that he started, right then and there, to toot out a little tune. He tooted loud. He tooted soft. He tooted long toots and he tooted short toots. He tooted and tooted and tooted. It was fun. And never had he tooted so well.

The Queen Mary listened to *Tommy the Tugboat*. Then she smiled. For right then and there, Tommy began to tremble all over and to blow smoke rings the size of cart wheels out of his stack.

Suddenly *The Queen* spoke to him.

"What rings, Tom! What rings!" she said. "Surely if you can do *that* you can handle—"

She broke off there and Tommy asked timidly, "Handle *what*, please, your highness?"

"Why handle *me*, of course," said *The Queen Mary.* "That is, the greater part of my weight. Why don't you try tonight? I'm sailing for Europe then, you know, with four thousand boys and girls and their fathers and mothers. Why don't you escort me out to sea?"

"C-c-c-c-could I?" stuttered Tom. "Oh, c-c-c-c-could I, your highness?"

The Queen Mary smiled down at the little tugboat. "Certainly you could," she told him again. "At least you could escort *most* of me. And what will the other tugs say to that? They won't think you can, but they'll see you with their own eyes. And your mother and father—how proud they will be! You, Tom, would be a hero!"

Tommy was so excited over the idea that he nearly burst one of his pipes in the LOUDEST TOOT you ever heard. Still he was shy. And *The Queen,* who noticed this, went right on.

"I'll tell you a secret," she whispered. "Just at midships on my port side under the waterline is my most *important* spot. You come to this place at seven tonight. I'll start my steam early and will get well heated up by then."

"W-w-when will the other tugs come? W-w-w-what will they say when they s-see me there?" stammered Tommy.

The Queen Mary smiled again. "The other tugs, including your mother and father, will arrive about quarter past seven," she said. "If you are noticed and if they talk about you, pay no attention to them. Just do your job. Remember, I'm counting on *you!*"

At exactly seven o'clock that night Tommy chugged over to *The Queen Mary.* And of course he found the important secret place she had spoken of—midships on her port side under the waterline.

Every nerve in his hull was tense. He was so excited.

231

And he kept saying to himself, "I-must-not-fail! I-must-not-fail! I-must-not-fail!"

Suddenly his engines sputtered. Suddenly his engines stopped, started again, STOPPED, started, S-T-O-P-P-E-D. . . .

And all the time Tommy kept saying to himself, "I-can't-start. I-can't-start. Or-can-I? Or-can-I? I-CAN'T-START!"

Poor Tom! He was SO shy!

The Queen tried to be patient. She waited five minutes. She waited ten minutes. She waited and waited and *waited.*

Finally, at seven-thirty *The Queen Mary* had to start. She sighed and gave the signal to the other tugboats, who were beside her now. And s-l-o-w-l-y she began to move up the river. Somehow that night she simply *could not* get her speed. There were one, two, three-four-*five* tugs pulling with all their might. And still no speed!

Suddenly Tommy took a deep breath. *The Queen* needed help. She needed *him*. That was all that mattered. He made sure he was in position, in just that secret place she had told him about—at midships, on her port side just *under* the waterline. Yes, he was there. He took another deep breath and made tug noises. "I-must-not-fail! I-must-NOT-fail. I must—push —push—push—PUSH!" said Tommy.

And he did!

The Queen smiled happily. "I'm FREE!" she cried. And she was. And there was Tom doing the best job of all.

"Whee!" cried the other tugs. "Look at Tommy! Look at Tommy! Would you *believe* it!" And they tooted the news all over the harbor.

The people on the decks of *The Queen Mary* and the people watching from the pier all cheered and cheered.

What a day for Tom! Now he was some use in the world, and it was *fun*. He smiled and smiled and smiled.

The Queen Mary smiled, too. "I knew it all the time! I knew he could do it!" she said. And as she sailed majestically up the harbor she let out one long toot for Tom!

Miriam Clark Potter

NINE RABBITS
AND ANOTHER ONE

ILLUSTRATED BY *Hazel Frazee*

OW one night when the rabbit family were getting ready for bed they heard a knock-knock-knock at their little grass-green door, and Mr. Rabbit said, "Someone is there . . ."

"Mother, Daddy, who do you think it is?" cried the seven little rabbits. "Is it company? Or a strange wild animal?"

Their father told them, "I will go, myself, and see . . ."

So he walked across the floor, *thump-thump-thump* in his garden shoes, and opened the door very quickly.

There stood a tall, scraggly rabbit with bent-over whiskers and tired eyes. His ears looked wilted, as though he had forgotten to water them. His suit needed pressing, too; and he had no hat.

"Good evening," said Mr. Rabbit.

"Good evening," said the scraggly one. "You couldn't take me in for the night, could you? I have come so far—and I still have miles to go."

"We haven't a single extra bed, I am sorry to say," Mr. Rabbit told him. "You can see for yourself how

234

many there are of us. My wife and myself and seven children; that makes nine. Our house is *full*."

The tall scraggly rabbit scratched his head and looked up at the sky. "That's bad news for me," he sighed. "It looks like wet weather, and I am tired way down to my toes. Well, if you don't mind, I'll just lie down here in your little front yard. You have some nice dry grass to stretch out on."

"Are you sure you'll be all right?"

"Oh, yes, thank you. Good night . . ."

"Good night," said the rabbit family, all together, for the rest of them had been watching and listening. But when the door was shut, Mrs. Rabbit said, "Poor thing."

"Yes, it's too bad," sighed Mr. Rabbit, "but what else could we do? We are quite crowded as it is, nine of us rabbits in this small house. Another one—that's just *too* many."

The children ran to the window.

"Now he's lying down," they said. "He has put his head on a stone."

Their mother thought a minute. Then she told them, "I do think he'd be more comfortable with a pillow. I can spare mine . . ."

She took it right out to him.

"Why, thank you," the scraggly rabbit said. "Now my head will be as cozy as a bird in a nest."

Mrs. Rabbit looked pleased.

"That was very kind of you, my dear," Mr. Rabbit said, when she came back into the house.

The children were still watching from the window.

"Now he's scattering grass all over his legs," they

said. "Only not enough . . . and his long feet stick out."

The smallest rabbits giggled at this, but the older ones said, "Don't laugh. He is a poor, scraggly rabbit without a bed."

"Grass really doesn't make a very good cover," said their father. "I have three blankets on my bed. I could spare *one*."

So he got a nice thick one with pink fuzz all over it and took it out the door.

The scraggly rabbit sat up so suddenly that the grass scattered in all directions. "Why, thank you," he said. "Now I shall be as snug as the root of a tree."

Mr. Rabbit smiled when he went back into the house. "That was very nice of you," said his wife.

Then the children called out, "Oh, it has begun to rain! Drops are coming down on his face, and he is wrinkling up his nose and opening and shutting his eyes. May we take him out the big, red umbrella?"

"That's very thoughtful of you, my bunnies," said their mother.

"Hurry it right out to him," their father told them.

So the seven little rabbits rushed out the door, carrying the big, red umbrella.

He put it right up. "Thank you," he said. "Now my face will be as dry as a pebble under a mushroom."

When the little rabbits came back into the house they looked delighted. "Now he is all fixed for the night," said Mr. Rabbit.

"With a pillow, and a blanket, and an umbrella," added his wife.

But while they watched, the scraggly rabbit dropped the umbrella!

Rain dribbled down on his face and on his shut-up eyes.

The family all hurried to the door, and called out, "The umbrella! The umbrella! You let go of it!"

The scraggly rabbit opened his eyes quickly. "Why, so I did," he said. "I wonder, how can I remember to keep on holding the handle when I drop off?"

"Drop off what?" asked the littlest rabbit.

"Why, to sleep, of course. If I stay awake, I hold up the umbrella; but the minute I start dreaming, I let go of it. What shall I do?"

None of the family knew what to say to this. Then Mrs. Rabbit suggested, "Why don't you come in and sleep on our floor in front of the fire? There is a good thick rug, and you can still have the pillow and the blanket."

"And in the house you will not need the umbrella at all," said Mr. Rabbit.

So very soon their company was stretched out on the floor. He looked up at them happily and said, "Now I am as nicely fixed as a turtle in a shell. I know I shall have a good night's rest. Thank you!"

"You are *very* welcome," said the family all in a row together, with a bow and a smile.

Then all the rabbits went to sleep, and soon the little house was quiet, with just the sound of the fire dying down, and the rain on the roof.

But when the family got up in the morning their company was gone!

The pink fuzzy blanket was neatly folded up. The pillow was on a chair.

"But why didn't he say good-bye?" asked the little rabbits, looking disappointed.

"He probably had to leave early, and didn't want to disturb us," their mother told them.

"But he might have said 'Thank you!' "

"Oh, he did that," said their father. "Why, for each thing that we did for him, he thanked us so nicely."

"Well, he might have left a note, or something," said the next-to-the-littlest rabbit.

But just then the very littlest one broke into a happy cry. "He did leave something! Look—on the mantel-shelf!"

And there was a row of nine perfectly lovely little baskets, all tied with gay bows; and each one was filled with candy eggs!

"Why, he was the Easter Bunny!" said Mr. Rabbit, looking surprised.

"And we didn't even suspect," said his wife.

"We should have taken him in right away if we had known. . . ."

Mrs. Rabbit smiled. "It was better this way," she said. "We thought he was just a strange, scraggly rabbit, and we made him comfortable, anyway. I am *so* glad we asked him in to sleep by our fire!"

"And it was fun," said all seven of the little rabbits.

THE BUNNY

Eleanor Underwood

There was a little bunny. He lived in a wood.
He waggled his ears as a little bunny should.
He hopped by a squirrel, he hopped by a tree,
He hopped by a duck, and he hopped by me.
He stared at the squirrel. He stared at the tree.
He stared at the duck, but he made a face at me!

Marjorie Barrows

MUGGINS MOUSE
AT THE SEASHORE

ILLUSTRATED BY *John Gee*

Once Muggins Mouse was playing
  A game of whisker-tap
And stopped to climb inside a pail
  To take a little nap.

But some boy took that pail along
  To play with by the sea.
When Muggins woke he jumped right out
  And squeaked excitedly,

For he saw sand and sand in front
  And sand behind his tail,
And sand on both sides of his ears—
  It turned his whiskers pale!

240

Then Muggins ran and ran and ran
  Until he couldn't stop,
And when he reached the ocean, why,
  He jumped right in ker-flop!

A big wave took him for a ride;
  He bobbed along—whee-eee!
And he bobbed up and he bobbed down
  'Til he felt all at sea.

He landed on an island where
  A lobster made him hop,
Because he grabbed his tail till Muggins
  Asked him please to stop.

Then Muggins straightened out his tail
    And somersaulted and
Just looked around until he found
    Some footprints in the sand.

He wondered who had made them
    And stood there, quite annoyed,
'Til someone cried, "Oh, Mouse ahoy!"
    And Muggins Mouse ahoyed.

He found a wooden sailor
    Half-buried in a hill.
"Please rescue me!" the sailor cried,
    And Muggins said, "I will."

So Muggins dug the sailor out
  And plunging through the foam,
He swam with him upon his back
  And took him to his home.

Then Muggins waved good-bye to him
  And followed his old trail
And came back where he started from
  And jumped inside the pail.

When home at last what tales he told
  To make mice quake and laugh!
And all his friends asked Traveler Muggins
  For his autograph!

Alice Dalgliesh

THE STORY OF DOBBIN

ILLUSTRATED BY *Ruth van Tellingen*

DOBBIN was a wooden horse. He belonged to Jane and Jerry, who were twins four years old. He had belonged to them ever since they were tiny babies, and they had played with him so much that now he was almost worn out. Poor Dobbin! One leg was broken, one eye was gone, and so were his mane and tail. The wheels had come off his little red wooden stand. Most of all Dobbin needed a coat of paint.

One evening Father brought home a new wooden horse. It was larger than Dobbin. It was all shiny with paint and had a fine black mane and tail. The twins were so pleased that they danced about and clapped their hands.

"What shall we do with Dobbin?" asked Jerry.

"I think we might send him to a little boy who has no toys to play with," said Mother. "But, of course, we can't send him just the way he is. We must paint and mend him."

So the twins helped Mother mend Dobbin. First they mended the broken leg and put four new wheels on his stand.

Then Mother let them take turns painting Dobbin a beautiful red and the stand bright red. Last of all Mother took the paintbrush and gave Dobbin two black eyes, a bridle, a black mane, and some black spots. With the red paint she gave him a red saddle.

"Now he is all ready," said Mother.

"But he has no tail!" said Jane.

Mother took some hairs from an old broom and glued them in the place where Dobbin's tail had been.

The hairs were quite short, and Dobbin's new tail was so straight and stiff that it made the twins laugh to look at it.

When all the paint was dry, Mother said, "Now we can wrap Dobbin up and send him to his new home." She found a large sheet of paper, stood Dobbin on it, and began to tie up the package. Jane and Jerry watched. Soon there wasn't any Dobbin to be seen— not even the straight, stiff, little tail.

"Oh, Mother," cried Jane, "we can't send Dobbin away. He's been with us such a long time."

"Send the new horse instead," said Jerry.

Mother looked surprised, but she opened the package and put the new horse in Dobbin's place.

Jane and Jerry hugged Dobbin. "We like you ever so much better than the new horse," they told him.

Then they took turns riding on his back as they had
always done.

"Gee up, Dobbin! Whoa, Dobbin!" they shouted.

Dobbin ran so fast on his little red wheels that it
seemed as if he knew he was to stay and play with
the twins for a great many more years.

THE CHIMNEY

Mildred Plew Meigs

Oh, the chimney sits on his perch so high,
And he winks at the world with a soot black eye;
And he roars out loud and he laughs when he winks,
For the poor old brick of a chimney thinks
That the big white clouds that blow through the blue
Are just little puffs of his smoke that grew.

Author Unknown

THE LITTLE STEAM ENGINE

ILLUSTRATED BY *Clarence Biers*

A LITTLE steam engine had a long train of cars to pull.

She went along very well till she came to a steep hill. But then, no matter how hard she tried, she could not move the long train of cars.

She pulled and she pulled. She puffed and she puffed. She backed and started off again. Choo! Choo!

But no! the cars would not go up the hill.

At last she left the train and started up the track alone. Do you think she had stopped working? No, indeed! She was going for help.

"Surely I can find someone to help me," she thought.

Over the hill and up the track went the little steam engine. Choo, choo! Choo, choo! Choo, choo! Choo!

Pretty soon she saw a big steam engine standing on a sidetrack. He looked very big and strong. Running alongside, she looked up and said:

"Will you help me over the hill with my train of cars? It is so long and heavy I can't get it over."

The big steam engine looked down at the little steam engine. Then he said:

"Don't you see that I am through my day's work? I have been all rubbed and scoured ready for my next run. No, I cannot help you."

The little steam engine was sorry, but she went on. Choo, choo! Choo, choo! Choo, choo! Choo, choo!

Soon she came to a second big steam engine standing on a sidetrack. He was puffing and puffing, as if he were tired.

"He may help me," thought the little steam engine. She ran alongside and asked,—

"Will you help me bring my train of cars over the hill? It is so long and so heavy that I can't get it over."

The second big steam engine answered,—

"I have just come in from a long, long run. Don't you see how tired I am? Can't you get some other engine to help you this time?"

"I'll try," said the little steam engine; and off she went. Choo, choo! Choo, choo! Choo, choo!

After a while she came to a little steam engine just like herself. She ran alongside and said,—

"Will you help me over the hill with my train of cars? It is so long and so heavy that I can't get it over."

"Yes, indeed!" said this little steam engine. "I'll be glad to help you, if I can."

So the little steam engines started back to where the train of cars had been standing. Both little steam engines went to the head of the train, one behind the other.

Puff, puff! Chug, choo! Off they started!

Slowly the cars began to move. Slowly they climbed the steep hill. As they climbed, each little steam engine began to sing,—

"I—think—I—can! I—think—I—can! I—think—I—can! I—think—I—can! I—think—I—can! I—think—I—can! I think I can—I think I can—I think I can I think I can—"

And they did! Very soon, they were over the hill and going down the other side.

Now they were on the plain again; and the little steam engine could pull her train, herself. So she thanked the little engine who had come to help her, and said good-bye.

And she went merrily on her way, singing:

"I—thought—I—could! I—thought—I—could! I—thought—I—could! I—thought—I—could! I thought I could—I thought I could—I thought I could—I thought I could—I thought I could I thought I could—"

CLARENCE BIERS

Margery Williams Bianco

MR. MURDLE'S
LARGE
HEART

ILLUSTRATED BY *Betty Carroll*

Ⅰ**N NEARLY** every town you will find one store which keeps all those foolish little things that the other stores forget, or are so apt to be out of.

Mr. Murdle's is just such a store. Many years ago, when Mr. Murdle was a round-faced little boy, he must have said to his mother: "When I grow up I'm going to keep a store!"

He had no idea at all of what he wanted to sell in his store; it was just going to be a store. And so it turned out. He started by buying a little bit here and a little bit there, just as he fancied, and all sorts of funny cardboard boxes began to pile up on his shelves. He thought of ginger ale and slate pencils and newspapers and paper clips, and of course candy; of little celluloid dolls and hairpins and pencil sharpeners, and ash trays with scalloped gilt edges and pictures on them, and lots and lots of cigars.

Mr. Murdle himself doesn't really know all that he has in his store, and certainly no one else does. But if ever it happens that you want to buy something that you cannot find in any of the other stores along the street, sooner or later someone will scratch his head and say,—

"Well, you *might* try Mr. Murdle, across the way!"

So across the way you go, and sure enough, after Mr. Murdle has stood for a moment thinking, he will rummage among his cardboard boxes and pull one of them out, and nine times out of ten there it is, the very thing you were looking for!

All this is wonderful enough, but it isn't the most remarkable thing about Mr. Murdle, by any means.

The most remarkable thing about Mr. Murdle is his Large Heart.

Everyone who knows Mr. Murdle will tell you what a Large Heart he has. And it is really true. I have seen it myself, hanging up at the back of Mr. Murdle's store. It is pink and purple, with yellow around the edges, and in the middle, which is white, there are rows of little elastic loops, which once upon a time held tiny bottles of pink and purple and yellow lozenges. Fairy lozenges, they must have been, but that is so long ago that no one knows what they really were like. But the Heart is still there.

It is a fine thing for anyone to have such a Large Heart. But there are disadvantages also, especially for anyone like Mr. Murdle, who is in business, and who really ought to be thinking of money every minute, as all the other storekeepers do. It makes it very nice of course for Mr. Murdle's customers, but it must be difficult for Mr. Murdle. That Large Heart of his is always getting in the way.

When a little girl comes into his store, for instance, and wants an ice-cream cone and has only three cents,

or when some little boy wants candy and Mr. Murdle knows perfectly well that he should only give him five chocolates for a nickel, then that Large Heart begins to whisper to him, and before Mr. Murdle knows it he has handed out the cone with an extra lump of strawberry ice cream on, or he has slipped seven chocolates into the bag instead of five.

And if you want some particular-sized envelopes, or some special kind of paper clip such as you bought three years ago and have never been able to find since, and Mr. Murdle has hunted through and through his cardboard boxes and finally found it, then as likely as not he will say: "Oh, I've had that in stock so long I wouldn't know what to charge you for it. We'll make it up next time!" And next time, of course, never comes.

Then there are the cats.

It began with one cat. She was a tortoise-shell cat, and she found that the pleasantest place to spend the morning was curled up in the sun, on top of Mr. Murdle's stack of daily papers, just inside the store. She spent every morning there, and usually the afternoon as well. Mr. Murdle used to give her the melted ice cream that was left over at night.

Presently she married and had a family, and they all came to live in Mr. Murdle's store. Several of her cousins came, too. Now there were eleven cats, and not nearly enough melted ice cream to go round. So Mr. Murdle—having such a Large Heart—took to melting the ice cream on purpose. He found that the cats liked vanilla best, so he always ordered more of the vanilla than of any other kind, and with it he gave them crumbled-up wafers and peppermint creams.

Early every morning when Mr. Murdle came to open the store, there were the cats waiting for him, and the very first thing he did was to look in the ice-cream can and see if there was anything left over from the day before. Usually there wasn't, and then Mr. Murdle would take eight pennies from the till behind the counter and go over to the grocery to buy milk for the cats' breakfast.

Everyone liked Mr. Murdle, including the cats, and Mr. Murdle himself was one of the happiest people in the world, and all on account of his Large Heart.

But there was one person who did not at all approve of Mr. Murdle's Large Heart. This was Mr. Murdle's aunt. It may seem funny for anyone like Mr. Murdle, who is at least forty and quite bald on the top of his head, to have an aunt; but he had, and

one fine day she came all the way from Vermont to
keep house for him. She was a busy, active sort of
woman, and not content with managing Mr. Murdle's
house for him, she soon began to think of managing
his store as well.

She didn't approve of the cats and she didn't approve of the little boys and girls. In fact, she didn't
approve of anything at all that Mr. Murdle liked and
least of all of the way he did business. She decided
that all that sort of thing must be changed.

At first she didn't have much success. Mr. Murdle
had been going along very comfortably in his own way
for so long that it wasn't easy, even for a determined
person like Mr. Murdle's aunt, to change him. But she
did her best, and as luck would have it, while she was
rummaging about and tidying the store up one day,
she came upon Mr. Murdle's Large Heart. She didn't
at all know what it was, but she certainly didn't like

254

the look of it. She leaned on her broom and stared.

"Now that's a foolish sort of thing," she said. "Cluttering the store up and taking space where it isn't wanted. I'm going to throw it out!"

And she did.

From that moment, a very dreadful change came over Mr. Murdle.

The aunt thought it was all due to her lecturing and her good advice. But it wasn't at all. It was just because Mr. Murdle had lost his Large Heart.

In two days you wouldn't have known Mr. Murdle's store.

Everything was tidy, and Mr. Murdle himself just as business-like as he could be. He knew the price of everything. When little boys came in and asked for a nickel's worth of candy, believe me they *got* a nickel's worth of candy, and not one speck more, and if the

little girls hadn't enough money for their ice-cream cones they might just turn right around and walk out again.

It was terrible, and as for the cats, they all left in a body and went to live with the fat lady at the delicatessen store across the way. Mr. Murdle said he couldn't afford to feed a lot of lazy cats that did nothing but sleep all day, and that moreover they mussed up his newspapers.

Can you *imagine* that!

All the little boys and girls were very upset. But luckily there was one little boy who had more sense than the rest.

He was loitering in the store one day. Mr. Murdle's aunt happened to be away shopping, or you may be very sure she would have chased him out. But there he was staring about him and trying to make out just why it was that everything should look so different. And all at once he realized that something was missing.

It was Mr. Murdle's Large Heart.

It wasn't there in its usual place above the counter, and it wasn't anywhere in the store, though he searched high and low. Being a clever little boy he soon put two and two together.

"I bet you," he said, "that mean old woman has thrown it out!"

He went straightway into the yard behind the store, where Mr. Murdle kept all his old boxes and empty crates, and began to hunt. And sure enough, after a little while there he found it, thrown out with a pile of rubbish and broken pasteboard boxes, waiting to be burned.

It was torn at one side and a bit crumpled, but he smoothed it out and carried it back to its old place on the wall behind the counter, and to make sure this time, he fetched a hammer and nails and he *nailed* it, all around the edge.

Not even Mr. Murdle's aunt could have torn it down again!

What's more, she never got a chance. For as soon as Mr. Murdle set foot in the store, now that his Large Heart was back in its right place again, he became just the same Mr. Murdle that he had been before.

The very first thing that he did was to send his aunt packing.

Then he telephoned for fresh ice cream—every kind he could think of—and he opened all the candy boxes and told the little boys and girls, who by this time had heard the news and had all come trooping round, that they might help themselves, and if they didn't have any money they could pay him next year.

And he dragged his old armchair out, and lit a big cigar, and settled down by the doorway, as happy as could be.

When the cats saw that, they all came trooping back again, too.

So today things are just as they used to be, and there is very little danger they will ever change again.

Not as long as Mr. Murdle's Large Heart stays there, right in its place, and that, you may be very sure, will be for a long time to come.

As for Mr. Murdle's aunt, she gave him up as a bad job and went back to Vermont, broom and all.

And if you don't believe me, all you need do is to walk into Mr. Murdle's store some fine morning, past the curled-up cats and the newspapers and ask for a nickel's worth of candy.

You will see how much you get!

MY PUPPY

Ellis Atkinson McDonald

When I go out
And take my pup,
His ears are glad
And sticking up.

His eyes are gay,
He tries to laugh.
His long tail wags
His whole back half.

Margaret Friskey

JOHNNY
AND THE MONARCH

ILLUSTRATED BY *Fiore Mastri*

OHNNY had a dog named Duke. He had a duck named Dora. He lived on a farm at the foot of a hill.

When it was time to hunt for eggs Johnny went through the woods and across the creek and up the hill to the henhouse.

One day Duke and Dora were going with him through the woods and across the creek and up the hill. Dora saw a butterfly on the path. Dora went after the butterfly.

"Oh, no!" cried Johnny. "The butterfly has hurt his wing." Johnny picked it up and put it on a milkweed plant.

The next day the butterfly was gone. It had left a little yellow-green egg on the milkweed leaf.

Johnny and Duke and Dora watched the egg.

One day it hatched into a caterpillar. The little caterpillar ate the milkweed leaves. It grew and grew. Its skin became so tight it split down the back and the caterpillar crawled out in a new skin. It shed its skin three or four times before it grew into a big caterpillar.

260

"No, no!" said Johnny to Dora. "You must not eat the caterpillar. It will turn into a butterfly."

Dora walked away down the creek. Johnny could not find her.

Every day Johnny and Duke went through the woods and across the creek and up the hill to look for Dora. They looked in the chicken yard. But Dora was not there. They looked back of the haystack. But Dora was not there.

All this time the caterpillar was busy. It spun a pad of silk and fastened it to the milkweed leaf. Then it hung head-down from the pad of silk, curled up, and spun a cocoon around itself. It was a green cocoon with gold dots.

"See!" said Johnny to Duke. "Now the caterpillar will sleep until it turns into a butterfly."

Days went by. But Johnny and Duke could not find Dora. They found some kittens in the barn. They found

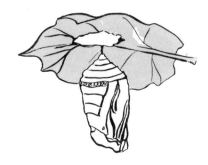

a wobbly calf. They found six baby pigs. They found two baby lambs.

The green cocoon turned muddy blue.

One day Johnny and Duke went through the woods and across the creek and up the hill to gather eggs. The cocoon was almost black.

"The caterpillar is almost a butterfly," said Johnny.

The cocoon split open. A Monarch butterfly with orange and black wings crawled out on a leaf. The wings were soft. It could not fly. The butterfly seemed to pump fluid into its wings from its body. The wings spread out, slowly, slowly. They moved up and down. Then the butterfly flew off.

"Look at it go!" cried Johnny.

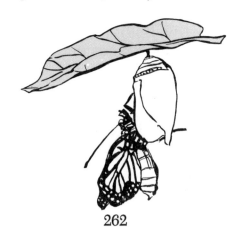

But Duke would not look. Duke was barking and running up and down the path. Johnny followed Duke around the bend. There was Dora coming up the path. Six little ducklings were following her.

"You had a hidden nest all the time," said Johnny.

Johnny put the ducklings in his egg basket. Then Johnny and Duke and Dora and the six little ducklings went down the hill and across the creek and through the woods and home.

WING DREAMS

Dixie Willson

I wish that I could dream me dreams
That magically come true—
Like fuzzy wuzzy wormy squirmy
Caterpillars do.
A caterpillar dreams himself
Right out of all his fuzz
And into lovely fairy wings.
I wonder how he does?

Alice Dalgliesh

LETTERS FROM THE SEA

ILLUSTRATED BY *Dorothy Short*

JEREMY lived by the sea. He lived in the little village of Sandy Cove, where the houses are white with gray roofs and where all the trees are evergreen trees.

Jeremy loved the sea. He liked to watch the gulls flying over the blue water and the boats rocking up and down on the waves. He liked to run on the long sandy beach and to feel the cool wet sand under his bare feet. He hoped when he grew up that he would be a sailor.

When the weather was fine Jeremy's mother would say, "This will be a good day at sea," and when it was stormy she would say, "It's a bad day for ships at sea." This was because Jeremy's uncle was a sea-captain. He was captain of one of the biggest boats that crossed the Atlantic Ocean. Jeremy wished that he could see his uncle.

At last one day the captain came home to Sandy Cove for a visit. He was a tall man with blue eyes and a friendly smile. He wore a gray suit and a gray felt hat.

"Oh, Uncle Ben," said Jeremy, "you don't look a bit like a captain. I thought a captain had gold braid on his clothes."

"So he does," said Uncle Ben. "But on shore he doesn't always wear his uniform. I'll show you how a captain looks."

He put on his uniform. It was dark blue with four bands of gold braid around the sleeve. There was gold braid around the edge of his cap.

"Now you look like a captain!" said Jeremy.

Jeremy and his uncle went for long walks together. They built sand castles on the beach. The night before Uncle Ben left, Jeremy was allowed to stay up very late. It was a cool clear night, and Uncle Ben built a bonfire with the big driftwood logs on the beach. The flames leaped into the air, and sparks flew up into the darkness. Uncle Ben told stories of exciting things that had happened to him at sea. He told of getting a radio message from a sinking ship and of hurrying to help the people who were on board.

"I wish you would send me a message from the sea," said Jeremy. "Send me a letter by radio."

"I'll send you two letters," said the Captain. "When I'm two days out I'll send you a radiogram. That will come very quickly, and you'll get it in just a few hours. Then when I'm halfway across I'll send you another letter. This one I'll put in a bottle, seal it up, and drop it over the side of the boat. Then perhaps the waves will bring it to you. Ships often used to send messages that way."

The next day the Captain went away. Jeremy could hardly wait for the messages to come. Two days after the boat sailed, the telephone rang.

"Jeremy!" said his mother. "You're wanted at the telephone."

Jeremy was so excited he could scarcely hold the telephone receiver. He heard the operator's voice say, "Radiogram for Jeremy Brown." Then came his uncle's message.

"Hello, Jeremy! Fine weather. Uncle Ben."

"Now the other letter will come," said Jeremy. Every day he went down to the beach and looked for a bottle.

The first day he found a bottle with nothing in it.

The second day he found a float from the fishermen's nets.

The third day he found the shell of a crab.

The fourth day he found a wooden box.

The fifth day he found two sea-urchins.

But the bottle from his uncle's ship did not come. Then there was a storm. The sea roared all night long, and the waves dashed on the beach. In the morning Jeremy hurried to the shore.

"*Now* I shall find the bottle," he said. "The storm will blow it in."

The beach was piled high with seaweed and there were all kinds of things that had washed ashore, but there was no bottle.

"I don't believe it will ever come," said Jeremy.

"Perhaps it has gone to a far-off country where no one could read the message," said his father. Jeremy felt very sad.

That afternoon Jeremy went to the village post office to get the mail. There were letters for his father and mother—and a package for him. What could it be? Jeremy raced home and ran into the house all out of breath.

"Look!" he shouted. "There's a package for me!"

"Why it's from Newfoundland," said his mother. "Whoever could have sent you a package from Newfoundland?"

"Let's open it!" said his father. So they untied the string and opened the paper. There was a bottle! Inside the bottle was a letter!

"Oh!" said Jeremy.

"There is a message on the outside of the bottle, too," said Father. He read it aloud.

I found this bottle on the beach and am sending it to the address given inside.

JIM HERSHEY, Fisherman.

"Why, it must be Uncle Ben's letter," said Jeremy. He took the letter out of the bottle. "Please read it."

The letter in the bottle said:

DEAR JEREMY:

This is a fine sunny day. We just sighted a whale and I wished you were here to see it.

I keep thinking of the good times we had in Sandy Cove.

I wonder how long the sea will take to carry you this message and where it will go ashore. I hope the person who finds it will send it to you.

Love from

UNCLE BEN

"It took a long time, but it *did* come," said Jeremy. "It's fun to get letters from the sea!"

Sterling North

THE FIVE LITTLE BEARS
HAVE THEIR PICTURES TAKEN

ILLUSTRATED BY *John Gee*

ONE morning Mamma Bear said to Papa Bear, "Abner, we should have our little bears' pictures taken 'so we can always remember just what they looked like."

"All right," said Papa Bear. "You get them ready while I start the car."

You couldn't tell which growled louder, Papa Bear or the self-starter of the old car. But finally the engine went POP—*POP—POP—POP*, and all the little bears jumped in the back seat, and Mamma Bear jumped in on top of them.

"Don't drive too fast," said Mamma Bear.

"Don't climb any telephone poles," said Eenie.

"Don't run into any policemen," said Meenie.

"Don't go through any red lights," said Meinie.

"Be careful on the curves," said Mo.

"Step on it, Daddy," said Nig.

269

And they rode, and they rode, and they rode, and after a while they came to a big tall building so high they couldn't see the top.

They got in an elevator and went up faster than any bear ever climbed a tree. They went up more stories than any of them could count, and when they reached the fifty-seventh floor they all got out.

Then they went into a room where there were bright lights and there was a man with his head in a big black box.

"Peek-a-boo!" said Eenie.

"What's he hiding for?" asked Meenie.

"Is he afraid of bears?" asked Meinie.

"Must be something to eat in there," said Mo.

"Maybe he's stuck," said Nig.

The man pulled his head out of the camera as quick as a jack-in-the-box, said, "How-do-you-do?" and made the little bears sit all in a row to have their pictures taken.

"Now look at the birdie," said the man.

"Let's get the birdie," said all the little bears, and they very nearly knocked the man and the camera over trying to catch the birdie.

"No, no, no!" shouted the man. "Sit up there and look pleasant, please."

"Like this?" said Eenie.

"Like this?" asked Meenie.

"Like this?" asked Meinie.

"Like this?" asked Mo.

"You mean this way?" asked Nig, trying to stand on his head.

"All right," said the man, who was now very angry.

270

"I'll show you little bears just how you look." He popped into the black box quickly, and then he popped out again, and he squeezed a little bulb that went

Pseeeeeeee

just like a water squirt-gun.

Then he hurried out of the room and came back in a few minutes with a picture of the five bears.

"Do I look like *that?*" said Eeine.

"Have I got dirt on my nose?" said Meenie.

"Am I cross-eyed?" said Meinie.

"Have I got a burr in my tail?" said Mo.

"That must be five other little bears," said Nig.

And Papa and Mamma Bear were so angry when they saw the picture that they told the little bears they couldn't have jam on their toast for a week.

"We'll be good," said Eenie.

"We'll look at the little bird," said Meenie.

"We'll look pleasant, please," said Meinie.

"We'll do anything the man tells us," said Mo.

"No toast on our jam for a week, eh?" said Nig.

And after Mamma Bear had wiped the dirt off Meenie's nose and taken the burr out of Mo's tail, they all sat up as nice as any little bears in the world.

The photographer took a picture and it was the best picture of five little bears you ever saw.

And the Mamma and Papa Bear both said at once, "You darling little bears, you can have all the jam you want on your toast every morning."

And this is the picture that the man took, up at the top of this story.

Margaret Baker

THE LOST
MERBABY

ILLUSTRATED BY
Decie Merwin

ONCE upon a time there were a
fisherman and his wife who lived in a little stone house
by the sea. It was only a tiny house, but that was no
matter, for it was so neat and pretty that no one could
wish it to be different. There was a creeper climbing
on the wall, and a pot of flowers in each little window;
and in the little kitchen there was a tall old clock, and
a dresser with rows of blue platters, and there were
two chairs and a round table and a carved oak settle,
and by the fireside was a wooden cradle.

But the cradle was empty.

"A baby would be so troublesome," said the fisherman's wife. "How would I keep my little house neat
and clean with a baby to mind?"

"A baby may be very well in its way," said the fisherman, "but we are happier as we are."

Every day the fisherman set the sails of his boat and
went out to sea, and every day his wife went busily
about and about the little house. And when her work
was done she took her knitting and sat beside the door.
She would watch the clouds wandering across the sky,
and the waves breaking on the sand, and the sea gulls
wheeling above the cliffs, and then at last she would see

the little boat come sailing into the bay, and she would run down to the beach to wave a welcome to the fisherman as soon as he should be near enough to see it.

"Who could be happier than we?" said they.

Now, not so very far away there was another little home, but it could not be seen from the fisherman's house however hard one looked, for it lay under the sea. It was only a sandy hollow among the rocks, but it was set about so prettily with seaweeds that it could not be bettered; and in the hollow lived four little mermaids and a merbaby.

The little mermaids loved the merbaby dearly, but for all that they often found her a great deal of trouble.

"Oh dear!" they would sigh, "how glad we shall be when she is grown up! She is sure to want us if we swim far away; and see how she plays with our seaweeds and spoils them, and how she disturbs the sand in our little hollow when we have taken care to make it smooth. She is the most beautiful merbaby that could be," said they, "but she is rather a nuisance sometimes."

Now it happened one day that they found a round basket, such as the fishermen use, floating on the waves.

"Here is a cradle for our baby!" cried they. "When we want to play we can lay her inside, and the waves will rock her to sleep."

So they took the basket and stopped up the holes and lined it with seaweed, and then they put the baby inside. The baby laughed and crowed with delight, and the mermaids swam to their home in the hollow among the rocks. They tidied the seaweed and smoothed the sand upon the floor, and when they swam back to the cradle and peeped inside the baby was fast asleep.

273

"See how useful a cradle can be!" they cried. "Now we can swim away to play, for she will not need us for a long, long time."

But the little mermaids had forgotten all about the wind and the tide, and while they were gone the basket was carried far away. It was carried so far that at last it came to the foot of the cliffs near the fisherman's house, and there it rolled over and the merbaby slipped into a rock pool among the anemones.

When the fisherman came sailing home he saw something shining at the foot of the cliffs, and as soon as he had brought his boat to land he went to find out what it could be. And it was the merbaby's hair shining like polished gold in the sun.

"Good lack!" cried the fisherman. "What have we here?"

The merbaby was very tired of being all alone and it held out its little arms and cried to be taken up.

What was there left for the fisherman to do but to lift the baby from the pool and hurry home with it as fast as he could?

The fisherman's wife was just as surprised as he. She took the baby in her arms and hushed it and sang to it and coaxed the smile back into its face.

"How it laughs and crows!" cried she. "Look! its eyes are the color of the sea, and what a dear little tail it has! It is nearly as beautiful as a real baby."

Then they pulled out the wooden cradle and put the baby inside, and there it lay crooning happily to itself. The fisherman's wife kept running to look at it and sing to it, and the baby laughed to see her and tangled its tiny hands in her hair; and the fisherman brought it

274

shells for toys and threaded them in a chain.

That was all well enough, but away under the sea things were not going well at all. The little mermaids had come back from their playing and were looking everywhere for the baby.

"Have you seen our baby?" they asked the plaice who were lying almost buried in the sand.

The largest plaice flicked the sand off itself, for it is not polite to speak to anyone with only your eyes showing. "I have not seen any merbabies for quite a long time," it said, "but that may be because I only see things that are above me on account of my eyes. Perhaps you have noticed my eyes are both on one side of my head," he said proudly; "we are not like other fishes."

"Our baby was in a cradle," explained the little mermaids. "It was only a round basket, but it rocked up and down on the waves and sent her to sleep as well as a real cradle could have done."

"Something that might have been your cradle floated overhead a little while ago," said the plaice. "That is the way it went. Now, if my eyes had been one on each side of my head I should never have seen it."

Away swam the little mermaids, but no sign of the merbaby could they find.

Presently they met a porpoise. "Have you seen our baby?" they asked, and told him all the tale.

"This is very sad business," said the porpoise. "Come with me and we will see what can be done."

So they swam away together and asked all the fishes they met for news of the merbaby. Not one of them had seen her, but they were so sorry for the little mermaids that they all joined in the search.

The fisherman stood at the door of his house. "There is no wind," said he. "But look how strangely the sea is tossing!"

How could he know the waves were made by the mermaids and fishes as they looked for the lost baby?

"Let us look for her in the rock pools under the cliffs," said the little mermaids.

The lobsters came out of their holes to see what was wanted.

"We have lost our baby," said the mermaids. "We used to think she was only a nuisance, but now she is lost we are sure we can never be happy until she is found." And they told them all about it.

The lobsters waved their legs in surprise. "How strange to mind losing a baby!" said they. "We never take any notice of our own."

The eldest lobster drew his claws thoughtfully among his feelers. "There is a nasty wicker thing over there that might be your baby's cradle," said he. "It looks too much like a lobster trap for my taste, but as you are not lobsters perhaps you will not mind going near it."

Away went the little mermaids, and among the rocks they found the basket they had used for a cradle. But there was no baby in it.

A big crab came sidling toward them.

"You look as unhappy as though you had just cast your shells," he said. "What can be the matter?"

Then the mermaids told their sorrowful tale all over again, and the crab was very sad for them. He went up and down the rock pools explaining what had happened to everything he met, to the fishes and the shrimps and the seahorses and the whelks, but not one of them could tell him anything.

At last he came to the anemones. "Have you seen the merbaby?" he asked.

"How could we see it?" asked the anemones. "We have no eyes."

"How dreadful to have no eyes!" exclaimed the crab, popping his own in and out with horror at the thought.

"No," said the anemones. "We have dozens of feelers. They are much more sensible than eyes, we think."

"But I can't help being sorry for you," said the crab. "Why, even if the mermaids' baby was here you could not see her, and she is worth seeing, they say. Her hair is golden yellow and her eyes are the color of the sea."

"What does it matter what color hair may be as long as it is hair?" said the biggest anemone crossly. "There is a piece twisted around one of my feelers now and it is most uncomfortable."

The crab brought the mermaids to look. He twiddled his eyes in great excitement. "See what I have found!" cried he.

One of the mermaids gently untangled the hair, and it was so fine and so shining that it could have belonged to no one but a merbaby.

"Our baby has been here," said they, "but where can she be now?"

The puffins came waddling along to see what was the matter. They looked very wise indeed when they heard all there was to be told.

"Now we come to think of it . . ." began one.

"We don't think often, you know," said the others. "But when we do, we think to some purpose."

"When we come to think of it," said the first puffin again, "we saw the fisherman pick a merbaby from that very pool where you were talking to the anemones."

"Oh, tell us what he did with her!" cried the little mermaids.

"He took it home, of course," said the puffins. "Your baby is not lost now because we have told you where she is."

And they waddled away.

"Alas!" cried the mermaids. "We are scarcely any better off than when we did not know where to find her. The fisherman's house lies far beyond the reach of the waves, and we can only go where the waves can carry us."

Then the mermaids lifted themselves out of the water. "Sea gulls! Sea gulls!" they cried. "Fly to the fisherman's house and tell us what has become of our baby."

So the sea gulls flew across the sand and round and round the fisherman's house.

"Surely there is a storm coming," said the fisherman, "else why should the gulls fly so near and cry so loudly?"

How could he know they had come to see what was done with the merbaby?

"The fisherman has put the baby in the cradle and his wife is tending it as though it was their own," said the sea gulls when they came back. Then the little mermaids began to weep. "If they grow to love our baby they will never give her to us again," they sobbed.

"How the sea moans tonight!" said the fisherman. "There is surely a storm coming."

But when the merbaby heard it she began to wail and would not be comforted. "Hush, hush!" soothed the fisherman's wife and ran to pick the baby out of the

cradle, but the baby only wailed the more pitifully.

"It is the moaning of the sea that distresses her," said the fisherman's wife. "I could almost weep myself for the sorrowful sound of it." And she shut her window.

How could she know the baby cried because she knew the sound was the mermaids' weeping?

Now, as was only to be expected, the news of the merbaby spread among the fisherfolk, and they one and all made some excuse to come tapping at the fisherman's door.

The fisherman's wife showed the baby proudly. "Look what beautiful eyes she has!" she would say. "And see her tiny hands and the shining of her hair!"

"Yes! yes!" said the fisherfolk, "but it is a great pity that she has a tail."

"It is a very beautiful tail," said the fisherman's wife. "And there are so many people with feet that to have a tail is to be quite distinguished."

"A tail will be very awkward when she grows up," said the fisherfolk shaking their heads. "Why don't you put her back in the sea?"

"How cruel that would be!" cried the fisherman's wife. "She is far too tiny to care for herself. Besides, we love her too much to part with her now."

So the merbaby lay from day to day in the wooden cradle and cooed and crooned to itself. The fisherman would leave the mending of his nets to play with it, and his wife sang it gay little songs as she went about her work and ran to kiss its tiny hands and cover it with caresses.

"How could we think a baby was too much trouble!" cried they. "A baby is the loveliest thing in the world."

But the little mermaids in their home among the rocks had no heart to tend the seaweeds, nor to smooth the sand upon the floor and make all neat and tidy; they had no heart to talk to the fishes, nor to play as they had done before.

"How could we think our baby a trouble?" cried they.

"Perhaps some day the fisherman's wife may tire of her," said the eldest.

So every day they swam to the foot of the cliffs. "Sea gulls! Sea gulls!" they cried. "Fly away and bring news of our baby!"

And every day the sea gulls told how the fisherman's wife was fondling the baby as though it were her own.

"Alas! Alas!" wept the little mermaids. "We shall never see our baby again."

And every day when the merbaby heard the sound of their crying it began to wail and would not be comforted.

Then the fisherman would shake his head and ponder. " 'Tis strange," said he, "the moaning of the sea is as the sound of someone weeping."

His wife, too, would ponder on the strangeness as she tried to hush the baby's crying, and she pondered so long that in the end she could not help but find the truth.

"Hark!" cried she. "The baby weeps in answer to the sound. It is no moaning of the waves we hear, but the sorrowing of those who have lost her."

Then she lifted the baby from the cradle, and kissed it on this cheek and that, and ran with it to the shore. There sat the little mermaids weeping, and when they saw the fisherman's wife they held out their arms.

"Give us our baby!" cried they. "We cannot play nor sing nor be happy till we have her again."

"Sorrow no more. Here is your baby," said the fisherman's wife, and she kissed it over and over and gave it to them.

But when she came back to the little house and saw the empty cradle she fell to weeping as sadly as ever the little mermaids had done.

"It is my turn to sorrow now," said she.

And the fisherman could find no words to comfort her, for he was as sad as she.

But the little mermaids were happier than they had ever been before, and they swam up and down with the baby to tell all the sea-creatures of their good fortune and to thank them for their help.

"You look much happier than you did," said the crabs, but, "It is rather hard to understand family life," said the puffins. "We think a great deal of our babies, but of course they are much nicer than mer-babies because they have down and feathers."

"And wings," added the sea gulls. "We cannot imagine what use arms can be."

The anemones shut up as soon as the mermaids came near. "We are glad you have found the baby, since it pleases you so much," said they. "But do take her away or we shall get hair all over us again."

The fishes looked at the merbaby very curiously. "Her tail is very fine," they said, "but a fin or two would improve her."

"Or having both her eyes on one side of her head," said the plaice.

"But of course if you are satisfied with her there is nothing more to be said," added the porpoise, and waved his flipper as he swam away.

The little mermaids hugged and kissed their baby. "Fancy thinking she is not perfect!" they cried. "Only the fisherman and his wife know how to love her as we do, and now they are sorrowful because we have taken her back again."

So sometimes they swam to the little bay and called, and the fisherman's wife would hear them and come running to the edge of the sea. Then the mermaids would give her the baby, and she would sit on the rocks to play with it and fondle it.

"It is so lonely now that the cradle is empty," she would sigh for sympathy. "We will come again soon," said they.

But one day when they swam to the bay, though they called and called, the fisherman's wife did not come running out to greet them.

"What can have befallen her?" they asked one another.

Then they lifted themselves out of the water. "Sea gulls! Sea gulls!" they cried. "Fly away across the sand and tell us why the fisherman's wife does not hear us calling."

So the sea gulls flew round and round the little house as they had done before.

"You need not sorrow longer for the loneliness of the fisherman's wife," said they. "There is another baby in the cradle; it has feet instead of a tail, and its eyes are the color of the sky, but she does not seem to mind, nor does the fisherman. They have not heard you call because they are too happy to hear anything but their own joy."

Then the little mermaids swam back to the hollow among the rocks.

"Now we can be happy all day long," said they, "for there is no one left lonely and sorrowing. And some day we will go again to the bay and the fisherman's wife will show us her baby and we will love it next to our own."

Malvin Wald

THE BOY WHO
OWNED AN ELEPHANT

ILLUSTRATED BY *Rosemary Buehrig*

ONE day Johnny went to the circus—
.a big, three-ring circus with clowns, acrobats, and animals. And in the middle of the center ring stood a large flop-eared elephant. It was the biggest living thing Johnny had ever seen.

That night, Johnny dreamed about elephants, and the next morning he said, "Mother, could I have an elephant for my birthday?"

"Maybe," replied his mother. "But you'll have to wait until your birthday on Sunday."

Sunday morning, Johnny asked for his elephant.

285

His mother told him to open a large box in the corner. Johnny did so and pulled out a gray toy elephant. It was two feet high and was mounted on little wheels.

Johnny thanked his mother. He played with the toy elephant for a while. Then he put it away.

"Don't you like it?" asked his mother.

"Oh, sure," mumbled Johnny. "But I wanted a real, live elephant. Like in the circus."

His mother didn't want him to be unhappy. But she couldn't get Johnny a real elephant, because elephants come from far-off Asia and Africa.

Then she remembered where there was the only elephant in the city.

"Johnny," she said, "get dressed. You're going to meet your elephant."

Fifteen minutes later they were in front of a huge cage in the city zoo. Inside the cage was a big, gray elephant, sound asleep.

"That's your elephant," said his mother. "His name is Butch."

Johnny's face lit up like a Christmas-tree bulb.

"Oh, thank you, Mother," he said. "I guess I'm the luckiest boy in the world with a mother like you and an elephant like Butch."

He shouted to the elephant, "Hello, Butch."

Butch kept on sleeping. And snoring, too. Loud.

"Poor ol' Butch," sighed Johnny. "I guess he's tired. Let's take him home."

"We can't," said his mother.

"Why not? He's mine, isn't he?"

Johnny's mother didn't want to tell him that Butch

belonged to the city. But, she thought, the city belonged to the people. Johnny was one of the people. So, in a way, Butch did belong to Johnny.

"Well, Johnny," she said, "we have no place to keep him. He's too big for any room in our house."

"I guess so, Mother," admitted Johnny. "He is awfully large for a pet."

"And he must have a tremendous appetite!" added his mother. "He'd eat up all our food."

"That would be bad," agreed Johnny. "What can we do?"

"Why not leave him here?" suggested his mother.

A small, thin man in a gray uniform came along, carrying a broom.

"That's Butch's keeper, Mr. Smith," said Johnny's mother. "He'll look after Butch and feed him and keep him clean. You can come back and play with Butch tomorrow."

"All right," sighed Johnny. "So long, Butch," he called out. "See you tomorrow."

Butch snored on.

The next day Johnny was in front of Butch's cage. Butch was snoring as usual, dreaming of his mighty ancestors in distant India.

"Hello, Butch!" Johnny called.

Butch snored on.

Then Mr. Smith came by.

"Hello, Mr. Smith," said Johnny. "What's the matter with Butch?"

"He's a bad elephant," declared the keeper.

Johnny couldn't believe it. "But he's my elephant," he said. "My mother gave him to me. For my birthday.

287

You'll take care of him, won't you?"

Mr. Smith smiled. "I'll do my best, son."

"My name's Johnny," said Johnny. "And I don't think Butch is bad."

"I don't know," sighed Mr. Smith. "He sits with his back to the public. Sleeps most of the time. Snores awful loud. And he squirts me with water when he drinks."

"But elephants are wonderful," argued Johnny. "They can't be bad."

"Then why does Butch act the way he does? Listen to him snore!"

"I know why," said Johnny. "No one ever taught him to behave."

"And you're going to teach him?" Mr. Smith wanted to know.

"Since he's my elephant," said Johnny, "I have to."

Every day Johnny came to Butch's cage. Butch got to know and like him.

Johnny would always shout, "Hello, Butch!"

Butch would shout back the way elephants do— sounding like a trumpet—"TA-RANT-ARAH!" In elephant talk this means, "Hello yourself!"

Johnny would talk quietly but earnestly to Butch. "Now listen, Butch. You gotta behave good. F'r instance, face the people. You're not very pretty from the back."

At first Butch pretended not to know what Johnny was talking about.

But one day he turned around. And he continued to sit that way every day.

People began to stop and admire Butch.

288

"What a handsome beast!" they would say.

"His name is Butch," Johnny would tell them. "He belongs to me."

"Really!" the people would remark. "That's a mighty fine elephant you have, my boy."

And Johnny would smile until his face would shine like a brand new penny.

Butch no longer slept all day. Now that people could see him, he would stand up—or walk about. Once in a while, he would even smile or bow his trunk, as if to say, "Howdy, folks. Nice day, isn't it?"

Johnny would talk to him, or yell at him suddenly, "Hello, Butch."

And Butch would trumpet back, "TA-RANT-ARAH!"

Johnny was more sure than ever that Butch was a good elephant.

"What about his squirting me with water?" argued Mr. Smith.

"Hook up a hose," said Johnny. "And leave the rest to me."

When Mr. Smith brought Butch his bucket of water, Johnny stood by. Butch took a trunkful of water and showered it on poor Mr. Smith.

"Butch," said Johnny, "that's not nice. Cut it out!"

But Butch was feeling very playful. "TA-RANT-ARAH!" he shouted. He squirted Johnny. Then the big elephant laughed with joy.

Johnny jumped out of the way of most of the water. Then he turned the hose on Butch.

The cold stream of water frightened Butch. He jumped back, shouting in fear until Johnny stopped.

"Aha, Mr. Butch," said Johnny. "It's not so funny when the shoe is on the other foot. From now on you will get soaked with this hose whenever you squirt Mr. Smith."

Butch backed up further in his cage.

"Don't be afraid, Butch," said Johnny. "We won't squirt you if you leave Mr. Smith alone. Promise?"

Butch nodded happily. He stuck his trunk through the bars and nuzzled it against Johnny's hand. They were friends again.

"Good boy," said Johnny. And he emptied a bag of peanuts into Butch's trunk.

Butch quickly put the nuts into his mouth and gobbled them down. "TA-RANT-ARAH!" he bellowed in sheer delight.

And so the bright golden summer passed. Johnny taught Butch to behave like a first-class elephant. Mr.

Smith was very pleased and let Johnny help him feed Butch.

Johnny was as happy as any boy could be, for he owned an elephant.

In September, Johnny went to school where there were other boys to play with. That was fun.

After school one day, the boys were boasting about things they owned.

"I got a bicycle," said a boy named Peter, "with real rubber tires."

"That's nothing!" said Arnold, another boy. "I got a white bulldog. The biggest one you ever saw."

"So what?" shouted Johnny. "I own an elephant."

"You're crazy," yelled Arnold.

The other boys laughed at Johnny. They didn't believe him.

"All right," said Johnny. "I'll show you."

Johnny took the boys to Butch's cage. Butch was sound asleep.

"My elephant," said Johnny proudly. "Name is Butch."

"G'wan," scoffed Arnold. "He ain't yours."

"He is, too," said Johnny. "Hello, Butch!" he shouted.

Butch woke up, reared on his two hind legs, and shouted back, "TA-RANT-ARAH!"

Johnny fed him peanuts. Butch went back to sleep. The other boys were amazed. All except Arnold.

"Nothin' special about that. That ol' elephant will do it for me, too." Arnold shouted, "Hello, Butch!"

Butch rolled over in his sleep without missing a snore.

"Hey, Butch," shouted Arnold again.

Still no answer from Butch.

"See," said Johnny triumphantly. "He's *my* elephant."

The other boys, including Arnold, were now sure Johnny was right.

"Golly," they said with envy, "he's swell. Who gave him to you?"

"He's a birthday present," replied Johnny. "From my mother."

The next morning Johnny's mother was called to school by Johnny's teacher. The teacher explained that all the boys in the class, except Johnny, wouldn't talk or laugh or sing. They just sat looking straight ahead. They were unhappy because they didn't own an elephant, like Johnny.

"I'm so sorry," said Johnny's mother. "What can I do?"

"Tell Johnny the truth," said the teacher.

Johnny's mother took him out into the school hall. She told him that Butch wasn't his elephant after all. Butch belonged to all the people in the city.

"Am I one of the people?" asked Johnny.

"Why, yes," admitted his mother.

"Then Butch does belong to me," concluded Johnny.

"In a way," admitted his mother. "But he also belongs to the other boys. You must tell them."

"Why?"

"Because they're unhappy. They want an elephant, too."

"But what's stopping them?" asked Johnny.

"Butch is the only elephant in the city," replied his mother. "It would be nice if you would share him with other boys."

"Butch and I are good friends," said Johnny. "We don't need anyone else."

Later, in the schoolyard, none of the other boys felt like playing. They sat down on benches and day-dreamed of owning an elephant.

Johnny tried to play alone. It wasn't fun.

Finally he sat down on a swing without moving.

That night he didn't want to eat his supper.

"What's the matter, Johnny?" his mother asked.

"No fun playing alone. The other boys won't play with me, because of Butch," Johnny sighed.

"Maybe you ought to show them that you're their friend," suggested his mother.

Johnny thought it over for a minute.

"Mother," he said, "would it work if I shared Butch with them?"

His mother smiled. "You might try."

The next afternoon Johnny took Arnold, Peter, and the others to Butch's cage.

"I understand," he said, "that you want elephants, too."

They nodded.

"Butch is the only elephant in the city," said Johnny. "I happen to own him."

"We know that, Johnny," said Arnold.

"But there's no reason why all of us can't sort of share him," said Johnny.

"He's big enough," agreed Peter hopefully. "And we're pretty small boys!"

"Sure," announced Johnny. "From now on, fellers, we all own Butch."

"You aren't kidding?" asked Arnold.

"I mean it," declared Johnny. "Butch really belongs to the people. That's us. All of us."

"But does Butch know?" asked Arnold.

"I'll tell him," said Johnny.

He shouted to Butch. "Hello, Butch!"

Butch reared on his hind legs and replied with his usual, "TA-RANT-ARAH!"

"This is very important," said Johnny. "These boys are your friends. They own you as much as I. We're all partners. Understand?"

Butch nodded his trunk.

"All right," said Johnny. "From now on, when they yell, 'Hello, Butch!' you're to shout, 'TA-RANT-ARAH' to them, too."

Johnny turned to the other boys. "O.K., fellers, go ahead!"

The boys hesitated. Then together, with a mighty

roar, they shouted, "HELLO, BUTCH!"

Butch looked at them for a long minute. The boys held their breaths.

Then Butch reared on his hind legs and trumpeted back, "TA-RANT-ARAH!"

Broad smiles covered the boys' faces.

"What did I tell you?" Johnny said excitedly. "Now we all own an elephant!"

"TA-RANT-ARAH!" said Butch, meaning he liked the idea very much.

THE SLIDE

Emily Hilsabeck

We climb to the top
Then DOWN we go,
As free as a plane or a bird;
And some of us laugh,
And some of us squeal,
And some of us don't say a word!
And every time that we swoop down,
The wind goes past our faces.
I think the wind is sliding, too,
And running races!

Mildred Lawrence

JANIE'S WISH

ILLUSTRATED BY *Janet Smalley*

JANIE thought that Aunt Emily's house in the country had everything that anybody could want—except one thing.

Kittens in the barn, roses on the trellis, an apple tree outside the bedroom window, and, best of all, tame ducks paddling in the water at the edge of the lake, which was Aunt Emily's backyard. But still there was one thing more Janie wanted.

Every morning she went out to the barn and said, "Good morning, kittens." Next, she hurried to the garden to sniff the roses. After that, she took a short trip up the apple tree and back down again. And then —and this was best of all—she went to see the duck family—Mr. Mallard with his beautiful green head, Mrs. Mallard neatly dressed in brown, and their seven babies diving gaily into the shallow water with their silly, webbed feet up in the air.

If they were not in the lake, they were crossing the road to their little yard, where Henry, Aunt Emily's hired man, filled their battered blue pan with shelled corn. Janie always knew when they were on the road because there was the surprised squeak of brakes and the sound of motor horns.

It was because of the ducks that Janie almost found the one thing which was lacking at Aunt Emily's. One day, when the ducks were crossing the road, a dark red car slowed up long enough for the tail of the last duck to disappear in the grass on the other side. Looking out of the side window was a little girl with fat yellow braids and big brown eyes. She was looking at the ducks and laughing, and then, as the car regained speed, she looked out of the back window at Janie and waved her hand.

"That is the little girl that I want for my friend," said Janie. "That is the one thing that I need at Aunt Emily's house—a friend to play with and talk to. I can play with the ducks and the kittens, but they never say anything but 'Quack!' or 'Mew, mew!' And the roses and the apple tree say even less."

It was true that the dark red car passed Aunt Emily's house nearly every day, and always the little girl with the yellow braids waved out of the back window, but the car never stopped.

"If only I knew some way to get acquainted!" Janie thought. "If only the car would stop!"

If Aunt Emily had anything to sell, like eggs or fresh vegetables, Janie could put up a sign and perhaps the little girl's mother would stop and buy some. But Aunt Emily used all her eggs and fresh vegetables herself.

"I wish you could help me," Janie told the sleepy kittens, "but I couldn't put you up for sale!"

Next, Janie climbed up in the apple tree.

"If only the apples were ripe, I could sell some of them."

But the apples were still only small, green nubbins. Janie went to look at the roses, too, but only a few were in bloom—not enough for a bouquet.

"No, none of them can help," Janie said. "Not the kittens nor the apple tree nor the roses. I might as well forget all about it and go to play with the ducks."

The ducks were playing follow-the-leader, with Mr. Mallard at the head of the procession, Mrs. Mallard next, and the seven babies tagging along behind like the tail of a kite. They were all quacking and talking to each other.

"Are you having fun?" asked Janie sadly. "At least you have somebody to talk to."

The ducks suddenly scrambled out of the water and waddled as fast as they could across the lawn.

"What in the world?" cried Janie. "Oh!"

Across the road, Henry was shelling corn into the blue pan.

"Quack, quack, quack!" said the ducks.

"Click, click, click," said the corn.

Janie wished very hard that the dark red car would come along, right this very minute! But no car at all came along.

"So you're no help, either!" said Janie, dragging her feet a little.

But later, when the ducks were back in the lake, Janie came briskly around the house, sat down on the

298

front steps, and began watching for the red car all over again. Beside her, under a bush, she was hiding something. After a long time, Aunt Emily came out.

"Don't you want to play with the old-fashioned doll?" she asked.

"No, thank you," said Janie. "Not just now."

After another long time, Henry came over from the barn.

"Don't you want to help me hunt eggs?" he asked.

"No, thank you," said Janie. "Tomorrow, maybe."

All the same, it would have been great fun, too, to help Henry hunt eggs, because Henry always looked in the most impossible places—like up on a rafter or at the bottom of the drainpipe—and then acted very much surprised not to find anything.

"Maybe I will help him, after all," Janie decided. "I don't believe—"

But then, coming slowly down the road, just as usual, Janie saw the dark red car. She picked up the secret which she had been hiding under the bush and hurried across the road. The secret was the ducks' blue pan, full of corn.

"Click, click, click!" said the corn as Janie shook it around in the blue pan.

"Quack, quack, quack!" said the ducks, rushing out of the lake and across the lawn.

"Not too fast," begged Janie, "and not too slow. Please make it be just right."

And, sure enough, just as the dark red car reached Aunt Emily's house, a long line of ducks was strung across the road. The car stopped, and out hopped the little girl with the yellow braids.

"Aren't they sweet? What's your name? Oh, I'm so glad the ducks were on the road! Do you have anybody to play with? My name's Marigold," she said, all in one breath.

"Oh, Marigold!" cried Janie. "I do want somebody to play with, and I do hope it can be you!"

By this time Aunt Emily was out on the steps, and Marigold's mother was out of the car.

"Those ducks!" said Aunt Emily. "They just won't keep off the road!"

"They're cunning," said Marigold's mother. "Now, where did that child go?"

"Do come in and sit down until Janie brings her back," invited Aunt Emily.

"It's all right!" said Janie, peering in the front door. "They like each other, too. Ask your mother if you may spend the day tomorrow."

When it was time to go, Marigold waved her hand at Mr. and Mrs. Mallard and their seven children.

"Good-bye," she said, "and thank you for crossing the road."

The next morning, extra-early, because Marigold was coming soon, Janie went to pet the kittens, who only rolled themselves into tighter balls and went to sleep again. She hurried to the garden to sniff the roses, still sparkling with dew. She climbed the apple tree and wondered when the first apples would be ripe. And then, best of all, she went to see the ducks, who were skimming in and out among the reeds. Janie reached out and gave each feathery back a grateful pat as it floated past.

"Today," she said, "I will tell Marigold how to make the ducks cross the road."

APPLE BLOSSOMS

Helen Wing

The apple blossoms grow so high
   Upon the branches of our tree,
I can't reach up to smell them; so
   They send their perfume down to me.

Laurence Housman

ROCKING-HORSE LAND

ILLUSTRATED BY *Ruth van Tellingen*

ITTLE Prince Freedling woke up with a jump and sprang out of bed into the sunshine. He was five years old that morning, by all the clocks and calendars in the kingdom; and the day was going to be beautiful. Every golden minute was precious. He was dressed and out of his room before the attendants knew that he was awake.

In the antechamber stood piles on piles of glittering presents; when he walked among them they came up to the measure of his waist. His fairy godmother had sent him a toy with the most humorous effect. It was labeled, "Break me and I shall turn into something else." So every time he broke it he got a new toy more beautiful than the last. It began by being a hoop, and from that it ran on, while the Prince broke it incessantly for the space of one hour, during which it became by turn—a top, a Noah's ark, a skipping-rope, a man-of-war, a box of bricks, a picture puzzle, a pair of stilts, a drum, a trumpet, a kaleidoscope, a steam engine, and nine hundred and fifty other things exactly. Then he began to grow discontented, because it would never turn into the same thing again; and after having broken the man-of-war he wanted to get it back again. Also he wanted to see if the steam engine would go inside the Noah's ark; but the toy would never be two things at the same time, either. This was very unsatisfactory. He thought his

302

fairy godmother ought to have sent him two toys, out of which he could make combinations.

At last he broke it once more, and it turned into a kite; and while he was flying the kite he broke the string, and the kite went sailing away up into nasty blue sky and was never heard of again.

Then Prince Freedling sat down and howled at his fairy godmother; what a dissembling lot fairy godmothers were, to be sure! They were always setting traps to make their godchildren unhappy. Nevertheless, when told to, he took up his pen and wrote her a nice little note, full of bad spelling and tarradiddles, to say what a happy birthday he was spending in breaking up the beautiful toy she had sent him.

Then he went to look at the rest of the presents, and found it quite refreshing to break a few that did not send him giddy by turning into anything else.

Suddenly his eyes became fixed with delight; alone, right at the end of the room, stood a great black rocking-horse. The saddle and bridle were hung with tiny gold bells and balls of coral; and the horse's tail and mane flowed till they almost touched the ground.

The Prince scampered across the room and threw his arms around the beautiful creature's neck. All its bells jangled as the head swayed gracefully down; and the Prince kissed it between the eyes. Great eyes they were, the color of fire; so wonderfully bright, it seemed they must be really alive; only they did not move, but gazed continually with a set stare at the tapestry-hung wall, on which were figures of armed knights riding to battle.

So Prince Freedling mounted to the back of his rocking-horse; and all day long he rode and shouted to the figures of the armed knights, challenging them to fight, or leading them against the enemy.

At length, when it came to be bedtime, weary of so much glory, he was lifted down from the saddle and carried away to bed.

In his sleep Freedling still felt his black rocking-horse swinging to and fro under him, and heard the melodious chime of its bells, and, in the land of dreams, saw a great country open before him, full of the sound of the battle cry and the hunting-horn calling him to strange perils and triumphs.

In the middle of the night he grew softly awake, and his heart was full of love for his black rocking-horse. He crept gently out of bed: he would go and look at it where it was standing so grand and still in the next room, to make sure that it was all safe and not afraid of being by itself in the dark night. Parting the door-hangings he passed through into the wide hollow chamber beyond, all littered about with toys.

The moon was shining in through the window, making a square cistern of light upon the floor. And then, all at once, he saw that the rocking-horse had moved from the place where he had left it! It had crossed the room, and was standing close to the window, with its head toward the night, as though watching the movement of the clouds and the trees swaying in the wind.

The Prince could not understand how it had been moved so; he was a little bit afraid and, stealing timidly across, he took hold of the bridle to comfort himself with the jangle of its bells. As he came close, and looked up into the dark solemn face, he saw that the eyes were full of tears and, reaching up, felt one fall warm against his hand.

"Why do you weep, my Beautiful?" said the Prince.

The rocking-horse answered, "I weep because I am a prisoner, and not free. Open the window, Master, and let me go!"

"But if I let you go I shall lose you," said the Prince. "Cannot you be happy here with me?"

"Let me go," said the horse, "for my brothers call me out of Rocking-Horse Land; I hear my mare whinnying to her foals; and they all cry, seeking me through the ups and hollows of my native fastness! Sweet Master, let me go this night, and I will return to you when it is day!"

Then Freedling said, "How shall I know that you will return; and what name shall I call you by?"

And the rocking-horse answered, "My name is Rollonde. Search my mane till you find in it a white hair; draw it out and wind it upon one of your fingers; and as long as you have it so wound you are my master; and wherever I am I must return at your bidding."

305

So the Prince drew down the rocking-horse's head; and searching the mane, he found the white hair, and wound it upon his finger and tied it. Then he kissed Rollonde between the eyes, saying, "Go, Rollonde, since I love you and wish you to be happy; only return to me when it is day!" And so saying, he threw open the window to the stir of the night.

Then the rocking-horse lifted his dark head and neighed aloud for joy, and swaying forward with a mighty circling motion rose full into the air and sprang out into the free world before him.

Freedling watched how with plunge and curve he went over the bowed trees; and again he neighed into the darkness of the night, then swifter than wind disappeared in the distance. And faintly from far away came a sound of the neighing of many horses answering him.

Then the Prince closed the window and crept back to bed; and all night long he dreamed strange dreams of Rocking-Horse Land. There he saw smooth hills and valleys that rose and sank without a stone or a tree to disturb the steel-like polish of their surface, slippery as glass, and driven over by a strong wind; and over them, with a sound like the humming of bees, flew the rocking-horses. Up and down, up and down, with bright manes streaming like colored fires, and feet motionless behind and before, went the swift pendulum of their flight. Their long bodies bowed and rose; their heads worked to give impetus to their going; they cried, neighing to each other over hill and valley, "Which of us shall be first? Which of us shall be first?" After them the mares with their tall foals came spinning to watch, crying, "Ah! which shall be first?"

"Rollonde, Rollonde is first!" shouted the Prince, clapping his hands as they reached the goal; and at that, all at once, he woke, and saw it was broad day. Then he ran and threw open the window and, holding out the finger that carried the white hair, cried, "Rollonde, Rollonde, come back, Rollonde!"

Far away he heard an answering sound; and in another moment there came the great rocking-horse himself, dipping and dancing over the hills. He crossed the woods and cleared the palace-wall at a bound, and floating in through the window, dropped to rest at Prince Freedling's side, rocking gently to and fro as though panting from the strain of his long flight.

"Now are you happy?" asked the Prince as he caressed him.

"Ah! sweet Prince!" said Rollonde. And then he said no more, but became the stock-still, staring rocking-horse of the day before, with fixed eyes and rigid limbs, which could do nothing but rock up and down with a jangling of sweet bells so long as the Prince rode him.

307

That night Freedling came again when all was still in the palace; and now as before Rollonde had moved from his place and was standing with his head against the window waiting to be let out. "Ah, dear Master," he said, as soon as he saw the Prince coming, "let me go this night also, and surely I will return with day."

So again the Prince opened the window, and watched him disappear, and heard from far away the neighing of the horses in Rocking-Horse Land calling to him. And in the morning, with the white hair round his finger, he called, "Rollonde, Rollonde!" and Rollonde neighed and came back to him, dipping and dancing over the hills.

Now this same thing happened every night; and every morning the horse kissed Freedling, saying, "Ah! dear Prince and kind Master!" and became stock-still once more.

So a year went by, till one morning Freedling woke up to find it was his sixth birthday. And as six is to five, so were the presents he received on his sixth birthday for magnificence and multitude to the presents he had received the year before. His fairy godmother had sent him a bird, a real live bird; but when he pulled its tail it became a lizard, and when he pulled the lizard's tail it became a mouse, and when he pulled the mouse's tail it became a cat. Then he did very much want to see if the cat would eat the mouse, and not being able to have them both he got rather vexed with his fairy godmother. However, he pulled the cat's tail and the cat became a dog, and when he pulled the dog's tail the dog became a goat; and so it went on till he got to a cow. And he pulled the cow's tail and it became a camel, and he pulled the camel's tail and it became an elephant, and still not being contented, he pulled the elephant's tail and it became a guinea-pig. Now a guinea-pig has no tail, so it remained a guinea-pig, while Prince Freedling howled at his fairy godmother.

But the best of all his presents was the one given to him by the King his father. It was a most beautiful horse, for, said the King, "You are now old enough to learn to ride."

So Freedling was put upon the horse's back, and from having ridden so long upon his rocking-horse he learned to ride perfectly in a single day, and was declared by all the courtiers to be the most perfect equestrian that was ever seen.

Now these praises and the pleasure of riding a real horse so occupied his thoughts that that night he forgot all about Rollonde, and falling fast asleep dreamed of nothing but real horses and horsemen going to battle. And so it was the next night too.

But the night after that, just as he was falling asleep, he heard someone sobbing by his bed, and a voice saying, "Ah! dear Prince and kind Master, let me go, for my heart breaks for a sight of my native land." And there stood his poor rocking-horse Rollonde, with tears falling out of his beautiful eyes on to the white coverlet.

Then the Prince, full of shame at having forgotten his friend, sprang up and threw his arms round his neck, saying, "Be of good cheer, Rollonde, for now surely I will let thee go!" and he ran to the window and opened it for the horse to go through. "Ah! dear Prince and kind Master!" said Rollonde. Then he lifted his head and neighed so that the whole palace shook;

and swaying forward till his head almost touched the ground, he sprang out into the night and away toward Rocking-Horse Land.

Then Prince Freedling, standing by the window, thoughtfully unloosed the white hair from his finger, and let it float away into the darkness, out of sight of his eye or reach of his hand.

"Good-bye, Rollonde," he murmured softly, "brave Rollonde, my own good Rollonde! Go and be happy in your own land, since I, your Master, was forgetting to be kind to you." And far away he heard the neighing of horses in Rocking-Horse Land.

Many years after, when Freedling had become King in his father's stead, the fifth birthday of the Prince his son came to be celebrated; and there on the morning of the day, among all the presents that covered the floor of the chamber, stood a beautiful foal rocking-horse, black, with deep-burning eyes.

No one knew how it had come there, or whose present it was, till the King himself came to look at it. And when he saw it so like the old Rollonde he had loved as a boy, he smiled, and, stroking its dark mane, said softly in its ear, "Art thou, then, the son of Rollonde?" And the foal answered him, "Ah, dear Prince and kind Master!" but never a word more.

Then the King took the little Prince his son and told him the story of Rollonde as I have told it here; and at the end in the foal's mane he found one white hair, and he wound it about the little Prince's finger, bidding him guard it well and be a kind master to Rollonde's son.

So here is my story of Rollonde come to a good ending.

THE GENIAL GRIMALKIN

J. G. Francis

There was an old Cat named Macduff,
Who could joke till you cried, "Hold, enough!"
His Wife and his Child so persistently smiled
That their cheeks got a permanent puff.

THE BARBER

J. G. Francis

A Lion emerged from his lair
For a short summer cut to his hair.
But the Barber he wept;
While his customers slept
As they waited their turn in the chair.

311

Florence Page Jaques

THE RUNAWAY BUS

ILLUSTRATED BY *John Gee*

HE WAS such a funny, sweet-tempered, jolly old motor bus, Number 999 was. He was so very wide and so very steady, and his bright paint always looked so fresh and shiny that you loved the first glimpse you had of him.

He never pretended not to see people when they wanted him to stop at a corner. He wouldn't have dreamed of such a thing! He always stopped and waited patiently till they got on with both feet. He never skidded sideways on slippery days, as some of the younger busses liked to do. He went rumbling straight along and never broke down.

Everybody liked Number 999; and Number 999 liked everybody, from the tiny little babies who looked so surprised to be there, to the old, old men who always carried their canes and their white whiskers with them.

But one morning Number 999 started out, and he didn't feel like himself at all!

It was a lovely, cold, snowy morning, with great white snowflakes like butterflies in the air, and a soft gray sky. And everybody seemed so happy, with bundles and holly and twinkles in their arms and buttonholes and faces.

There were round green wreaths and bright red ribbons on doors and bells jingling down the streets. The shop windows were packed with scarlet and green

312

and gold, and there was a smell of pine trees in the air which made Number 999 feel like a little play bus again, somehow. "Why do I feel like that?" he wondered. "It smells like—like Christmas trees!" And just then a gay little boy's voice said, "It will be a snowy Christmas tomorrow, Daddy!"

"Why," said Number 999 to himself, "it's the day before Christmas!"

Now, Number 999 always worked harder at Christmas time than any other time. Everybody in the world was scurrying around then, shopping at the last minute, and losing their packages, and having to go back again, and going to see their grandmothers and cousins and children and aunts and mothers and fathers, (according to their age, you know), and carrying big parcels with exciting ends sticking out, a doll's foot or a velocipede handle or a long scarlet candle. Number 999 had very heavy loads.

But he adored Christmastime just the same. And best of all he liked the day before Christmas. It seemed the gayest and the most adventurous, and the fullest of delightful secrets of all the days!

But this particular day before Christmas, as I said, Number 999 felt very odd. He had never felt just this way before in his whole life! Somehow he didn't want to carry everybody back and forth to their merry Christmases. He wanted to have a day before Christmas himself!

All at once, there in the middle of the street, he gave a jump, up in the air, with all four wheels. "I'm *going* to have a Christmas myself," he said. "I'm going to run away!"

And without even thinking another minute about it, he started off! He ran down the snowy street just as fast as he could, and though there was a nice old lady waiting for him on the very first corner, he didn't even wink! He just tossed his head, and laughed deep down in his radiator, and ran on faster than ever.

He had never done that before! He had always stopped for everybody.

He was as bad as he could be, that day before Christmas. He ran all over town, and nobody could stop him! He didn't pay the least attention to the traffic cops—he ran around just as he liked!

He got the street cars and trucks all mixed up by running down the wrong side of the street. He tooted his horn unexpectedly at people and made them jump out of their rubbers. He stood up on his back wheels and *lunged* at a very fat young man, with a flower in his coat and a beautiful new hat. And the very fat young man ran and lost his flower *and* his hat. And Number 999 laughed till he choked. Yes, he did—good old Number 999, who had always been so kind!

314

He picked up a holly wreath with a big bright ribbon bow and stuck it over one ear. Then he looked at himself in a big store window and pranced in the street, because he was so proud. Then he started off to run faster than ever! Nobody could do one thing with him!

The Policeman tried to stop him; so did the Chief of Police; so did the Mayor. But Number 999 just laughed and blew his horn and ran around the corner.

At last the Mayor ordered *all* the police, especially the two on horseback, and *all* the fire department, especially the hook and ladder, and the band, and the patrol wagon, to assemble in the square, by the big outdoor Christmas tree.

"We'll have to catch Number 999 and put him in jail," the Mayor said sternly.

Number 999 decided, suddenly, that he had played long enough in the city. So he ran away, out into the country.

Oh, what a good time he had out there! For he was a city bus—he had never been in the country before—and he *liked* running along a country road in the snow, with no one else in sight, and his horn sounding so loudly in the still blue air. He felt more and more excited.

Then he found a steep hill, and he lay down on his back with his wheels in the air and slid down it! Then he rolled over and over in the fluffy snowdrifts, first taking off his holly wreath and hanging it up on a tree.

Then he found a little river all covered with ice, and he slid up and down it for a long time. Then he went back to find his holly wreath, and he put it on and

315

started down the winding road again. He skipped.

After a while he saw the high and mighty walls of a castle, up on a hilltop. He stopped a green wagon which was ambling slowly by.

"What is that, on that hill, over there?" he asked.

"What?" said the wagon.

"That castle on the hill—what is it?" Number 999 asked the green wagon a second time.

"It's a castle," said the wagon.

"Of course it is, old slab sides," said Number 999, laughing. "But who lives there?"

"The Lord of the Castle lives there," said the wagon slowly, after a long silence. "All alone he lives, since his daughter married the piper, and he sent them away."

"I'll just run up and see him," said the motor bus.

"I'll watch for you to come down," said the green wagon. It gave a low, deep chuckle, and started slowly on again.

Number 999 ran up the steep hill to the castle gates. He had to go so fast to get up the hill at all that, when he ran inside the castle gates, he couldn't stop. He ran on, through the castle door, and—*bang!*—into the great crystal mirror in the Hall of State, and he shattered it to bits. Nothing was left but the gold frame, and it was hanging around Number 999's neck!

The Lord of the Castle came rushing out from lunch with a blueberry muffin in his hand. Oh, how angry he was! He threw the muffin violently at Number 999, and he called to all his soldiers, "Arrest that motor bus!"

Number 999 ran round and round the Hall of State, and the soldiers ran after him, tripping on the crimson cord that hung from the mirror frame.

But at last Number 999 crashed into a marble column accidentally—a muffin crumb had gone in his eye—and he sat down with a thump. Then all the soldiers seized him (he was so stunned by the crash that he couldn't even wiggle), and they *threw* him out of the castle gates and he rolled down the steep castle hill.

Number 999 heard a faint giggle as the green wagon passed slowly behind a hill in the distance.

The soldiers had barred the gates, and the Lord of the Castle stood on the gray wall in his purple cloak and shook his fist at Number 999, who sat in the ditch and rubbed his forehead and straightened his holly wreath.

"If you ever come back again," said the Lord of the Castle, "I'll have you chopped up in little pieces. In pieces!"

The motor bus climbed stiffly out of the ditch and started off again. All at once he began to laugh. "I wish I could have seen myself falling down the hill!" he said.

By this time it was almost dark. It was very quiet

along the country road, and the snow lay white on the hills, and the great silver Christmas star shone in the sky. "It's Christmas Eve," said the motor bus to himself softly, and suddenly all the mischief left his heart, and something else came into it. He looked up at the Christmas star again, shining in the dark, clear sky.

"It's Christmas Eve," said the motor bus, and he began to sing a Christmas carol. But he stopped soon, for he loved music.

Then he heard a real Christmas carol coming through the air. And he followed the singing, and at last, just as it was really dark, he came to a little brown house, almost covered with snow. Round and round he prowled, till he found a window with a shade only half pulled down. Then he kneeled down on his front wheels and peeped through the window.

There was a rosy fire in the fireplace of the little house, and sitting before it was the loveliest lady he had ever seen, with three little girls on one side of her, and three little boys on the other. And they were all singing Christmas carols. The motor bus liked listening to their songs.

At last the lovely lady said, "Now, darlings, you must run away to bed. And remember, though tomorrow is Christmas Day, there won't be any Christmas presents. Are you *sure* you won't mind?"

"Of course, we won't mind, Mother," said the oldest little boy sturdily. "We think you're wonderful. You've made enough money sewing to get our bread and milk, even though you do have to work all the time." Number 999 looked, and indeed the lovely lady was sewing even then.

"We all think the Christmas carols are a lovely Christmas present," said the middle boy.

"Are you sure the Lord of the Castle won't send Christmas presents?" said the littlest little boy wistfully.

"Of course, he won't," said the oldest little girl. "He doesn't know that Daddy had to go way off to the other side of the world to get money enough for us."

"I know," said the littlest girl, "how you can give us a Christmas present tomorrow, Mother. You can tell us about the wonderful Christmases you had when you were the Lord of the Castle's little girl!"

"That's what I'll do," said the lady, laughing. But when all the children were asleep, she cried because there were no Christmas presents for them.

Oh, the motor bus simply couldn't bear to see the lady crying! It hurt him somewhere inside. And when he thought of all the things the Lord of the Castle had, it made him so mad that his engine whirred faster and faster. Then, all at once, he had a wonderful idea!

It was such a good idea that Number 999 could hardly keep from sounding his horn. He could hardly keep his wheels still. But he waited patiently till the lady went to sleep, there by the fire.

Then—he slipped around to the front of the house, and he pulled a strong rope out of the tool box, and he tied one end of it around the little brown house, and the other around his waist, and he began to pull the little brown house down the snowy road!

Down the road they went and through the snow, till they came to the Castle hill. The bus had a dreadful time pulling the little brown house up that steep hill! But at last he did.

319

Then he opened the castle gates gently, and he left the little brown house in the courtyard. He went on into the castle—only carefully this time, so that he wouldn't break anything—and into the banquet hall where the Lord of the Castle and all the soldiers were having a feast.

"There's that ridiculous motor bus," shouted the Lord of the Castle angrily. "Didn't I tell him I'd have him chopped up in little pieces if he ever came back?"

"Well, you can have me chopped up in little pieces," said the motor bus bravely, though his windows shook at the thought. "But first I have something to show you."

So he led the Lord of the Castle out into the courtyard and showed him the little brown house, and the three little girls and the three little boys asleep in their beds, and their mother asleep by the fire, and not a single Christmas present in the house.

The Lord of the Castle wanted to cry, but he couldn't, because he was Lord of the Castle. So he walked up and down the courtyard very fast, stamping his feet. Then he slapped the motor bus on the side.

"You're a good old bus, after all," he said. "Thank you for bringing them up."

Then he called to his soldiers, and everyone hurried.

In the morning, when the lady and the children woke up, it seemed unusually warm in the little brown house, which was most frightfully cold on winter mornings. And when they looked out a window, they seemed to see walls and banners instead of snow and fields! It seemed queer. So as soon as they were dressed they opened the door.

The little brown house had been moved again in the night. It was inside the Hall of State, which was big enough to hold ten little brown houses!

When the lady and the children walked out of the front door, there was a great fireplace with a huge fire roaring in it, and a stocking apiece hanging, crammed full! In one corner was an enormous Christmas tree, green and silver and sparkling, with playthings, and candy and nuts, and every single thing a Christmas tree should have, hanging on it. And in the other corner was the motor bus, still with his holly wreath on, and Christmas tree ornaments all over him to make him look gay, and the biggest smile on his face that you ever did see! And there was a lovely turkey-cranberry-ice-cream-plum-pudding smell coming around the corner!

And best of all, there was the Lord of the Castle, with open arms, in front of the fireplace!

The lovely lady laughed and cried and laughed again, and the Lord of the Castle hugged her and each little girl and each little boy. And then they had the stockings and then breakfast, and then the tree, and then dinner, and everybody said it was the nicest Christmas ever!

Forever after, the lady and her three little boys and three little girls lived with the Lord of the Castle, and when her husband, the piper, came back from the other side of the world, he lived there, too.

And Number 999? Why, of course, he stayed! They all loved him as hard as they could. He had a green wreath to wear every day, and a gold one for Sundays. And he asked them if they would call him Jimmy once in a while, and they did! And he never had to carry anyone around unless he wanted to, except the Lord of the Castle when he went into town to call on the Mayor. And he liked that.

The motor bus has been very happy ever since. But once in a while when he gets tired of playing around the castle, he goes down into the city and pretends to be a regular hard-working bus. Maybe you've ridden on him sometimes! He likes specially to take children and he likes the most specially of all to take them at Christmastime!

Dr. Seuss

McELLIGOT'S POOL

ILLUSTRATED BY THE AUTHOR

"Young man," laughed the farmer,
"You're sort of a fool!
You'll *never* catch fish
In McElligot's Pool!

"The pool is too small.
And, you might as well know it,
When people have junk
Here's the place that they throw it.

"You might catch a boot
Or you might catch a can.
You might catch a bottle,
But listen, young man. . . .

"If you sat fifty years
With your worms and your wishes,

You'd grow a long beard
Long before you'd catch fishes!"

"Hmmm . . ." answered Marco,
"It *may* be you're right.
I've been here three hours
Without one single bite.
There *might* be no fish. . .

". . . But, again,
Well, there *might!*
*'Cause you never can tell
What goes on down below!*

"This pool *might* be bigger
Than you or I know!

"This MIGHT be a pool, like I've read of in books,
Connected to one of those underground brooks!
An underground river that starts here and flows
Right under the pasture! And then . . . well, *who knows?*
It *might* go along, down where no one can see,
Right under State Highway Two-Hundred-and-Three!
Right under the wagons! Right under the toes
Of Mrs. Umbroso who's hanging out clothes!
It *might* keep on flowing . . . perhaps . . . who can
  tell? . . .
Right under the people in Sneeden's Hotel!
Right under the grass where they're playing croquet!
Then under the mountains and far, far away!

This *might* be a river,
Now mightn't it be,
   Connecting
    McElligot's
    Pool
     with
      the
       sea!
Then maybe some fish might be swimming toward me!
(If such a thing *could* be,
They certainly *would* be!)
Some very smart fellow might point out the way
To the place where I'm fishing. And that's why I say

If I wait long enough; if I'm patient and cool,
Who knows *what* I'll catch in McElligot's Pool!
I might catch a thin fish,
I might catch a stout fish.
I might catch a short

or

a

long,
long
drawn-out fish!

Any kind! Any shape! Any color or size!
I *might* catch some fish that would open your eyes!

326

I won't be surprised if a *Dog Fish* appears!
Complete with a collar and long floppy ears!
Whoofing along! And perhaps he might chase
A whole lot of *Catfish* right straight to this place!
I might catch a fish
With a pinwheel-like tail!
I might catch a fish
Who has fins like a sail!
I might catch some young fish,
Some high-jumping friskers.
I might catch an old one
With long flowing whiskers!

I might catch a fish
With a long curly nose.
I might catch a fish
Like a rooster that crows.
I might catch a fish
With a checkerboard belly,
Or even a fish
Made of strawberry jelly!
I might catch a Sea Horse.
(Now mightn't I now . . .?)
I might catch a fish
Who is partly a cow!
Some fish from the Tropics, all sunburned and hot,
Might decide to swim up!
         Well they might . . .
         Might they not?
Racing up north for a chance to get cool,
Full steam ahead for McElligot's Pool!
Some Eskimo Fish
From beyond Hudson Bay
Might decide to swim down;
Might be headed this way!
It's a pretty long trip,
But they *might*
And they *may*.
I might catch an eel . . .
(Well, I might. It depends.)
. . . A long twisting eel
With a lot of strange bends
And, oddly enough,
With a head on both ends!
One doesn't catch *this* kind of fish as a rule,

But the chances are fine in McElligot's Pool!
I might catch a fish
With a terrible grouch . . .
Or an Australian fish
With a kangaroo's pouch!
Who wants to catch small ones like mackerel or trout!
SAY! I'll catch a Saw Fish with such a long snout
That he needs an assistant to help him about!
If I wait long enough, if I'm patient and cool,
Who knows *what* I'll catch in McElligot's Pool!
Some rough-neck old Lobster,
All gristle and muscle,
Might grab at my bait,
Then would I have a tussle!
To land one so tough might take two or three hours,
But the *next* might be easy . . .
. . . The kind that likes flowers.
I *might* catch some sort of a fast-moving bloke
Who zips through the waves with an overarm stroke!
(I *might* and I *may* and that's really no joke!)
A fish even faster!
A fish, if you please,
Who slides down the sides
Of strange islands on skis!
He *might* ski on over and pay me a visit.
That's not impossible . . . really, now is it?
Some Circus Fish!
Fish from an acrobat school,
Might stage a big show in McElligot's Pool!
Or I might catch a fish
From a stranger place yet!
From the world's highest river

In far-off Tibet,
Where the falls are so steep
That it's dangerous to ride 'em,
So the fish put up chutes
And they float down beside 'em.
From the world's deepest ocean,
From way down below,
From down in the mud where the deep-divers go,
From down in the mire and the muck and the murk,
I might catch some fish who are all going, "GLURK!"
            WHALES!
I'll catch whales!
Yes, a whole herd of whales!
All spouting their spouts
And all thrashing their tails!
I'll catch fifty whales,
Then I'll stop for the day
'Cause there's *nothing* that's bigger
Than whales, so they say.
Still, of course,
It *might* be . . .
. . . that there IS something bigger!
Some sort of a kind of
A THING-A-MA-JIGGER!!
A fish that's so big, if you know what I mean,
That he makes a whale look like a tiny sardine!
Oh, the sea is so full of a number of fish,
If a fellow is patient, he *might* get his wish!
And that's why I think
That I'm not such a fool
When I sit here and fish
In McElligot's Pool!"

Catherine Woolley

THE PUPPY
WHO WANTED A BOY

ILLUSTRATED BY *Clarence Biers*

ONE day Petey, who was a puppy, said to his mother, "I'd like a boy for Christmas."

His mother, who was a dog, said she guessed he could have a boy if he was a very good puppy.

So the day before Christmas, Petey's mother asked, "Have you been a very good puppy?"

"Oh yes!" said Petey. "I didn't frighten the cat."

"You *didn't?*" asked Petey's mother.

"Well—a—I just frightened her a *little,*" said Petey, "And I didn't chew any shoes."

"Not *any?*" said his mother.

"Just a teeny-weeny chew," said Petey. "And I remembered—well, practically always—to bark when I wanted to go out."

"All right," said his mother. "I guess you've been good. Anyway, you're awfully little. I shall go out and get you a boy for Christmas."

But when Petey's mother came back, she looked very much worried.

"How would you like a soft, white rabbit with pink ears for Christmas?" she said to Petey.

"No thanks," said Petey.

"Don't you want a lovely canary?"

332

"No, I just wanted a boy."

"How about some guppy fish? They're nice," said Petey's mother.

"I don't like fish," said Petey. "I'd like a boy."

"Petey," said his mother, "there are no boys to be had."

"No boys?" exclaimed Petey in dismay.

"Not one could I find. They're terribly short of boys this year."

Petey felt as if he couldn't stand it if he didn't have a boy.

Finally his mother said, "There, now, there must be a boy somewhere. Perhaps you could find some dog who would give his boy away."

"Do you think I could?" asked Petey.

"It wouldn't hurt to try."

So Petey hopefully started off.

It wasn't long before he saw a collie racing with a boy on a bicycle. Petey trembled with joy.

"If I had a boy on a bicycle," said Petey, "I could run like everything! I'll take a little run right now," he thought, "and I'll ask the collie politely if he'll give his boy away." So Petey leaped after the bicycle. He called out to the collie, "Excuse me. Do you want to give your boy away?"

But the collie said *no*, he definitely *didn't*, in a dreadful tone of voice.

Petey sat down. He watched the collie and his boy on a bicycle until they were out of his sight.

"I didn't really want a boy on a bicycle anyway," said Petey.

After a while he saw a big setter playing ball with

a boy. Petey was just delighted. "If I had a boy to play ball with," said Petey, "I'd catch the ball smack in my mouth. I'd like to catch the ball now!" he thought.

But he remembered how cross the collie had been. So he sat down on the sidewalk and called out politely, "Excuse me. Do you want to give your boy away?"

But the setter said *no,* he definitely *didn't,* in a terrifying tone of voice!

"Oh, well," said Petey, trotting off, "I don't think playing ball is much."

Soon Petey came to a bulldog, sitting in a car with a boy. Petey was pleased, for he was getting a little tired from so much walking.

"If I had a boy in a car," said Petey, "I'd laugh at walking dogs. I'd like a ride right now," he thought.

So he called out loudly, but very politely, "Excuse me. Do you want to give your boy away?"

But the bulldog said *no*, he definitely *didn't*, and he growled in Petey's face.

"Oh, dear!" said Petey. He ran off behind a house and stayed there until the bulldog and his boy drove away.

"Well, who wants to go riding in a car? Pff! Not me!" said Petey.

He thought he'd just rest a while, though. He had come a long way for such a little dog. He was limping a little when he started off again.

After a while he met a Scotty, walking with his boy and carrying a package in his mouth.

"Now that is a good kind of boy!" said Petey. "If I had a boy to take walks with and carry packages for, there might be some dog biscuit or cookies in the package. I'd like a cookie this minute!" he thought, for he hadn't had a bite of lunch.

But he remembered how cross the collie and the setter and the bulldog had been. So he stayed across the street and shouted at the top of his lungs, but polite as could be, "Excuse me. Do you want to give your boy away?"

The Scotty had his mouth full of package. But he managed to say *no*, he definitely *didn't*, and he showed his sharp teeth at Petey.

"I guess that wasn't the kind of boy I wanted either," said poor Petey. "But my goodness, where *will* I find a boy?"

Well, Petey went on and on. Up busy streets, dodging the cars and looking in stores and round corners, down quiet lanes where dogs rushed to their fences and yelped at him.

He saw Irish terriers, Scotch terriers, Skye terriers. He saw foxhounds, greyhounds, wolfhounds. He saw pointers, setters, spaniels, beagles, chows.

He asked every dog politely. But he couldn't find a single dog who would give his boy away.

Petey's ears began to droop. His tail grew limp. His legs were *so* tired. "My mother was right," he thought. "There isn't a boy to be had."

As it was getting dark, he came to a large building on the very edge of town. Petey was going by, very slowly because his paws hurt, when he saw a sign over the door. The sign said:

ORPHAN'S HOME

"I know what orphans are," Petey said to himself. "They're children who have no mother, and no dog to take care of them either. Maybe I could find a boy here!"

He padded slowly up the walk of the Orphan's Home. He was so tired he could hardly lift his little paws.

Then Petey stopped. He listened. He could hear music. He looked. Through the window he could see a lighted Christmas tree, and children singing carols.

Petey looked some more. On the front step of the Orphan's Home, all by himself, sat a boy! He was not a very big boy. He looked lonely.

Petey gave a glad little cry. He forgot about being tired. He leaped up and landed in the boy's lap.

Sniff, sniff went Petey's little nose. Wiggle, wag went Petey's tail. He licked the boy with his wet tongue.

How glad the boy was to see Petey! He put both

his arms around the little dog and hugged him tight.

Then the front door opened. "Goodness, Dickie," a lady said, "what are you doing out here? Come on in to the Christmas tree."

Petey sat very still.

The boy looked up at the lady. Then he looked down at Petey. Petey began to tremble. Would the boy go in and leave him?

But the boy said, "I've got a puppy. Can he come, too?"

"A puppy!" The lady came over and looked down at Petey. "Why," she said, "you're a nice dog. Wherever did you come from? Yes, bring him in."

"Come on, puppy," said the boy, and in they scampered.

A crowd of boys was playing around the Christmas tree. They all rushed at Petey. They all wanted to pick him up. They all wanted to pet him.

Petey wagged his tail. He wagged his fat little body. He frisked about and kissed every boy who came near.

"Can he stay?" the boys asked.

"Yes," said the lady, "he may stay."

"Come on, puppy," Dickie said. "Get your supper."

"We'll fix you a nice warm bed!" cried another boy.

"We'll all play games with you," said a third.

Petey wriggled away from the hands that petted him. Dickie was the one he loved best!

"But who ever would think," said Petey to himself, "that I'd get *fifty* boys for Christmas!"

SAID THE SANDMAN

Helen Wing

"Someone is staying up late tonight,"
Said the Sandman.
"Someone's forgetting to turn off the light,"
Said the Sandman.
"Someone is needing attention from me,
I'd better find out what the trouble may be,
Perhaps I can think of the right remedy,"
Said the Sandman.
"Somebody soon will be nodding his head,"
Said the Sandman.
"Somebody soon will be wanting his bed,"
Said the Sandman.
"I'll show him a meadow of little white sheep,
Who jump through the fence where the daisies are
    deep,
And the next thing you know he'll be sound, sound
    asleep,"
Said the Sandman.

ADAPTED FROM *Hans Christian Andersen*

THE FIR TREE

ILLUSTRATED BY *Ruth van Tellingen*

DEEP in the forest stood a little fir tree. The sun shone down on him, and on his tall companions, the pines and firs. But the little tree was not happy. He wanted to be tall, too.

Sometimes children would go into the forest to search for strawberries. Often they would sit down near the fir tree, and say, "Oh, isn't that a pretty little tree!" And the tree did not like to hear that at all.

"Oh, if I were only as high as the others!" sighed the little tree. "Then I could spread out my boughs. Then I could look out into the wide world. Birds would build nests in my branches. And when the wind blew, I could bow with dignity, too."

339

The little tree took no pleasure in the singing birds, or in the sunshine that drifted over him.

Sometimes in winter when the snow sparkled on the ground a rabbit would come along and hop right over the little tree. Oh, how embarrassed he felt! But after two winters the tree had grown so large that the rabbit could no longer jump over it.

"Oh, if I could only grow *very* tall!" thought the little fir. "That would be the most wonderful thing in the world!"

The next autumn the woodcutters came to cut down some of the largest trees. The young fir shuddered when the great stately trees crashed to the ground. After their branches were chopped off, the trees looked long and bare. Then they were placed on carts and horses dragged them away.

"I wonder where they go. I wonder what becomes of them," said the little fir tree to himself.

In the spring, when the swallows and storks came, the tree asked them, "Do you know where the tall trees have been taken? Have you seen them anywhere?"

The swallows knew nothing about it, but one of the storks, after thinking for a moment, nodded his head and said, "I think I saw them as I flew out of Egypt. I believe they are now great masts on some new ships. They are still fragrant firs—and they are still majestic."

"Oh, I wish I could sail over the ocean!" said the fir tree. "What is the ocean? What does it look like?"

"That would take too long to explain now," said the stork. And he flew away.

The wind kissed the tree. And the sunbeam said, "Be glad you are young." But the fir would not listen.

340

When Christmastime came many beautiful trees were cut down. Some were even smaller and younger than the fir tree. But none were as restless as he to leave their forest home. These trees kept all their branches. They were placed on carts, and horses drew them away.

"Where are they going?" asked the young fir. "They were no taller than I. One was even shorter. And why do they still have all their branches?"

"We know!" sang the sparrows. "We know where they're taken. We have peered into the houses in the town and have seen them. They are dressed up and look very beautiful. They stand bearing gilded apples, honey cakes, and toys, and they twinkle with a hundred lights."

"Then?" said the fir tree and he trembled. "Then? What happens then?"

"We did not see anything more," said the sparrows, "but they were beautiful."

"I wonder if something like that could ever happen to me!" cried the fir. "That is better than crossing the ocean! Wouldn't it be wonderful! Oh, I wish I were standing in a warm room, all atwinkle with lights, waiting for something still more exciting to happen!"

"Be happy here in the woodland!" said the air and the sunlight. "Rejoice in your youth!"

But the tree did not rejoice. There in the forest he grew and grew. And soon another year had passed.

At Christmastime the fir tree was the first to be chopped down. The fir fell to the earth with a sigh. Already he was sorry to leave his forest home, and the pines, and the birds.

341

But when he was unloaded in a large courtyard and heard a man say, "That is the finest tree. That is the one we want," the fir trembled with pride. Then two servants carried the fir tree into a warm and beautiful room. He looked around him and saw portraits hanging on the walls. Near the white porcelain stove stood two large Chinese vases with lions on the covers. There were large rocking-chairs, silken sofas, tables full of picture-books and toys worth hundreds and hundreds of crowns—at least the children said so.

The fir tree was placed upright in a wooden tub that was filled with sand, but no one could see that it was a tub, for green cloth was hung around it, and it was placed on a large, gaily colored carpet. Oh, how the tree quivered! What was to happen?

Young girls decorated it. On one branch there hung little bags cut out of colored paper, and each bag was filled with candy. Among the other boughs gilded apples and walnuts were suspended, looking as though they had grown there, and little blue and white candles were placed among the leaves. Dolls that looked like real babies swung among the foliage. At the very top a large star of gold tinsel was fixed. Oh, how beautiful he was!

"Oh!" they all said. "How it will shine this evening!"

"Oh," thought the tree. "I wonder what will happen now! Perhaps the other trees from the forest will come to look at me! Perhaps the sparrows will come, too. I wonder if I shall take root here and, winter and summer, stand covered with ornaments!"

At last evening came and the candles were lighted. How bright they were! How beautiful! The tree trembled so with joy in every bough that one of the candles fell and set fire to a green twig. "Help! Help!" cried the girls, and they quickly put out the fire.

Now the tree did not even dare tremble. The fire had frightened him, and he was afraid of burning. Suddenly both folding doors opened, and a number of children rushed in as if they would upset the tree. The older people followed quietly. The little ones stood quite still, but it was only for a moment. Then they shouted so that the whole place re-echoed with their laughter; they danced around the tree, and one present after another was pulled off.

"What are they doing?" thought the tree. "What is to happen now?" And the lights burned down to the very branches, and as they burned down they were put out, one after another.

"A story! A story!" cried the children, drawing a little fat man towards the tree. He seated himself under it, and said, "Now we are in the shade, and the tree can listen, too. But I shall tell only one story. Now which will you have; that about Ivedy-Avedy, or about Klumpy-Dumpy, who tumbled down the stairs, and yet, after all, came to the throne and married the princess?"

"Ivedy-Avedy," cried some; "Klumpy-Dumpy," cried the others. There was a great crying and shouting. The fir tree alone was silent, and he thought to himself, "Am I not to cry out also? Am I to do nothing whatever?"

The man told about Klumpy-Dumpy, who tumbled down, but notwithstanding, came to the throne, and at last married the princess. And the children clapped their hands, and cried out, "O go on! Do go on!"

343

The fir tree stood quite still: the birds in the woods had never told such tales as this. "Klumpy-Dumpy fell downstairs, and yet he married the princess! Yes, yes! that's the way of the world!" thought the fir tree, and believed it all. "Well, well! Who knows? Perhaps I may fall downstairs, too, and marry a princess!" And he looked forward eagerly to the next evening, when he hoped to be decked out again with lights, playthings, fruits, and tinsel.

"I won't tremble tomorrow!" thought the fir tree. "I will enjoy myself. Tomorrow I shall hear again the story of Klumpy-Dumpy, and perhaps that of Ivedy-Avedy, too." And the tree stood still all night, quiet and thoughtful.

In the morning, the servants entered and walked towards the tree.

"Now, then, the splendor will begin again," thought the fir. But they dragged him out of the room, and up the stairs into the attic. There in a dark corner, where no daylight could enter, they left him.

"What am I to do here? What shall I hear now, I wonder?" He leaned against the wall, and thought and thought. Days and nights passed, and nobody came up. When at last somebody did come, it was only to put some great trunks in a corner out of the way. The tree stood quite hidden; it seemed as if he had been entirely forgotten.

"It is now winter outside!" thought the tree. "The earth is hard and covered with snow; men cannot plant me now, and, therefore, I have been put up here under shelter till the springtime comes! How thoughtful that is! How kind everyone is, after all! If only it were not

so dark here, and so terribly lonely! Not even a rabbit. Out in the woods it was so pleasant when the snow was on the ground, and the rabbit leaped by; yes—even when he jumped over me, though I did not like it then. It is really terribly lonely here!"

"Squeak! squeak!" said a little mouse at the same moment, peeping out of his hole. Then another little one came. They sniffed about the fir tree, and crept among the branches.

"It is dreadfully cold," said the mouse. "Otherwise it would be comfortable, old fir, wouldn't it?"

"I am by no means old," said the fir tree. "Many a tree is older than I am."

"Where do you come from?" asked the mice, "and what can you do?" They were extremely curious. "Tell us about the most beautiful spot on the earth. Have you ever been there? Were you ever in the storeroom where cheeses lie on the shelves, and hams hang from the ceiling? Where one dances about on wax candles,— that place where one enters lean and comes out again fat and portly?"

"I know no such place," said the tree, "I know the wood, where the sun shines, and where the little birds sing." Then he told them all about his youth. The little mice had never heard the like before, and they listened and said, "Well, to be sure! How much you have seen! How happy you must have been!"

"Happy?" said the fir tree. "Yes, really, those were the happy times." And then he told about Christmas Eve, when he was decked out with cakes and candles.

"Oh," said the little mice, "how fortunate you have been, old fir tree!"

"I am by no means old," he said. "I came from the wood this winter; I am in my prime, and am only rather short for my age."

"What delightful stories you know!" said the mice.

The next night they came with four other little mice, to hear what the tree told; and the more he told, the more plainly he remembered everything himself, and it seemed as if those times had really been happy ones. "But they may still come—they may still come. Klumpy-Dumpy fell downstairs, and yet he got a princess!" And he thought at the moment of a pretty little birch tree growing out in the woods; to the fir that would be a charming princess.

"Who is Klumpy-Dumpy?" asked the mice. So then the fir tree told the whole fairy tale, for he could remember every single word of it, and the little mice jumped for joy up to the very top of the tree. Next

night two more mice came, and on Sunday two rats;
but they said the stories were not interesting. This
bothered the little mice, who were beginning to tire
of the tales themselves.

"Do you know only one story?" asked the rats.

"Only that one," answered the tree. "I heard it on
my happiest evening; but I did not then know how
happy I was."

"It is a very stupid story! Don't you know one about
bacon and tallow candles? Can't you tell any pantry
stories?"

"No," said the tree.

"Then good-bye," said the rats, and they went home.

At last the little mice stayed away also.

"It was very pleasant when the merry little mice sat
around me and listened to what I told them," the tree
sighed. "Now that, too, is over. But I will take good
care to enjoy myself when I am brought out again. Oh,
when is that to be?"

One morning people came to work in the attic. The
trunks were moved, the tree was pulled out and thrown
—rather hard, it is true—down on the floor, but a servant
dragged him towards the stairs, where the daylight
shone.

"Now a merry life will begin again," thought the
tree. He felt the fresh air, the first sunbeam, and soon
he was out in the courtyard. All passed so quickly, and
there was so much going on around him, that the tree
quite forgot to think about himself. The court was close
to a garden; everything was blooming and fragrant.
The lindens were in blossom. The swallows flew by
and sang a spring song.

"Now I shall really enjoy life," said the fir tree joyfully, and spread out his branches. But oh, they were withered and yellow! He lay in a corner among the weeds and nettles. The golden star of tinsel was still on the top of the tree and glittered in the sunshine.

In the courtyard some of the merry children, who had danced at Christmas around the fir tree, were playing. One of the youngest ran and tore off the golden star.

"Oh, look what is still on the ugly old Christmas tree!" he said, trampling on the branches so that they all cracked beneath his feet.

The tree saw all the beauty of the flowers, and the freshness in the garden; he saw himself, and wished he had remained in his dark corner in the attic; he thought of his early days in the wood, of the merry Christmas Eve, and of the little mice who had listened with so much pleasure to the story of Klumpy-Dumpy.

"It is over—it is past!" said the old tree. "If I had only been happy in those days! But now it is too late!"

And the gardener's boy chopped the tree into small pieces, until it was a heap of wood. The wood flamed up, and as it rose it seemed to sigh deeply!

The children played about in the court, and the youngest boy wore on his chest the gold star that the tree had worn on the happiest evening of his life. However, that was over now—the tree gone, the story at an end. All, all was over; every tale must end at last.

Charles Tazewell

THE LITTLEST ANGEL

ILLUSTRATED BY *Katherine Evans*

ONCE upon a time—oh, many, many years ago as time is calculated by men—but which was only Yesterday in the Celestial Calendar of Heaven—there was, in Paradise, a most miserable, thoroughly unhappy, and utterly dejected cherub who was known throughout Heaven as *The Littlest Angel.*

He was exactly four years, six months, five days, seven hours and forty-two minutes of age when he presented himself to the venerable Gate-Keeper and waited for admittance to the Glorious Kingdom of God.

Standing defiantly, with his short brown legs wide apart, the Littlest Angel tried to pretend that he wasn't at all impressed by such Unearthly Splendor, and that he wasn't at all afraid. But his lower lip trembled, and a tear disgraced him by making a new furrow down his already tear-streaked face—coming to a precipitous halt at the very tip end of his small freckled nose.

But that wasn't all. While the kindly Gate-Keeper was entering the name in his great Book, the Littlest Angel, having left home as usual without a handkerchief, endeavored to hide the telltale evidence by snuffing. A most unangelic sound which so unnerved the good Gate-Keeper that he did something he had never done before in all Eternity! He blotted the page!

From that moment on, the Heavenly Peace was never quite the same, and the Littlest Angel soon became the despair of all the Heavenly Host. His shrill, ear-splitting whistle resounded at all hours through the Golden Streets. It startled the Patriarch Prophets and disturbed their meditations. Yes, and on top of that, he inevitably and vociferously sang off-key at the singing practice of the Heavenly Choir, spoiling its ethereal effect.

And, being so small that it seemed to take him just twice as long as anyone else to get to nightly prayers, the Littlest Angel always arrived late, and knocked everyone's wings askew as he darted into his place.

Although these flaws in behavior might have been overlooked, the general appearance of the Littlest Angel was even more disreputable than his deportment. It was first whispered among the Seraphim and Cherubim, and then said aloud among the Angels and Archangels, that he didn't even look like an angel!

And they were all quite correct. He didn't. His halo was permanently tarnished where he held onto it with one hot little chubby hand when he ran, and he was always running. Furthermore, even when he stood very still, it never behaved like a halo should. It was always slipping down over his right eye.

Or over his left eye.

Or else, just for pure meanness, slipping off the back of his head and rolling away down some Golden Street just so he'd have to chase after it!

Yes, and it must be here recorded that his wings were

351

neither useful nor ornamental. All Paradise held its
breath when the Littlest Angel perched himself like an
unhappy fledgling sparrow on the very edge of a gilded
cloud and prepared to take off. He would teeter this
way—and that way—but, after much coaxing and a few
false starts, he would shut both of his eyes, hold his
freckled nose, count up to three hundred and three, and
then hurl himself slowly into space!

However, owing to the regrettable fact that he always forgot to move his wings, the Littlest Angel
always fell head over halo!

It was also reported, and never denied, that whenever he was nervous, which was most of the time, he
bit his wing-tips!

Now, anyone can easily understand why the Littlest Angel would, soon or late, have to be disciplined. And so, on an Eternal Day of an Eternal Month in the Year Eternal, he was directed to present his small self before an Angel of the Peace.

The Littlest Angel combed his hair, dusted his wings, and scrambled into an almost clean robe, and then, with a heavy heart, trudged his way to the place of judgment. He tried to postpone the dreaded ordeal by loitering along the Street of The Guardian Angels, pausing a few timeless moments to minutely pursue the long list of new arrivals, although all Heaven knew he couldn't read a word. And he idled more than several immortal moments to carefully examine a display of aureate harps, although everyone in the Celestial City knew he couldn't tell a crotchet from a semi-quaver.

But at length and at last he slowly approached a doorway which was surmounted by a pair of golden scales, signifying that Heavenly Justice was dispensed within. To the Littlest Angel's great surprise, he heard a merry voice, singing!

The Littlest Angel removed his halo and breathed upon it heavily, then polished it upon his robe, a procedure which added nothing to that garment's already untidy appearance, and then tiptoed in!

The Singer, who was known as the Understanding Angel, looked down at the small culprit, and the Littlest Angel instantly tried to make himself invisible by the ingenious process of withdrawing his head into the collar of his robe, very much like a snapping turtle.

At that, the Singer laughed, a jolly, heartwarming sound, and said, "Oh! So you're the one who's been making Heaven so unheavenly! Come here, Cherub, and tell me all about it!" The Littlest Angel ventured a furtive look from beneath his robe.

First one eye.

And then the other eye.

Suddenly, almost before he knew it, he was perched on the lap of the Understanding Angel, and was explaining how very difficult it was for a boy who suddenly finds himself transformed into an angel. Yes, and no matter what the Archangels said, he'd only swung once. Well, twice. Oh, all right, then, he'd swung three times on the Golden Gates. But that was just for something to do!

That was the whole trouble. There wasn't anything for a small angel to do. And he was very homesick. Oh, not that Paradise wasn't beautiful! But the Earth was

beautiful, too! Wasn't it created by God, Himself? Why, there were trees to climb, and brooks to fish, and caves to play at pirate chief, the swimming hole, and sun, and rain, and dark, and dawn, and thick brown dust, so soft and warm beneath your feet!

The Understanding Angel smiled, and in his eyes was a long forgotten memory of another small boy in a long ago. Then he asked the Littlest Angel what would make him most happy in Paradise. The Cherub thought for a moment and whispered in his ear.

"There's a box. I left it under my bed back home. If only I could have that?"

The Understanding Angel nodded his head. "You shall have it," he promised. And a fleet-winged Heavenly messenger was instantly dispatched to bring the box to Paradise.

And then, in all those timeless days that followed, everyone wondered at the great change in the Littlest Angel, for, among all the cherubs in God's Kingdom, he was the most happy. His conduct was above the slightest reproach. His appearance was all that the most fastidious could wish for. And on excursions to Elysian Fields, it could be said, and truly said, that he flew like an angel!

Then it came to pass that Jesus, the Son of God, was to be born of Mary, of Bethlehem, of Judea. And as the glorious tidings spread through Paradise, all the angels rejoiced and their voices were lifted to herald the Miracle of Miracles, the coming of the Christ Child.

The Angels and Archangels, the Seraphim and Cherubim, the Gatekeper, the Wingmaker, yes, and even the Halosmith put aside their usual tasks to prepare their gifts for the Blessed Infant. All but the Littlest Angel. He sat himself down on the topmost step of the Golden Stairs and anxiously waited for inspiration.

What could he give that would be most acceptable to the Son of God? At one time, he dreamed of composing a lyric hymn of adoration. But the Littlest Angel was woefully wanting in musical talent.

Then he grew tremendously excited over writing a prayer! A prayer that would live forever in the hearts of men, because it would be the first prayer ever to be heard by the Christ Child! But the Littlest Angel was lamentably lacking in literate skill. "What, oh what, could a small angel give that would please the Holy Infant?"

The time of the Miracle was very close at hand when

the Littlest Angel at last decided on his gift. Then, on that Day of Days, he proudly brought it from its hiding place behind a cloud, and humbly, with downcast eyes, placed it before the Throne of God. It was only a small, rough, unsightly box, but inside were all those wonderful things that even a Child of God would treasure!

A small, rough, unsightly box, lying among all those other glorious gifts from all the Angels of Paradise! Gifts of such rare and radiant splendor and breathless beauty that Heaven and all the Universe were lighted by the mere reflection of their glory! And when the Littlest Angel saw this, he suddenly knew that his gift to God's Child was irreverent, and he devoutly wished he might reclaim his shabby gift. It was ugly. It was worthless. If only he could hide it away from the sight of God before it was even noticed!

But it was too late! The Hand of God moved slowly over all that bright array of shining gifts,
        then paused,
            then dropped,
                then came to rest
on the lowly gift of the Littlest Angel!

The Littlest Angel trembled as the box was opened, and there, before the Eyes of God and all His Heavenly Host, was what he offered to the Christ Child.

And what was his gift to the Blessed Infant? Well, there was a butterfly with golden wings, captured one bright summer day on the high hills above Jerusalem, and a sky-blue egg from a bird's nest in the olive tree that stood to shade his mother's kitchen door. Yes, and two white stones, found on a muddy river bank, where

he and his friends had played like small brown beavers, and, at the bottom of the box, a limp, tooth-marked leather strap, once worn as a collar by his mongrel dog, who had died as he had lived, in absolute love and infinite devotion.

The Littlest Angel wept hot, bitter tears, for now he knew that instead of honoring the Son of God, he had been most blasphemous.

Why had he ever thought the box was so wonderful?

Why had he dreamed that such utterly useless things would be loved by the Blessed Infant?

In frantic terror, he turned to run and hide from the Divine Wrath of the Heavenly Father, but he stumbled and fell, and with a horrified wail and clatter of halo, rolled in a ball of consummate misery to the very foot of the Heavenly Throne!

There was an ominous and dreadful silence in the Celestial City, a silence complete and undisturbed save for the heart-broken sobbing of the Littlest Angel.

Then, suddenly, The Voice of God, like Divine Music, rose and swelled through Paradise!

And the Voice of God spoke, saying, "Of all the gifts of all the angels, I find that this small box pleases Me most. Its contents are of the Earth and of men, and My Son is born to be King of both. These are the things My Son, too, will know and love and cherish and then, regretful, will leave behind Him when His task is done. I accept this gift in the Name of the Child, Jesus, born of Mary this night in Bethlehem."

There was a breathless pause, and then the rough, unsightly box of the Littlest Angel began to glow with a bright, unearthly light, then the light became a lustrous flame, and the flame became a radiant brilliance that blinded the eyes of all the angels!

None but the Littlest Angel saw it rise from its place before the Throne of God. And he, and only he, watched it arch the firmament to stand and shed its clear, white, beckoning light over a Stable where a Child was Born.

There it shone on that Night of Miracles, and its light was reflected down the centuries deep in the heart of all mankind. Yet, earthly eyes, blinded, too, by its splendor, could never know that the lowly gift of the Littlest Angel was what all men would call forever

"THE SHINING STAR OF BETHLEHEM!"

Rachel Field

ALL THROUGH THE NIGHT

ILLUSTRATED BY *Helen Sewell*

ALL that day the Inn Yard had been thronged with people coming to pay their taxes in the town of Bethlehem. The small sturdy watchdog who slept in the stable and picked up what food he could find had never before seen such a crowd of travelers.

When night fell he was tired from barking at so many strangers and their beasts, and with scurrying out of the way of feet and hoofs. But for all the barking and running about it had been a good day. The Inn had overflowed into the yard. There had been a fire there with meat roasting over it and pots that sent out clouds of savory steam. Many a rich morsel had fallen his way, so he felt well content as he crept into his corner of the stable near the oxen's stall.

He and they greeted each other and exchanged news of the day.

"Yes, we, too, have been busy," the oxen told him. "Heavy loads for us since daybreak and the roads round Bethlehem so choked with carts and caravans and herds and flocks we could hardly move sometimes."

"And rude, stupid creatures they were to meet!" the ass put in from her corner. "With no manners at all or sense enough to follow their own noses. Some even dared to dispute the right of way with me, but I held my ground."

"I have no doubt you did," said the dog, for he knew

360

the ass was not one to be persuaded against her will. He turned himself round and round in a pile of straw to make himself comfortable and fell to licking a bruised spot on his leg.

"There must have been many sheep," the old ewe joined in from her pen. "I could not see them because I was shut in here with my two lambs, but I could tell by their voices that some came from places farther away than Judea. I should have liked to see them."

"Well," the dog told her, "I found them a dusty, frightened lot. I was thankful not to have their herding in my charge. And the goats were no better," he added, that the bearded gray goat might be sure to hear. He and the goat were not upon friendly terms and took pleasure in tormenting each other.

"Peace and quiet. Peace and quiet at last," the doves cooed from the rafters. "Peace and quiet till morning, that is all we ask."

The hens made soft clucking sounds to show that they were in complete agreement.

But the cock with his scarlet comb and burnished tail feathers, stepping about in search of stray kernels, was of a different mind. "I like noise and bustle myself." He voiced his opinion loudly. "Peace is all very well for those who haven't the spirit for something better. Now I can hardly wait for morning."

"Everyone to his own taste," the mild-eyed cow put in her word, shifting her cud deftly and flicking her tail as she did so. "If it were always day or always night we should not all be satisfied."

"Well said. Well said," the doves agreed in drowsy unison from the dimness of the eaves.

Darkness gathered there first. The swallows were already seeking their nests, while the bats were beginning to stretch and unfold their lean, black wings.

Night was coming fast and all the birds and beasts and insects of the stable knew that it belonged to them. The world was theirs as the world of day could never be. When the sun rose man would be their master again. They would carry his burdens or feed or serve him according to their different gifts. But night was their own, when they might move or fight or take counsel together without man's interference. It was good that this should be so, the little dog thought, as he burrowed deeper into the straw.

His sworn enemy the cat slid by. She moved like a shadow with fiery-green eyes ready to pounce upon the mice who were already squeaking and scampering at their play. But the dog was too tired and comfortable to give chase, so for once he let her pass unmolested. All about him crickets chirped in rusty chorus and sometimes a bat swooped so low he could feel the stir of its wings. The darkness was warm and alive with the familiar scents of fur and feathers and grain and straw.

"Rest well. Rest well. Rest well." The doves cooed sleepily, making a soft sound in their throats that was like the bubbling of a well-filled pot over a fire.

Night had come to Bethlehem. The Inn had been full hours ago. The dog could hear late travelers being turned away. The stable door was securely bolted against intruders, and the wind was rising, frosty and keen. Through an opening in the roof a star shone bright as purest silver.

"I never saw a star look so large or so near," the cock observed as he moved about with his spurred, high-stepping walk. "Somehow it makes me very restless, and there is something strange in the air. Perhaps you have felt it, too?"

But the dog made no answer. He yawned and laid his pointed muzzle on his paws and prepared himself for sleep.

He woke at the sound of voices outside and roused himself to bark. But though the hair rose along his back, no sound came rumbling from his throat. The bolt was drawn and the stable door opened to lantern light and the dim shapes of two men and a donkey on whose back a woman sat, wrapped in a heavy cloak.

"Well"—the voice of the Inn Keeper sounded short and impatient—"if you cannot go on, there is only the stable to offer. Coming as you have at such an hour, you are fortunate· to have this shelter till morning."

"The roads were crowded," the Man answered him, "and our pace was slow because of my wife. You can see that she is nearly spent."

"Yes, yes." The Inn Keeper was already shutting the door. "I am sorry for your plight, but I tell you there is no room left."

The dog was on his feet. He could hear the other animals rising about him, yet not one of them uttered a sound. Their throats were as silent as his own.

In the flickering lantern light he watched the Man lift the Woman from the donkey's back and set her upon her feet. She was so weary she would have fallen but for the Man's arms.

"Joseph," she said, "you must not be troubled for me,

363

even if it should be that the time has come. . . ." She rested her head on the Man's shoulder and sighed so softly it might have been one of the doves in the rafters drawing closer to her mate.

"But, Mary," the Man went on, "it is not right and fitting that it should be here,—not in a stable among the beasts."

"Who knows," she comforted him, "what is to be? These beasts are more kind than men who kill and hurt one another. I am glad to be here. Their warm breath comforts me. Their straw is clean and soft to rest upon."

Everywhere beyond the ring of light that the lantern made, bright eyes were upon the strangers. Furry ears and quivering noses pointed, alert and watchful.

The strange donkey, freed of his load, found a place beside the ass. He sank down, too tired to drink water from the trough or reach for a mouthful of hay.

A hush was on the stable. Not only were all throats silent, but no wings stirred; no claws scratched and not a hoof pounded. And in that hour nothing died. The young swallows and mice were safe from their enemies, for a mystery greater than death held them all in its power.

The lantern flickered and went out.

"Our oil is gone!" the Man cried out in distress.

"There will be light enough." The Woman spoke in a faint voice, and as if in answer the star in the roof gap shone brighter than before.

How long it was after that the little dog could not tell. Morning was still far off, yet the cock suddenly lifted up his voice, so shrill and clear it seemed he would split himself in two. It was not like any other

364

cockcrow since the world began, and it rose higher than the rafters and mounted to heaven itself. At the same instant each creature found voice and joined with him. Every living thing in the stable had a part in that swelling chorus of praise. Even the bees hummed till their hive throbbed with music, sweeter than all its store of honey.

"What manner of place is this?" the Man cried out. "What beasts are these who have the tongues of angels?"

But the Woman answered him softly out of the shadows. "It was they who gave us shelter this night. Let them draw near and be the first to worship."

She drew aside the folds of her cloak and light filled the stable even to the farthest corners. The dog cowered before such strange brightness. When he dared to look more closely he saw that it encircled the head of an infant, new born.

"There is no bed for him to lie upon," the Man sighed. "Only this"—and he pointed to the manger.

"Bring it here," the Mother said. "My heart tells me there will be nights when he will have no place at all to rest his head."

So the Child lay quiet in the straw-filled wooden manger and all the animals came to view him there— the oxen, the cow, the ass and the donkey, the ewe and her lambs, the gray goat, the dog, the hens and the proud cock ruffling his feathers. The cat left off her prowling to join them and the mice ran beside her without fear. The crickets came, too, drawn from the comfort of their warm straw; the bees, from their snug hive. The tireless ants and spiders left their toil to draw near.

The swallows in the eaves flew down; the bats bent low on their dark wings, and the doves came closest of all with their soft murmurs above the manger. When they had all seen the Wonder they returned to their places and were quiet again.

All but the dog. He could not rest as he had before. He stretched himself beside the manger and lay with his head on his folded paws, his eyes wide and watchful as the hours passed.

Long before sunrise the door opened without sound of bolt being drawn, and a band of Shepherds came in. They bore a strange tale on their lips and they also worshiped on bended knees. One carried a lamb in his arms, and the Child answered its bleating with a smile.

"Behold the Lamb of God," they said one to another as they turned to go back to their flocks on the hills.

The star grew pale, and through the gap in the stable roof morning showed rosy in the east. Even before the cock hailed it, the dog knew that the sun was up. But he did not move lest he rouse the three in his care. It was then that he saw a strange thing.

The rafters high above cast their shadows as the rising sun struck through. Two of the beams crossed in sharp black bars that fell directly across the sleeping Child. The little dog could not tell why the sight should make him cower in sudden fear.

Then the cock crowed three times, and the first sounds of people stirring in the Inn and yard began.

He watched the Man and the Woman preparing to go. He saw the donkey being watered and fed and the blanket fitted in place. He saw the Mother wrap her Son warmly against the cold before the Man set them upon the donkey's back and lifted a heavy bundle on his own.

"Come," he said and opened the stable door. "We must make haste."

Stiff from his long vigil, the dog rose and followed them to the door. He watched them cross the Inn yard in the early light and join other travelers who were already thronging the roads leading to and from Bethlehem. Soon they would be lost to his sight, those Three whom he had guarded through the hours of darkness.

"Ah," cried the cock, preening his burnished feathers, "what a morning!" He strutted over to where bits of food and grain lay scattered and began to forage for stray morsels.

The dog lifted his head and sniffed hungrily. He could tell that pots were already on the fires. The sharp morning air brought the savory news to him and he knew that by keeping close to the kitchen he would soon be well filled. He remembered a bone he had buried yesterday in a secluded spot. Yet he did not seek it. He trotted past the kitchen doors, and though his nose twitched at the smells that he was leaving he kept it pointed straight ahead.

"Wait. Wait." His bark rang out sharp and determined, and his paws clicked over the stones as he ran.

He did not pause till he had caught up with the Man who led the plodding donkey and his burden along the dusty road.

"Here I am!" He barked again as he fell into step beside them. "Let me come with you."

Index